Bride by the Book

KATHRYN BROCATO

Author of *The Look-Alike Bride* and *The Counterfeit Cowgirl*

CRIMSON
ROMANCE

F+W Media, Inc.

Published by
Crimson Romance
an imprint of F+W Media, Inc.
10151 Carver Road, Suite 200
Blue Ash, OH 45242. U.S.A.
www.crimsonromance.com

ISBN 10: 1-4405-8237-8
ISBN 13: 978-1-4405-8237-0
eISBN 10: 1-4405-8238-6
eISBN 13: 978-1-4405-8238-7

Cover art © 123RF/David Maixner

This book is dedicated to Dolores Brocato.

Chapter 1

Angie Brownwood looked around her office in search of items to toss into the cardboard box she was using to pack her personal belongings prior to leaving her job at BrownWare Business Software Company. She found almost nothing to pack, other than her personal coffee cup and her personal coffee maker, which were already lovingly settled in the box.

After spending a grand total of five years working at BrownWare, you'd have thought she would have at least two cardboard boxes full of miscellaneous personal items. Angie looked around regretfully and shook her head. She had no life, and that was the whole problem. Apparently, if you had a life, you collected personal items as something to show for all the time you spent in a location.

"He's on his way here, Ang." One of her colleagues from the software development lab stuck his head in her door. "He's really gone ballistic this time."

Angie shrugged. She was so tired, she literally no longer cared. "It doesn't matter. I'm on the way out the door. In case he hasn't heard, I quit."

Her friend glanced over his shoulder. "He's heard. See you."

Angie watched the young man dart off. A fraction of a second later, her father appeared in the doorway.

"You can't quit," he snapped. "For your information, I've already fired you."

Angie looked at him in wondering silence. Five years of striving to excel, striving to win his approval, and what did she have to show for it?

Not much, if she counted the contents of her cardboard box. She had been such a disappointment to him, he even used her one spectacular success to fuel his anger at her.

"You think that stupid game has made you somebody," he raged, as if he read her thoughts. "Everything you know, you learned here, and now you think you can take over my company. The company *I* founded."

There was more, but Angie tuned out and cast her gaze around her office. Nothing else caught her eye, so she folded in the cardboard tabs and picked up the box.

"Since I no longer work here, you should have nothing further to complain about," she said. "Maybe you can get back to business instead of fighting with me and Peter."

"You're darned right you don't work here anymore. You're fired!" her father yelled.

Angie rolled her eyes and headed out the door for the last time. "Bye, Daddy."

He didn't follow her as she had feared. Angie exited the building that housed BrownWare and another software company and headed for the parking lot. To her own surprise, every step away from BrownWare caused a corresponding surge of energy and a lift in her spirits. She had been so tired, she figured she'd need a nap before she could begin implementing her plans.

She intended to get a new life, and she had laid careful plans as to how to go about it. The first step involved updating her wardrobe. The second step involved moving halfway across the country to the house she had just inherited. The third step involved readying herself to step into a whole new career.

The further she got from BrownWare, the more Angie could hardly wait to get started.

• • •

Garner Holt stared, temporarily stunned, at the sheet of paper he had just extracted from an envelope and unfolded. In spite of his recent trials and tribulations, hope sprung eternal within his breast.

"Oh, Lord," he breathed prayerfully. He pressed the paper flat and pushed it across the diner booth toward his brother-in-law, Clifford Jones. "What do you think, Cliff?"

The two men shared office space in a house across the street from the New South Diner and had formed the habit of meeting for breakfast every morning. Cliff, a short man with curly, blond hair and a tendency to gain weight easily, cast a swift glance over the elegantly typed résumé.

"Sounds like your salvation, buddy." He grinned. "It also sounds too good to be true. A Stanford grad who wants to be a legal secretary?"

Garner frowned and studied the résumé once more, then shrugged. "As long as she can type, file, and is willing to clean up some of the mess in my office, I don't care if she went to clown college."

"Hire a maid," Cliff recommended. "It's a lot safer. How much would you like to bet this is Mindy Adams using some phony name to get to you? I heard she took some computer course once upon a time." Cliff regarded the résumé suspiciously. "I've been wondering why Mindy hasn't pretended she was a legal secretary and applied for a job in your office before this."

Garner tried in vain to imagine the spoiled daughter of the town judge at a computer for longer than five minutes at a time. "Mindy would fall apart the minute she was expected to do more than type her name. According to this, the woman is new to the area. Look at these skills." Garner grew almost reverent when he reread the sheet. "I'll bet she's middle-aged and tough. Just what I need to chase off husband-hunters like Mindy."

In spite of having lived in Smackover most of his life, Garner still wasn't accustomed to the attention he received from the single women in town. He definitely wasn't rich, he didn't consider himself particularly handsome, and he wasn't a man who enjoyed much of a social life. In fact, he'd have said he was a poor risk for marriage, considering his past romantic experience and his tendency toward suffering every stress-related illness in the medical texts. But he was single, and apparently that was all that counted these days.

Yes, a tough, efficient, battle-axe of a woman who could keep his business in order was just what the doctor ordered.

"Yeah," Cliff said, chuckling. "Just what you need. A secretary who'll organize you like you were a kid in grade school."

"Who cares? I could use a little organizing, and I need a secretary. *This* secretary."

"You could use some organizing, all right," Cliff agreed, with sinister emphasis.

Garner flushed but said nothing. During the two years he'd been practicing law in his hometown of Smackover, Arkansas, he'd let more than a few things slide. Although he never neglected his clients, his entire attitude about life had undergone a major readjustment.

For instance, he was no longer a fanatic about anything except his physical well-being, and that had become second nature. Garner had learned first-hand what stress could do to a man. For that reason, he avoided many situations and cases that might raise his stress levels, and in spite of that, he still found himself overwhelmed with work.

"I don't know what happened to you in Dallas, and I'm not sure I want to," Cliff muttered. He glared at his plate. "But I'll tell you this much. Chicken breast was never meant to be a breakfast food."

Since Cliff had put on a few pounds recently, he was allowing Garner to dictate his choice of food.

"Shut up and eat. Your stomach doesn't know it's getting chicken," Garner said without taking his gaze off the thick sheet of paper in his hand.

"My nose and my mouth sure know they're getting chicken instead of bacon with buttered toast and two eggs over easy." Cliff studied his plate with a definite lack of interest then lifted his guileless, brown gaze to focus on something behind Garner. "Wow. Get a look at that. There's someone new in town."

Smackover was small enough that any stranger was instantly noticed. Garner twisted in the narrow booth to look at the woman entering the diner. This particular stranger was more visible than most. Every male in the small diner took careful note of her.

She was a leggy, young girl of average height with a mass of pale blond hair floating around her shoulders. She could have done with a judicious application of makeup, thanks to the excessive paleness of her skin and the big, dark circles beneath the most beautiful, innocent blue eyes Garner had ever seen. She wore a pair of white Bermuda shorts and a shocking-pink blouse that attracted any eye not already focused on her. She created a welcome splash of exotic color in the small cafe.

But the most striking thing about her was the fascinated way she gazed at everything and everybody. She seemed enthralled by each item her gaze fell upon, including the waitress, crusty old Dolly Sims.

Garner, who had forgotten what it was like to greet each day with eager expectation, paid special attention to the girl's enthusiastic expression. It made him feel extra-old on this particular morning.

Too bad she was still in her teens, he thought cynically, watching the girl approach. He knew from experience that once a woman got older, she lost her enthusiasm for life and centered on one thing—herself. Garner let himself enjoy the gentle sway of her hips and the tiny waist above them. Some lucky male would probably snap this one up the minute she turned twenty.

The girl walked to the booth behind Garner with the springy, elastic step of youth. When she passed their booth, she cast a happy smile in their direction. A fresh, lemony scent that reminded Garner of a spring meadow followed her.

"Now there's a darned good-looking woman for you," Cliff said, lowering his voice. "She reminds me of Laura. It's that look of happy expectation."

"That'll change," Garner predicted with disgust. "What do you expect from a sixteen-year-old?" He studied the résumé again—the résumé that promised salvation. "I'd better call this number first thing. She's bound to be in huge demand."

"Your sister hasn't changed." Cliff peered over Garner's shoulder. "She's still got that joy in life that first attracted my attention, and we've been married three years now. Three *great* years, by the way." He watched the girl a moment. "What makes you think she's sixteen?"

"She looks sixteen, therefore, she must be sixteen." Garner studied the résumé again, conscious of his brother-in-law's steady gaze. He knew Cliff was curious about his time in Dallas and his failed marriage. Even after two years, Garner still didn't care to tell anyone, including his relatives, what a fool he'd been. "If you're through torturing that chicken, let's get back to the office so I can hire my new secretary."

"But I haven't had anything to eat," Cliff said plaintively He picked up his knife and fork and bravely attacked the chicken breast. "Calm down, Garner. She's probably sitting by her phone, waiting for calls.

"Her phone has probably been ringing since six this morning if she sent résumés to every lawyer in town." Garner plucked a pen from his shirt pocket and circled the phone number. "Let's hope I'm the only one who needs a secretary."

Dolly Sims, the crotchety waitress who had been at the small diner since it was the Old South Cafe, stalked past them with a glass of water and a menu in her hands. She glared at the girl.

Garner bit back a smile and wondered if the girl's expression of enthusiasm would dim in the face of that glare.

"Don't mind Dolly." Cliff smiled past Garner's shoulder. "She always looks like she just finished eating a sour pickle."

Dolly sniffed and ignored Cliff. Garner bit back a laugh, knowing that Dolly disapproved of Cliff's diet and would likely retaliate by setting a dish piled high with butter before him.

Garner turned. He might have known his kind-hearted brother-in-law would be unable to resist soothing the stranger in their midst. In spite of knowing she was too young to rate serious interest on his part, Garner couldn't resist basking in such youthful vivacity. The girl smiled. Garner almost flinched in the face of that beaming smile directed at Cliff.

"Thank you." The girl smiled up at Dolly when the glass of water plunked down on the table. "If it isn't too much trouble, may I please have some fried eggs and hash browns?"

"Ain't no hash browns in this place," Dolly said, with enormous contempt for the very concept of hash browns. "You'll eat grits with breakfast like everyone else, or you'll eat nothin'. "That's the menu. Take 'em or leave 'em."

"Grits," the girl repeated. Another beaming smile spread over her face. "I'll take them. Thank you so much for mentioning them."

Dolly glowered. "Shouldn't have to mention grits on a breakfast order."

"Come on, Dolly," Garner coaxed. "Can't you see she's a Yankee? How's she supposed to know every breakfast down here comes with grits and only grits?"

Dolly scowled, but her voice lost some of its bite.

"She could look at the menu for starters," she said and stalked back to the counter.

To Garner's surprise, the girl's dancing blue eyes followed Dolly. Her mouth twitched with enjoyment. The realization that this girl had the most kissable lips he'd ever seen was like a kick in the gut to him. Since when had he gone around ogling teenyboppers?

The girl's laughing gaze met his, then Cliff's, and the two broke into outright laughter. Garner wondered what it would feel like to be able to laugh like that. He was surprised to note he felt mildly jealous of Cliff, because Cliff could laugh so easily with this young girl.

"Is she always like that?" the girl asked.

"I've lived here five years," Cliff said solemnly, "and she hasn't changed a bit during that time."

"I've lived here most of my life, and she hasn't changed since I was a kid," Garner agreed, studying the girl closely.

She smiled back at him. Her eyes widened, but to give her credit, she employed no coy come-ons. Garner frowned, remembering how he'd caught a glimpse of himself in the bathroom mirror that morning and had decided he was beginning to look saturnine. In his opinion, there was nothing about him worthy of feminine admiration. A wise female would leave him alone.

"She must own the place," the girl said. "By the way, how does one eat grits?"

"It depends on how thick they are," Garner said. "The proper consistency of grits is a philosophical matter of great seriousness to connoisseurs of Southern cooking."

She gave him a beaming smile. "I can't wait to try them. This is so exciting."

Exciting? Eating grits? Garner studied her again. There was such a thing as an excess of enthusiasm. Especially when it made a man in his early thirties feel like a dour sixty-year-old.

Still, she appeared to be enjoying the exchange for what it was worth, and to have no feminine designs on him. Or was she just being exceptionally clever?

"Not getting any grits at all is a matter of even greater seriousness," Cliff said, looking regretfully at his plate.

"Shut up, Cliff," Garner said. "When you've taken off those ten pounds, you can have grits again. But I'd advise you to leave off the butter—"

"Not now," Cliff said, groaning. "This is my brother-in-law, Garner Holt, the resident health nut. If he mentions butter one more time in my hearing, I'm going to go berserk."

The girl smiled sympathetically. "I know exactly what you mean. I'm from California, and everyone there is counting fat or carb grams except me. You can't even buy a hamburger without being made to feel guilty by all the vegans." She rolled her eyes. "And don't get me started on the no-gluten freaks."

"No wonder I'm always on a guilt trip." Cliff fixed a meaningful stare on Garner. "Hamburgers are my favorite food, and my brother-in-law here acts like I'll die tomorrow if I eat one."

Garner ignored him and focused on the girl's delicious gurgle of laughter. Her unbridled joy in life made him long for something he had lost years ago. He stared at her full, smiling lips and wished she was old enough to date. He hadn't been interested in a woman in the past two years, but he'd love to spend some time in this girl's company, getting his battery recharged, so to speak.

The girl looked at Garner reproachfully. "I used to leave pizza boxes and French-fry cartons lying around my office in hopes that they'd keep the resident health freaks on the other side of my door."

"Did it work?" Cliff asked.

"Does it work with him?" she asked, nodding at Garner.

"It gets me a nice lecture on the fat and salt content of French fries and pizza slices," Cliff said mournfully. "What kind of work did you do in California?"

"I was a ... an office worker." Her smile bloomed forth once more. "I do hope they have lots of offices around here. I'm looking for a job."

That did it. Garner slid out of the booth, clutching the envelope with its precious contents. "See you later, Cliff. I've got to get busy on some telephone calls."

"I'm coming. I'm coming." Cliff cast one more glance of dislike at the remains of the chicken breast on his plate. "It was nice meeting you. You've just moved here? We hope you enjoy living in Smackover."

"Oh, I love it already," the girl said, beaming at them. "I adore the flowers and the big shade trees. Now, if I can just find a good job … "

"Try one of the employment agencies in El Dorado," Garner recommended. "We'll be seeing you around, I'm sure."

He paid his bill, feeling vaguely guilty about his curt behavior. He had to squelch the desire to go back and say something friendly by reminding himself she was far too young for a man who felt as ancient as he did this morning.

"You're in another weird mood," Cliff complained. "That was the nicest-looking woman to come along in years, and you hardly gave her the time of day. What the hell happened to you in Dallas that made you hate women so much?"

Garner felt vaguely ashamed of himself. "I don't hate women." He glanced at the ad in his hand. "Although I'll have to rethink that statement if this résumé turns out to be from Mindy Adams."

Cliff shrugged good-naturedly. "Why not hire Mindy and be the boss from hell?"

"Because I'd have to spend a few minutes with her before I could fire her." Garner headed out the diner's glass door.

"Why not give our little friend a try?" Cliff nodded toward the wide, picture window. "She does office work."

Garner glanced back as they waited on the curb for a car to pass before they could cross the street. The young blond was sipping her water. Garner noted she wasn't watching them and felt vaguely surprised, both because she wasn't watching them, and because she was enjoying Smackover water. Garner had thought he was the only person who liked the strong sulfur taste.

"She probably answered the phone for her daddy during Spring Break," he said.

"Well?" Cliff grinned at him, brown eyes twinkling. "Wouldn't getting your phone answered help you out some?"

Garner laughed and slapped his brother-in-law's back. "You have a point there. If this ad doesn't pan out and your young friend shows up looking for a job, I'll let her take Mindy's calls. That'll get Mindy off my back, at least."

"You ought to take Mindy out a couple of times." Cliff pretended to have a great interest in Garner's battered green Blazer as they approached the driveway of the house that contained their offices. "You could stand a little social life, and Mindy would probably never bother you again once she finds out what a bear you really are."

"Come on, Cliff." Garner paused at the sidewalk leading to the front door. "Mindy's convinced she can make me over into a society lawyer, but I didn't know you and Laura thought I needed making over, too."

"We don't." Cliff headed down the driveway to the front door of his own office and said over his shoulder, "We just think it's time you quit mourning over whatever happened in Dallas and start living again."

Garner remained on the sidewalk with his mouth half-open and no retort available while Cliff opened a door at the side of the house and disappeared from sight.

Garner shoved his hands in his pockets. So. Everyone thought he was mourning his dead marriage and his dead corporate law career. Maybe it was time he did something about that misconception.

But not with Mindy Adams.

The young blond in the diner across the street passed fleetingly through his mind. Garner took wistful note of the faint desire to get to know her better. It was too bad she was so young. By the time she was old enough for Garner to ask out, she'd have lost that attractive zest for life.

Garner entered the small front room that served as a reception area, refusing to glance toward the unoccupied secretary's desk that held central position. He went into his own office, tossed the résumé down on the desk in the single bare spot he maintained for actual work, and studied it once more.

He dialed the number, conscious of a curious feeling of impending … something. He couldn't call it disaster. It was more like fate, or destiny, or some other approaching event that would change his life forever.

He ignored the craven impulse to hang up the phone. He had to have a secretary, at least for long enough to clean up some of the paperwork inundating him.

While he waited, he surveyed his surroundings. If he wanted impending disaster, he need look no further than his own office. Papers, legal tomes, and thick file folders representing current and settled cases were stacked everywhere. The wastebasket brimmed over with his aborted attempts at typing his own documents.

Also, the floor could use a good sweeping, and every surface needed dusting. Garner shrugged. If he managed to get a secretary, he'd be able to rehire his old cleaning service. The service had quit a month ago because of the impossibility of cleaning around the stacks of books lining the floor of his office.

Garner had only been practicing law in his hometown of Smackover, Arkansas, for two years, but a visitor to the office would have thought it far longer. Never a neatness fanatic, Garner preferred to stack things where he could lay his hands on them. The problem was, many of the surrounding stacks contained folders and papers he no longer needed to lay his hands on.

Garner studied the résumé once more as he counted the third ring. It was amazing how three months without a secretary could back things up, even in a small office like his.

And now he'd received this résumé with its promise of succor. Garner held his breath while the other phone shrilled a fourth time.

You'd have thought secretaries were available for hire, even in a small place like Smackover, Garner thought resentfully. But that wasn't the way things were. People who claimed to be secretaries these days couldn't type, couldn't spell if they could type, and as for asking them to file a folder away in alphabetical order, forget it. In the past weeks, he'd given up on finding someone with computer skills or the ability to use a dictating machine. He was now willing to settle for a person who could use the old typewriter he kept for addressing envelopes.

The phone rang another ten times before Garner gave up at last and picked up the file of a case he needed to work on. After twenty futile minutes spent on that, when he realized the amount of typing that was going to be required before he could file the necessary motions, he tried the number once more.

On the third ring, a woman answered the phone in crisp, businesslike tones. "Miss Angelina Brownwood speaking."

In spite of himself, Garner's hopes rose. At least the woman knew how to answer the telephone, and she didn't mind having everyone know she was a "Miss" rather than a "Ms."

"I'm calling about the résumé you sent out," he said. "I'm a lawyer in need of a legal secretary who knows how to use a computer."

He sounded too eager. He should have beat around the bush a little and tried to feel out her skills and experience.

Miss Angelina Brownwood was silent a moment. Just as he was about to ask if she was the person who had sent out the résumé, she spoke.

"I'm a secretary who knows how to use a computer, although I've never done legal work before," she said, in cool, even tones. "May I know to whom I'm speaking, please?"

Garner concentrated hard on her voice but found himself unable to identify her accent. She was definitely what Southerners called a "Yankee," but that term was liberally applied to accents hailing from New England and the Midwest, all the way to California.

"I'm Garner Holt. My office is located on West Hickory Street, across the street from the New South Diner."

"I've seen the diner," she said, still cool and precise. "Very well, Mr. Holt. I'd better come in and discuss the job requirements with you. When would you like to see me?"

Just like that, Garner thought, amazed. No nonsense. No equivocating. His heart beat fast with hope. But she was bound to be in enormous demand with some of the local business offices.

Unless she was an ax murderer. Garner looked around his dusty, cluttered office once more. But if she could clear up some of this mess …

"How long have you been a secretary, Miss Brownwood?"

"Five years," she said. "How long have you been a lawyer?"

Garner blinked at the wall, which held his framed diplomas and certifications. "About seven years," he said drily.

Having her as his secretary was probably going to be like having a tough maiden aunt who saw through you to the bone, Garner decided. No matter how much you loved her, you were always terrified she was going to take you over, body and soul.

In the corner, a tottering pile of old newspapers and legal briefs suddenly gave up the good fight and spilled onto the floor.

Maybe someone needed to take him over. Or, at least, take his office over.

She was perfect. He was tempted to offer her the job right now, but supposed he should at least ask about her skills to try to preserve some dignity. "Do you know how to use VP-Base and Microsoft Word?"

"Of course," she said. She recited an entire list of other programs she used, including two he had never heard of before.

"Oh." Garner wondered what they were for and decided not to ask.

He glanced at the résumé more carefully. To his surprise, it stated that she'd graduated college—Stanford University, at that—six years ago. Younger than he'd expected. At twenty-seven she was old enough to have some sense, and young enough to have some stamina. But why would an Ivy League grad be looking for a secretarial position?

"I didn't realize they taught secretarial courses at Stanford," he commented. "No wonder you have so many computer-related skills."

She coughed delicately. "Exactly." Was that relief he heard? "Stanford is rather … computer-oriented. Don't worry, Mr. Holt. I'm quite skilled at what I do."

He blinked at her silky-voiced assurance and wondered briefly what Miss Brownwood looked like. Not that it mattered. He had three cases coming to trial in the next few weeks, and needed help. He didn't care what the woman—or man—he hired looked like if they could type at least 50 words per minute.

"I'm sure you are, Miss Brownwood," he said. "That's all I need to know for right now. I'll see you at two o'clock sharp on Wednesday. Bring another copy of your résumé along, please."

It wasn't until he'd hung up that Garner realized she had sounded a bit eager to bypass any further discussion of her academic career.

Perhaps she had flunked. Perhaps she had never received a degree. Surely a place like Stanford didn't have the associate degree programs popular at many community colleges.

What did he care? Garner asked himself and decided against calling Stanford. Lots of good secretaries had never gone to college at all. Either she could do the work, or she couldn't. In the meantime, he needed a secretary, and Miss Angelina Brownwood was a secretary.

Garner opened a desk drawer and dropped the résumé into the overflowing desk drawer. God bless the United States Postal Service, he thought, grinning at his own silliness. Just when he'd given up hope, the solution to his problem appeared in an ordinary envelope in the day's stack of mail.

He peered over the tall stack of folders on his desk at the crumpled paper lying on the floor beside the trash can. A man who'd been without a secretary for three months had a right to act a little silly, but in the meantime, maybe he'd better do a little picking up and straightening. He didn't want to make a bad impression the minute she walked in.

He opened the drawer and gazed at the résumé once more. If Miss Angelina Brownwood worked out, he was having that sucker framed, by God.

Chapter 2

"Good secretaries are always in demand."

Angie Brownwood walked up the sidewalk to Garner Holt's office reciting the quote from one of her ten well-studied secretarial manuals. Her stomach persisted in experiencing a bad case of butterflies in spite of this assurance of her desirability as an employee.

She knew the man might take one look at her and realize she'd lied about almost everything in her exquisitely typed résumé—especially if he realized he'd already met her that morning and had been vastly unimpressed. Thank goodness she had noted the house the two men had entered across the street and the names on the two signs outside it. Otherwise, she might have been caught by surprise.

"The professional secretary takes care to always dress in a professional manner."

She'd violated that one right off the bat, forgetting how noticeable she, a stranger, would be in a town of only a couple of thousand inhabitants.

But Angie Brownwood of the shorts and unstyled hair had metamorphosed into the glamorous Miss Angelina Brownwood, Executive Secretary. If her luck held, Garner Holt might never connect her with the woman he'd met that morning in the diner.

Angie took a deep, steadying breath and studied Garner Holt's office. The small wood frame house, typical of the area of mixed businesses and residences, was newly painted. Angie found it enchanting and homelike.

If she hadn't had that two o'clock appointment, she'd have stood outside and admired the bed of wildly blooming salvia and larkspur along the front of the house. She breathed in the summer-scented Arkansas air and enjoyed a sense of peace she'd never experienced before.

A battered green Chevrolet Blazer was parked in the driveway, with a red bicycle parked beside it. Two discreet signs hung on a wrought-iron post, one directing her toward the front door of the house to Garner Holt, Attorney-At-Law. The other directed her around the side of the house to the office of Clifford Jones, Certified Public Accountant.

Cliff had been sweet and friendly, but Garner had behaved as though he had a chronic case of indigestion, especially when he looked at her. Angie couldn't blame him. She had looked like a high-school refugee with no taste and less intelligence.

Angie pushed open the front door and stepped inside, blinking rapidly behind her new eyeglasses. She had dreamed of an executive suite in a corporate high-rise, where she could glide softly across thick, muted carpets and deliver cups of steaming coffee and perfectly typed documents on watermarked paper to distinguished businessmen and women behind glass-topped executive desks in wide, spacious offices.

Instead, she stood in the domain of a pack-rat. It looked like a records dump instead of an office. Once the living room of a residence, the outer office featured a desk obliterated by stacks of files and books, and two large file cabinets. Even the leather sofa and the two easy chairs for clients held stacks of books.

The professional secretary values order and her surroundings reflect that.

So much for that one. If she had any sense, she'd flee the scene and go home to await another call.

A movement to her left caught her eye. She turned toward a smaller room just off the larger room she stood in. The small room had probably once been the master bedroom of the house. It now served as her would-be employer's inner sanctum. She watched as a man arose from behind mountains of books.

And all her senses screamed: *Abandon hope, all ye who hang out here.*

•••

Garner heard the door open and close.

"Come in," he said, and rose swiftly. He had to stand so he could see over the stacks.

Before he could do more than think, *At last*, Miss Angelina Brownwood turned fully toward him.

Garner couldn't believe his eyes. He'd prayed for a secretary, and God had delivered him a super-secretary, at least judging from her appearance.

Angelina Brownwood wore a white linen suit with a pale blue silk blouse, along with high-heeled brown pumps and a jewel-toned scarf knotted at her throat. Her pale blond hair was pinned in a precise French twist at the back of her head. Her face was exquisitely but delicately made-up, and her short nails were painted a pale, unobtrusive pink. The crowning touch to her appearance was a pair of thin-rimmed, tortoise-shell glasses that added to the impression of elegant, businesslike efficiency.

She was perfect, Garner realized in stunned silence. Too perfect. She was so beautifully precise, she took his breath away. He could tell by looking at her that he probably couldn't afford the salary she'd request, and a woman like her would never consent to do something about his piles of books and folders. She'd tell him to hire a maid.

Damn.

She was here though. Garner supposed he might as well interview her. He cleared his throat.

• • •

"Mr. Holt?" Angie asked, lifting delicate brows.

Her heart fluttered. Why didn't he say something? After all the time and effort she'd put into choosing clothing that projected the image of a top-flight executive secretary, she couldn't imagine why he looked so stunned.

Maybe he recognized her. Angie's breathing went shallow. Her palms felt clammy. Her heartbeat probably showed through the discreet blue silk of her blouse.

He reached for a chair near his desk. Angie breathed easier. He wasn't going to throw her out. She thanked the impulse that had guided her to add a pair of glasses to her secretarial outfit.

"Come on in and sit down, Miss Brownwood."

He smiled, and the brooding look she was beginning to think was his habitual expression vanished, replaced by a formidable charm. It was as if the sun had come out and chased off the clouds.

Respect your employer. The professional secretary does not allow a warmer attraction to develop.

Angie tried not to stare. Her ten well-studied secretarial manuals had been clear on the point of romances between secretaries and bosses, but recalling quotes on the subject of romantic feelings wasn't much help in getting her careening thoughts back under rigid control.

"I suppose you can see why I'm needing a secretary," he went on.

She forced her frozen fingers to release the doorknob and walk toward him. When she'd fantasized about her new career, she had imagined a boss exactly like the man facing her. He was tall and leanly built, and his shoulders were broad and well-muscled. Instead of a business suit, he wore a blue work-shirt, a pair of old jeans, and a pair of scuffed cowboy boots. His golden tan signified he spent as much time as possible outdoors. His thick, brown hair was brushed casually back from a high forehead. Broad, dark brows framed eyes that were the silver-gray color of a rain pool reflecting sunlight, and his wide, mobile mouth was grooved at the sides.

She even liked his slow Southern drawl, so different from her own crisp diction. She could listen to him all day.

If she got the chance.

If she could persuade him to hire her. She thought how she could project an attitude of dignified desire for the job.

His desk sat in a light-filled room lined with crowded bookshelves. The desk was heaped with precise stacks of file folders and more books. Garner retained a couple of empty square feet in the center of the desk. She seized on that.

"It looks more as though you need an expert file clerk." Angie's gaze wandered suggestively around the room. "I'm very good at … sorting files."

Her gaze focused on the computer on his desk. Within seconds, she had calculated its speed, power, and memory and pronounced it outmoded. But she could deal with an old computer. A good secretary such as she intended to be could deal with anything.

"Is it that obvious?" He laughed and gestured at a chair, not noticing at first it was piled high with books. He lifted the books off and placed them carefully on the floor beside his desk. "I'll do anything before I start filing folders. As for the books." He gestured at the books piled everywhere. "An elderly friend retired and gave me his law library. Unfortunately, I have yet to get around to buying shelves for it."

His eyes, she saw, were focused upon her white linen suit. Perhaps he was thinking he needed a secretary who would roll up her sleeves and do some house-cleaning in addition to her secretarial chores. Angie hastened to suggest she was the woman for the job.

"We'll have to order some shelves right away," she said.

The professional secretary's attitude should include an enthusiasm for taking on new assignments.

But not this much enthusiasm, Angie added privately. She strove to keep her eagerness in check. At the moment, she wasn't sure why she wanted this job. She only knew she wanted it.

She seated herself gracefully. "Once we get those books and folders off your furniture, you'll have more space for work."

Being a secretary was going to be more fun than she'd thought. She'd enjoy bringing order to this scene of chaos. She'd enjoy basking in this man's rare smiles when she did her job well. And she intended to do her job very well indeed.

"Did you bring another copy of your résumé?" Garner went to sit behind his desk, still staring at her.

Angie wondered again where she'd gone wrong. Nothing could have been more businesslike than the white linen suit and the pale blue silk blouse. She wore unobtrusive tiny, gold balls in her earlobes and a single gold seal ring on her right hand. Even her watch was a masterpiece of plain gold simplicity.

Although she had been guilty of enhancing the color of her hair before she left California—if he considered the lightening of one's hair a crime—it had been an expert job. Angie had checked herself time and time again in her full-length mirror and could find no fault in her appearance.

But maybe Garner did. She swallowed hard. If he refused to hire her, she'd lose a job she already coveted with all her heart. She reached inside the flat, leather briefcase she'd brought in lieu of a purse.

Her hand shook so badly, she could hardly produce the sheet of paper that had been the object of more research and more creativity than anything she had ever written in her life. What if the woman outlined on this résumé came across as overqualified for the job? Garner received the single, exquisitely printed sheet, still staring at her. "This may seem a little personal, but what brings you to Smackover? You look like someone who's used to big-city life."

"Oh, I can fit in everywhere." Angie gave him a hopeful smile then caught herself and smoothed out her expression. "My great-aunt died and left me her house here in Smackover. About that time, I was … I decided to leave my job in Palo Alto. It seemed a good time to make a major change." Angie had no intention of telling him just how major the change had been. "I love it here. Everyone has been so friendly."

Garner blinked and shook his head. "Who was your aunt?"

"She was actually my father's aunt. Her name was Loretha Culp."

"Of course. Miss Culp was a friend of my grandfather's." Garner sounded surprised. "My sister and I were sorry to hear of her passing."

Angie inclined her head. "Thank you. She used to send me dolls every Christmas during my childhood."

Now why had she told him that? Angie asked herself. It was that voice of his, slow and hypnotic. If she didn't watch out, he'd soon hypnotize her into telling him a lot of other things he didn't need to know.

"So tell me about your previous job." Garner stared down at her résumé in a baffled way. "What kind of work did you do?"

"I did … the usual secretarial work," Angie said, thrown off balance. "The filing was much like what you need done—lots of books and folders that needed organizing. Organizing files is my specialty."

It wasn't exactly a lie. Angie crossed her fingers in her lap and hid them with her other hand.

"Is that right?" Garner sounded as if he couldn't believe his ears. "What business was the company in?"

Angie had prepared herself thoroughly for this question. "The only companies I've ever worked for have been software companies." She managed a deprecating shrug. "A lot of the industry in Palo Alto revolves around computer technology."

"'Van Holden Software,'" Garner read aloud thoughtfully. "What programs do they put out?"

"Oh." Angie thought fast. "Mr. Van Holden used to be the chief systems programmer with BrownWare, but he left them several months ago. He's working on an—er—advanced grammar checking program."

"BrownWare? Isn't that the big database company?"

Angie wished she'd never mentioned BrownWare, but it was too late to take it back. "Yes, it is. Mr. Van Holden got fed up with databases and decided to do something about grammar. He said it's terrible the way people have let their grammar skills deteriorate."

She winced inwardly. Peter Van Holden had never typed a sentence correctly in his entire life. He hadn't needed to. But she'd caught a glimpse of a box on Garner's shelf that contained a grammar-checking program. She didn't dare tell him Van Holden Software's true goal in the business world, which was to claim half the assets of BrownWare and half-interest in the copyright to BrownWare's major programs.

Garner stared at her a moment, then looked back at her résumé. Angie had spent many loving hours on that résumé. It was professionally printed on heavy bond paper, and she hoped just the look of it would convince a prospective employer of the quality of her secretarial skills. So far, she couldn't decipher the expression on Garner's face.

"Before Van Holden Software, you were with Glen Goodwin Enterprises. I see Goodwin is now a full-time professor at California Institute of Technology. What sort of work did you do for him?"

Angie caught her breath. Why on earth had she mentioned Cal Tech?

Because she had no other job references she could trust to say what she instructed them to say, that was why, and she had to list some phone numbers. Glen couldn't give her a reference unless her prospective employers could get hold of him.

"Mr. Goodwin was a graduate student—um—researching electronic networking at the time." Angie could have groaned aloud at this lame explanation and hoped Garner was as ignorant as most people of the more arcane elements of computer technology. "I kept him organized, typed his notes—um—filed his correspondences … that sort of thing."

She hadn't realized how hard it was to be creative with her job experience in spite of having practiced her spiel. She hadn't expected Garner's interest, or that she'd be rattled enough to mention BrownWare. Angie could have kicked herself.

"Both these guys are known computer wizards," Garner said. "I suppose you picked up all sorts of computer tricks ordinary people wouldn't know."

"Oh, yes." Angie was almost overcome with gratitude. "I did. They were always looking over my shoulder and trying to show me better ways to do things on the computer."

That was more like it. Angie cast a beaming smile at Garner. Now she had a ready explanation if Garner should catch her doing something esoteric with his computer.

Garner seemed to freeze. Then he quickly dropped his gaze to the résumé on his desk before he once more studied her from the top of her shining, pale-blond head to the tips of her equally shining brown pumps.

"Is something wrong?" She watched him with outward concern while she berated herself for that smile. Trust something so silly to give her away.

"Wrong?" Garner coughed. "Not at all. That is … No, nothing's wrong. How many years' experience did you say you have?"

Angie paled. Just as she'd feared, he had recognized her. She had added a year to her work history so she could say she'd been a secretary for five years, assuming she had graduated from a college secretarial course at the age of twenty-two. She had calculated everything very carefully. What had tipped him off to that extra year?

"Five years." She drew herself up and tried for a hint of frost. "Didn't I remember to state that clearly?"

After all the calculation she had done, she knew she had. Part of the problem centered around the fact that she began college at the age of sixteen, which she knew was unusual. She had planned her résumé to project a woman who was thoroughly normal, but highly skilled.

"Here it is. Sorry." Garner looked at her with that rising-sun smile. "You have such a youthful air I thought you were much too young to have this much experience. Although, I'm sure you're very qualified. That is—" He stopped and stared at her.

Angie sucked in her breath. She'd lost the job, and all because he had recognized her. Her heart sank to her feet. Her first interview and she had already failed to impress her prospective employer because she'd been dumb enough to appear in a public place wearing shorts and no makeup.

The secretarial manuals were right. A professional secretary could never let down her guard.

"I *am* qualified, Mr. Holt." She rose with an attempt at dignity. "I'd have worn a gray wig and orthopedic shoes if I'd realized you wanted someone over sixty for the job."

Garner shot to his feet. He reached toward her and knocked a stack of books off his desk. "Wait. Where are you going? We haven't even discussed salary yet."

"Yee-ow!" Two heavy tomes landed on her right foot.

Off-balance already because of her high-heeled pumps, she jumped back and staggered into the stack of books Garner had transferred off her chair. The stack toppled onto her left foot. She tumbled backwards, amid the books and folders, and a cloud of dust rose about her. Her glasses flew off her face and skidded across the room.

"Oh, Lord." Garner rushed around to help her up. "Are you hurt?"

Angie propped herself up on her elbows and looked at the papers scattered around her. "I'm okay, but your folders aren't." She sneezed violently and shoved down her skirt, which had hiked up to expose a good portion of her thigh and her lacy slip.

Two of the file folders had spilled their contents on the floor around her. Angie sneezed again and reached for one.

"I'll take care of it," Garner said. "Here. Let me help you up."

Her head spun when he lifted her to her feet in one smooth motion. She swayed, conscious of her foot and ankle.

"Easy," he said. "I've got you."

He did, Angie realized wildly. She rested in his arms. It was a moment frozen in time, something she'd never experienced before. In her usual textbook manner, Angie tried to sort out, analyze, and explain the feelings rioting through her.

She had been kissed before, on rare occasions, and had experienced her share of hugs. Yet, those feelings weren't the same. She felt … helpless. She found herself paralyzed by an emotion she tentatively defined as a desire to stay right there.

Her face was pressed against his chest. Angie felt the scratch of his white cotton shirt against her face and breathed in the scent of fresh starch mixed with a unique odor of male and spicy aftershave.

She'd thought the scents of Arkansas roses and pine trees were the most invigorating scents on earth, but it seemed she'd been mistaken. This particular combination of scents made her feel strange, as if she wanted something badly, but she didn't know what it was she wanted.

What was more, she could hear his heart beating beneath her ear, a strong, steady, reassuring sound, and Angie discovered the sound gave her tremendous comfort.

What she couldn't understand was why this combination of scents and sound and feelings was creating such a clamor of longing and emotion inside her. Worse, she wanted him to hold her even closer. She wanted to *kiss* him.

What, she wondered, did an ethical professional secretary do now?

Withdraw her application so she could feel free to kiss him, thus losing a perfectly good job opportunity?

Strive for high standards always, her manuals said.

Angie sighed. High standards were such a pain.

Garner set her back on the chair, frowning. Angie glanced up cautiously. Garner's face was set in the familiar, brooding expression once more. She rubbed her throbbing foot and noticed a patch of dirt decorating her formerly pristine white linen skirt.

"You know, you really do need to do something about these books," she said. Since she wasn't going to get the job, she might as well let him know what he was missing. "They're a menace to your clients. Besides, it's a crime to treat valuable books like that. I'd have all those books on shelves by tomorrow afternoon." She glanced down. "And just look at this floor. You ought to be ashamed of receiving clients in a room that looks as though it hasn't been swept in a month."

Garner cast a glance at her white linen outfit. "Legal work generates a lot of dust, and I've been too busy to sweep lately."

She sneezed. "I'm surprised you haven't succumbed to a major allergy attack."

"Uncle," Garner said, grinning that sunrise grin of his. "The job is yours. If you want it."

"Of course, I want it." Angie sneezed violently and dusted at her skirt. "Why do you think I'm here?"

She was past caring about the bland facade the perfect executive secretary was supposed to maintain. That fall had done something to her attitude and made her revert back to type. She had better go home and get herself back into correct professional order before she showed up to assume her duties.

"Point taken." He hesitated, staring at her face. "Are you sure you're over sixteen?"

"I'll have you know, I am twenty-si—seven years old. Furthermore, I am a graduate of Ca—Stanford University's business assistant program. I have been out of school and in the job market for five years."

Garner actually took a few steps back. Angie almost bit her tongue in order to stop herself from giving him the lecture that wanted to burst forth about the length of her experience, including the truth she was determined to hide.

"I believe you," he said hastily. "It's just that you look a lot younger than your age without your glasses."

"My glasses." Angie looked around for them. She wasn't used to wearing glasses and had temporarily forgotten about them. "They must have slid underneath something when I fell."

"Here they are." Garner located the glasses in the rear corner of his office behind his desk. He studied the lenses a moment then brought them over and placed them in her hand. "Aren't you going to ask me about the salary?"

Angie stuck the glasses on her nose. "What salary are you willing to pay?"

She didn't care. She needed a job, and she wanted *this* job.

Besides, she didn't need to work, at least not right away, thanks to a computer game she had sold that was currently generating huge royalties. She could afford to wait for exactly the right job, and so far as she was concerned, this was the job.

Garner named the salary, described the conditions under which she'd earn a bonus, detailed the job requirements, and went into detail about vacation time.

Angie knew the salary was far below her former pay, but she also figured the peace of mind was more than worth it. "Fine. I'll take it. When can I start?"

"Tomorrow morning." Garner looked at her with a strange combination of suspicion and eagerness. "Be here at nine."

"Are you sure? Don't you get here earlier?" She recalled that Garner and Cliff had been eating breakfast in the café at seven that very morning.

"I do, but there's no reason why you should." He looked closely at her eyes. "You look as if you could use a little extra sleep."

Angie ignored that in favor of casing his office and listing in her mind where she intended to begin. "We have a lot of work to do if we want to improve your efficiency."

Garner leaned back in his chair, studying her. "Calm yourself, Miss Brownwood. You don't want me to think you're too enthusiastic, do you?"

"I've always enjoyed setting things right." Angie struggled to rein herself in. "Before any secretarial work can be done, the office will have to be straightened. It's a challenge, but one that I can meet."

Garner looked at the books and folders scattered over the floor. "I'll admit that this office is a challenge, but I'm surprised a professional of your obvious caliber would be so eager to tackle what amounts to heavy-duty housework."

"I've never minded rolling up my sleeves and doing a little physical labor." Angie hoped she sounded sufficiently haughty. "In this case, I'm considering it part of the job."

Garner looked at her as though he wondered about her sanity. Or maybe her motives, Angie thought. Not that she cared. This job marked the beginning of a whole new life for her, and she did not intend to muff it. This was going to be *fun*.

"I'll be here when you are," she said. "The first thing I'll need to do is get some shelves delivered."

Garner gave her a silky smile. "Oh, no, you don't. The first thing you'll need to do, my dear Miss Brownwood, is type a few letters."

Angie blinked at him and felt a huge smile coming on in spite of her efforts to tame it down. Trust her to almost forget her true calling as a secretary in the midst of her desire to tackle the mess in Garner's office.

"Certainly, Mr. Holt," she said, with formal emphasis. "In fact, maybe I'd better get started on the office this afternoon so I'll have a suitable space cleared on the desk for actual secretarial work."

"Also," he added, frowning, "I can't go around calling you Miss Brownwood unless clients are present. Do you go by Angelina?"

Maintain a professional relationship with your employer at all times.

Angie blinked, nonplussed. She'd love to have this man call her Angie. Besides, this small-town law office didn't really require the formality of a big-city corporation.

"You can call me Angie," she said, smiling agreeably.

The manuals were right about one thing. Having her employer call her Angie definitely led to unprofessional thoughts. But he was the boss, she reminded herself. She was paid to do as he requested.

He regarded her again with that peculiar mix of suspicion and eagerness. Maybe he wondered if she could even type.

Angie smiled at him cheerfully. She'd show him. She'd show everybody, including certain persons left behind in Palo Alto, California.

"I'll be back in half an hour," she said. "If we're going to get a space on my desk cleared off by tomorrow, I'll need to get started right away."

Chapter 3

Angie went home and gleefully changed clothes. This was an opportunity to wear the beautiful trousers that went with the linen suit. They were much more suitable for the afternoon's activities than a business suit.

Actually, the only thing suitable for the afternoon she planned was a pair of old jeans and an equally ancient T-shirt, but not for anything was Angie going to let down her professional guard. Never again, she vowed. Only in her own yard would she wear casual clothes. Her days of going to work in comfortable jeans and T-shirts were over.

She had chosen the large bedroom at the back of the old-fashioned little house. She liked it because it looked out at the sunny backyard. Angie had discovered she loved sitting on the back steps gazing at her own yard. Owning property was a new sensation in her young life, and she mentally thanked Great Aunt Loretha for making it possible.

Casting a possessive glance at the backyard, Angie plucked her secretarial manuals from their place of honor on the bookshelves. Thanks to them, she knew everything necessary to build a satisfying new career upon the foundation of the computer skills she already possessed.

She opened each manual and reviewed the section on professional relations with her boss. She hadn't expected any problems, but then, she hadn't expected a boss like Garner Holt. In hopes of increasing her professionalism, she polished the plain glass lenses of her glasses and centered them carefully on her nose.

She returned the manuals to their shelves and went into the master bedroom, where she'd temporarily set up her laptop computer on the old-fashioned dresser, and her laser printer on top of an antique chest-of-drawers.

She stepped around boxes packed with her collection of books and textbooks and flicked on the computer. When it had booted, she brought up the inter-office messaging program she had used in Palo Alto and paged her friend, Fonda Clancy.

When Fonda answered, she typed hastily, *Guess what? I just landed a job.*

That fast? Fonda returned. *I didn't even know they had your kind of job in a town that little. Or are you still intending to be a secretary?*

Angie debated telling Fonda all about her new job and her handsome boss, but something told her to keep that quiet for the time being. Fonda did not believe in mixing business with pleasure and would consider the handsome boss a liability.

If anyone asks, she typed, *tell them I've got a job with an Arkansas-based computer chip maker, and I'm seeing to it that BrownWare and VP-Base are blacklisted with every major Arkansas business I can locate.*

Fonda returned: *His Highness actually told Ripplecroft he'd personally pull VP-Base from every computer they manufactured if they hired you. Johnny Croft is so mad, he wants to hire you on the spot. Are you sure you want to go through with leaving your whole life behind like this? Maybe you should talk to Johnny, just in case.*

I was never more sure of anything in my life, Angie typed back, more certain than ever she'd been right to leave BrownWare and her former career far behind.

She had left California in the nick of time. Apparently, her father had gone ballistic, but she wasn't there this time to bear the brunt of his fury.

Here's the latest update on the situation, Fonda typed, and proceeded to fill Angie in on developments at BrownWare, which Angie had left barely one week ago.

Angie wasn't interested in hearing the increasingly acrimonious hell-raising at BrownWare. She had more important things to do, but Fonda was a good friend. She exclaimed suitably then logged off with relief.

She swiftly scanned the messages in her e-mail inbox. Thank goodness she'd had the foresight to tell everyone at BrownWare to e-mail her. Since her cell phone had no service here, she'd bought a new smart phone with local service, but no way was she giving the new number to anyone in Palo Alto.

"Got a phone call yesterday from some guy looking for you," Peter Van Holden had written. "It wasn't a prospective new employer, I hope. He didn't call back."

Angie replied that she'd just been hired by one Garner Holt, attorney-at-law, and reminded Peter of every favor he owed her from the five years of their association. Rereading Peter's message, she noted he'd misspelled several words and had left out most of the punctuation.

"Angie, darling, I'm worried about your father's attitude," her mother had written. "Are you sure you don't want to come back home? I'll insist Vernon rehire you, or else Stanford will reevaluate the use of VP-Base in their computer training courses."

Celia Brownwood, a full professor, taught radiation-physics at Stanford, and her recommendations carried a lot of weight among the senior faculty.

There was a lot more, but Angie scanned it swiftly and shuddered. She wrote Celia that VP-Base had enough troubles without being kicked off the Stanford campus and said she loved her new home in Arkansas. As for her father's attitude, she no longer found it bothersome.

There were several other messages from her former colleagues at BrownWare. Each told of a new and different atrocity perpetrated by Vernon Brownwood, who seemed to be on a tear now that he'd fired his own daughter and accused her of disloyalty to the firm he'd sweated blood to found.

Angie thanked each writer and privately wished they'd make their complaints to a major computer publication. *She* was no longer interested, especially when she knew they hoped she'd return and draw Vernon's fire once more, thus smoothing the waters for them.

Thank goodness she had an interesting new job and a glamorous new career. She shut down her computer and sailed out the door happily, pausing only to exchange insults with a resident mockingbird that had taken exception to Angie's arrival. She even loved the hostile Mr. Mockingbird today, the first official day of her new life.

• • •

Garner looked up, surprised, when Angie walked back into his office. He was grumbling at his computer, cursing the fact that he needed the letter he was typing yesterday, and that his computer had picked today to act up.

"I'll need to know where you want me to buy the shelves." Angie fairly brimmed with enthusiasm. She cast a proprietary glance over the outer office. "By the time they're delivered, I should have the front office cleaned and ready for them."

Not unless she intended to clean all night, Garner thought grimly. He felt like an elderly curmudgeon in the presence of so much youthful joy and vigor.

He said nothing aloud, but his thoughts probably showed on his face as he assimilated the crisp, white linen trousers she wore. Obviously she didn't intend to do any real cleaning. Not in that outfit.

"I've got a better idea," he said. "Why don't you type this letter while I go buy the shelves?"

Angie came around his desk to peer over his shoulder at the computer screen. Her excitement, if anything, increased. "Is there a copy to follow?"

Garner gestured at the hand-scribbling that decorated a yellow legal pad. "Think you can read my writing?"

She smelled like lemon flowers. He stifled an urge to turn and pull her down onto his lap and absorb both her scent and her joyous spirit.

"Of course." Angie surveyed the hieroglyphics masquerading as handwriting with undimmed confidence.

He studied the glasses she wore and wondered again if they were real. When he had looked through them earlier, he'd have sworn they were plain glass. And if they were not real, then why on earth was she wearing phony glasses?

Maybe he'd better not worry about it until after she'd proven whether or not she could actually do secretarial work.

"Damned computer." Garner punched the save command, but the machine proved recalcitrant. If he wound up having to take the thing to the shop now of all days ...

"Here," Angie said. "I'll deal with it. I'm good with computers. You go buy those shelves. Tell them you want delivery tomorrow morning at nine o'clock on the dot."

Garner turned to look at her. He closed his mouth firmly on the urge to salute and say, "Yes, ma'am."

Angie smiled kindly at him. "You could probably use an afternoon out of the office. It's beautiful outside."

On that, Garner found himself in total agreement. "Angie ... "

He gave up. Telling his new secretary he was the boss when she'd ordered him to do exactly what he wanted to do probably wasn't the way to begin a working relationship. He got to his feet, stretched, and wondered if she really intended to clean his office in the two hours before five o'clock.

Angie settled in the chair before the computer. "If I can't do anything with this one, I'll use the one on my desk." She stared at the screen a moment then looked up at him. "The computer out front is a working computer, isn't it?"

"It was working when I last had a secretary." Annoyance at himself for noticing how well she filled out her trousers led him to attempt reclaiming his authority. "Clean off that desk of yours, first. It looks like a rabbit warren."

On that, he fled the office.

•••

Angie whipped around but all she saw was his back. She shrugged and returned her attention to the computer. She fully intended to clean the entire office. The desk would have to wait its turn. She had her own schedule.

As she had suspected, Garner had no idea how to treat a computer. The data on his hard disk was hopelessly fragmented, and the drive held no software with which to defragment it. Moreover, it was probably clogged and cluttered with temporary files from every website he had ever visited.

Clicking her tongue in disapproval, Angie opened never-before-touched programs on his hard drive and did what she could to remedy the problem. Then she returned to his word processing program to type his letter.

She printed it out proudly after cleaning and adjusting the printer, which wasn't in prime working condition, either. Then she printed out an envelope and called it quits. Even she had to admit she'd done a beautiful job. Her first secretarial duty, and she had succeeded. Angie printed a duplicate copy and stowed it in her briefcase as a memento.

Since there was so much to be done, she cleared the top of the desk that was to be hers, placing everything on the already crowded sofa. She might as well get the computer in order, since she was the one who was going to use it. Cleaning and defragmenting the hard drive would take a couple of hours at least, and that could be done in the midst of other cleaning chores.

Garner walked in two hours later and found her attacking the floor against the far wall with a broom. She nodded and smiled at him, then wondered why he seemed so fascinated by the computer screen.

She had no idea why. The computer was so old, it ought to be junked. She might have to start bringing her laptop to work if she hoped to get anything done, especially if her boss wanted her to research anything online.

Garner stared at the elderly computer. "How did you get that thing online? I thought it gave up the ghost a couple of years back."

"It's old, but it's not dead." Angie surprised herself, defending the old computer. "Part of the problem is that you don't have any of the latest Windows XP updates, including Service Pack Three. So I'm putting it on for you. Plus the hard drive was so full and so fragmented, it was lucky it could even boot up."

"I see."

Angie bit back a grin because it was obvious he didn't see at all.

He actually leaned over to stare at the winking pixels and squares that bounced around the screen. "What are you doing now?"

"I'm sweeping the floor."

"This is amazing," he said, indicating the screen. "Are you some sort of computer genius or something?"

Angie flushed. She could only feel thankful he was watching the computer screen rather than her. She had never dreamed he'd assume she had computer expertise just because she knew the basics of operating Windows XP.

"Not at all. I just opened the programs that are available on Windows and put them to work. We … er … learn this sort of thing at secretarial school, since computers are the office machine of choice these days."

"I was never able to figure out how to keep this computer running. In fact, my last secretary quit because of it." He looked up at her and grinned. "Among other things. She said the computer was the last straw."

"You should have ordered a new computer," Angie said. "Desktop models are really cheap now."

Garner said nothing. Angie bit back a smile upon realizing a new computer would not have changed the secretary's mind.

"I'll bet you keep up with all the new developments in computer technology," Garner said, still watching the computer screen as if mesmerized. "Do you own one of those smart phones that goes online for e-mail and social networking?"

"Cell phones are necessities these days." Angie said nothing about the state-of-the-art smart phone that currently resided in her purse and made a deprecating movement with her shoulders. "Mine is … reasonably smart."

"What about a Facebook page or a Twitter account?"

She gave him her best "Are you kidding?" look and reminded herself to change her Facebook page status to friends only. She had almost forgotten the fun prospective employers could have with would-be employees' Facebook pages.

Not that Garner would see anything entertaining on her page. He would, however, find out about the trouble at BrownWare that had resulted in her recent firing. Or her grand exit, depending on whose side you were on, she thought with wry humor.

Maybe she ought to take down her old Facebook page, just in case.

At least she'd had the good sense not to fool with a Twitter account, even though she knew all too well that the other

BrownWare engineers and employees were tweeting away about the latest fireworks in the upper echelons of management.

She so did not want to know what was happening at BrownWare. At the moment, she had too many other things to do and experiment with.

Except cooking, she reminded herself. She had just put a new app on her phone that promised to deliver recipes for whatever she wanted to cook. A good secretary, Angie figured, ought to know how to cook. Why she had decided this, she wasn't sure, other than the fact that Fonda, her father's secretary and her good friend, was an excellent cook. Therefore, she would learn how to cook, also. How hard could it be?

She glanced again at the computer on her desk that her boss still stood before in mesmerized silence. From the look of things, she might need the phone's capabilities just to do her daily work.

Either that or she would need an alternate computer. The small notebook computer she had bought last year for use in meetings would be perfect. It would fit in her briefcase.

On that thought, she turned a considering gaze upon the printer hooked to the desktop computer. It looked even more archaic than the computer, but if it worked, she could deal with it. Hopefully, she could find some drivers that would allow her notebook to control it. If not, she would get a cheap little inkjet printer.

She moved her broom closer to the desk and hovered there, all too conscious of the spicy scent of his aftershave, and watched Garner as he watched his old computer. His long, elegant fingers with their almond-shaped nails rested on the desktop, and she astonished herself by wondering what those fingers would feel like if he should stroke them over her skin.

Angie caught herself. A good secretary never fantasized about her boss. Or she didn't on her first day on the new job.

"What are you going to do to it after this?" Garner asked.

"Reboot and run a couple of other disk-fixing programs." Angie made a couple of half-hearted attempts at sweeping under the desk. "By the time I get through with it, it should be running as well as it's capable of running."

"I believe you." Garner turned to give her a respectful glance. "It seems I remember something about disk-maintenance programs. But that was a hundred years ago, and I expect the computer to just keep on running."

"Right. Like your car. No maintenance required."

"Not much, anyway," Garner said, grinning.

"You'll need to start running several programs on your computer every day when you finish your work. Otherwise, it'll quit on you when you need it most. I'll show you how." Angie ignored the advice from her secretarial manuals about taking too much authority upon herself, especially in front of the boss. It was obvious he needed help badly when it came to computers. "By the way, a Ms. Mindy Adams is supposed to call you back right about now."

On cue, the telephone on Angie's desk rang.

Garner regarded it with dislike. "Tell her I'm not expected back this afternoon."

"Is this a case where the secretary is expected to lie through her teeth for the boss?"

"Consider it the truth." He checked his watch. "The office just closed. This over-worked lawyer won't be in again until tomorrow morning."

"I don't think she's interested in legal advice." Angie picked up the phone. "Mr. Holt's office. Yes, Ms. Adams, I informed him of your call. He won't be in the office until tomorrow morning. Yes, I certainly will give him the message." She hung up. "There's a message on your desk. Ms. Adams is giving a party a week from Friday, and she isn't taking any excuses. You're expected to attend."

"Is that right?" Garner eyed the computer screen wistfully. "How about showing me how to operate the program you're running."

"Tomorrow," Angie said firmly. Tonight, she needed to reread the sections in her manuals about the awful things that happened to secretaries who fell for their bosses. "We're cleaning tonight, remember?"

Garner leaned back in the chair and studied her. "Didn't they teach you in secretarial school about the importance of catering to your boss?"

"My boss has already given me an ultimatum about cleaning this desk and this office."

She made herself ignore his silver-gray eyes and sensitive, bracketed mouth. She had a job to do, an interesting job. She had no time to dream about good-looking bosses.

"Now, Angie . . .

"Sorry, boss. This is a lot of dirt, and tomorrow morning, they're delivering those shelves. They *are* delivering the shelves tomorrow, aren't they? Then kindly vacate that desk, because this floor is about to be mopped."

"I don't believe this." Garner left the chair reluctantly and moved aside so she could attack the floor beneath the desk vigorously. "Are you really intending to stay here until this floor is clean?"

"Hey, Garner, I just got a call from Mindy Adams," Cliff Jones called from the front door. "Oh. Hello, ma'am. I didn't know Garner had anyone in here."

"Come on in and meet my new secretary." Garner backed off from Angie's ferociously wielded broom. "Miss Brownwood, meet my brother-in-law, Cliff Jones."

Cliff came in, eyeing Angie's elegant figure appreciatively. "Wow. A woman with a broom. This is a terrifying setup, Garner.

Miss Brownwood, you're the answer to a great many prayers, let me tell you."

Angie stopped sweeping long enough to shake his hand. "This office is a true challenge for a secretary with a passion for cleanliness and order. When we get the shelves in tomorrow, you won't recognize this office."

Cliff's jaw dropped.

"She's got all the computers cleaning and defragging," Garner said, indicating the desktop computer. "She actually got this one working again."

"Is she the one from the résumé?" Cliff stared at Angie, who went back to sweeping. "She looks familiar somehow."

Great, Angie thought, chastising herself yet again. One public appearance in shorts, and everyone of any importance in her new life saw and remembered the event.

• • •

Garner shook his head at Cliff. He'd already seen Angie didn't want him recognizing her. Why antagonize the secretary-from-heaven before she'd had a chance to straighten out his office and teach him a few things about computers?

"On the other hand," Cliff said swiftly, "I've been known to lose bits and pieces of my mind at odd times. At least, now I know why Mindy bothered to call *me*."

"Show us how to call up that disk-cleaning program, Angie," Garner urged. "I want Cliff to see this."

"Tomorrow," Angie said firmly. "Tonight, I have more important things on my mind, like getting ready for those shelves. Excuse me, please. I'll shut down the computer."

Garner swiveled to watch her fingers fly expertly over the keys, before hitting the master switch of an electrical strip. "Where'd you find that?"

"You had it stored in the bottom desk drawer." She indicated the drawer with a stern gesture. "What I want to know is why haven't you been using it?"

Garner glanced up in time to see his brother-in-law's silent whistle. "Darned if I know. Well, carry on, Angie. Come on in my office a minute, Cliff."

"Pleasure meeting you, Miss Brownwood." Cliff smiled at her. "I can see you're just what this office needs."

Cliff followed Garner into the other office, and Garner half-closed the door. "Well, what do you think?"

"Are you sure you want to know?" Cliff nodded his head at the door. "That one is a force to be reckoned with, mark my words. If you're not careful, she'll be going to court in your place. Have I seen her before?"

"That bad?" Garner laughed. "She does seem a mite determined for such a young thing, doesn't she?" He grinned and added, "Remember that young girl you were so impressed with this morning? The one who was tasting her first serving of grits?"

"You're kidding." Cliff whistled again. "So she's the one from the résumé."

"She does appear to know a lot about computers." Garner settled behind his desk and cast an indifferent glance at the three messages from Mindy Adams Angie had left for him. He picked up the letter Angie had typed and admired the beautiful formatting. "I figure she has an agenda of her own. Why else would she want this job?"

"Why, indeed?" Cliff took the other chair. "Now that we know she's a stranger in town—"

"Look at her, Cliff." He gestured toward the outer office. "Why would a woman like that take on a job in this picayune office?"

Garner dearly loved his sister and thought Cliff was the perfect man for her, but sometimes he found Cliff's complete lack of suspicion toward strangers a bit naïve.

"Yeah, and with a sleazy shyster such as yourself as boss. I guess I can see your point." Cliff leaned back, yawning. "Lord, I'll be glad when the quarter is over. These quarterly reports are killing me."

Garner reminded himself of the help Cliff had given him, unasked and without asking awkward questions, when he left Dallas and moved back to Smackover, not to mention the way he had stuck by Garner and Laura during the death of their father that occurred around the same time.

"Seriously, why would she take this job?" he argued, seeing Cliff was unconvinced. "That outfit she's wearing probably cost what she'll make in a couple of weeks working for me."

"Didn't she say she just moved here from California? Salaries were probably a lot higher out there." Cliff ran a hand through his curly hair and yawned again.

"She's up to something." Garner reread the letter she had typed. "She even used the printer to address the envelope. I've never figured out how to—Huh." He thrust the letter at Cliff. "Instead of 'arbitration,' she's got 'Arbitron.' Instead of 'abate,' she's got 'Seagate.'"

"Isn't Seagate one of those companies that make hard disk drives for computers?" Cliff took the sheet and read it swiftly. "Beautiful job otherwise. Are you sure she didn't type it off something you hand-wrote? Because if so…"

"Go ahead." Garner took the letter back. "Insult my writing. Seriously, Cliff. Take a good look at her and tell me why you think she's in this office."

"I already told you." Cliff looked over his shoulder obligingly but Angie wasn't visible. "She just moved here and she needed a job. It's probably as simple as that. And no one but you can read your handwriting."

Garner wished he could feel as sanguine. The feeling that there were major chunks missing from Angelina Brownwood's professional résumé had been growing all day. Her peculiar choice of words to fill spots where she couldn't read his writing added to the feeling.

"Then you don't think she took the job just to get the inside tips on one of my cases?" he asked. "I have that big case coming up in a couple of months—"

Cliff stared at him. "Inside tips? Jeez, Garner, are you defending Mafia dons or something? One of these days, you're going to have to tell me just what the hell happened in Dallas. You're going paranoid, buddy."

Garner felt faintly foolish. "Can you blame me? Why would a woman like her take a job here, unless she's a reporter? Either she's on the run, or she wants inside info."

"If it's a choice between the two, she must be on the run," Cliff said. "You ought to be glad you're so desirable and in the right business. Otherwise, you might never have gotten a good secretary."

"It isn't a joking matter," Garner said. "Who knows? She might be into white-collar crime."

"Yeah," Cliff dead-panned. "Hold onto your bank account."

As his bank account wasn't worth a decent white-collar criminal's attention, Garner felt even more foolish. But he still wondered just what Miss Angelina Brownwood was up to, and why she'd picked his office to do it.

•••

Just outside the door, Angie paused, broom in hand, and dropped all pretense of working. Who on earth did Garner Holt think he was?

If there hadn't been a grain or two of truth in his speech, Angie wouldn't have been nearly so angry. As it was, she swelled with righteous indignation and thought about marching in and telling him what he could do with his filthy office.

Instead, she turned and silently walked back to the other end of the room. Not for anything would she let him realize she'd overheard this conversation.

That did it. She'd allow herself to work for him for three months; she'd seek employment elsewhere after that. By then, she'd have gained enough new skills to call herself a legal secretary.

Garner was suspicious, which meant he would probably research her name on the Internet. Then he would find out she'd been fired from BrownWare for "official misconduct." Angie now had no doubt he'd believe the worst of her.

The secretarial manuals were right. She had no business developing romantic feelings for her boss.

Angie began sweeping vigorously, raising clouds of dust with each push of the broom. She'd show him. She'd show everyone, including her father, who had told her she'd come crawling back home within six weeks, begging to have her job back.

Never, Angie declared silently. She wasn't going back to California, and she was never working for BrownWare again, she didn't care if she starved.

Not that she would starve, thanks to her alternate source of income, but the principle remained. Not for anything was she ever returning to Palo Alto or to BrownWare.

Angie listed what she probably needed to learn in order to call herself a legal secretary. The first item on the list was the ability to understand legal terminology. Angie resolved to look into some books on the subject. She was a quick study. In three months, she would be on her way out Garner Holt's door, with skills she could use to get a job almost anywhere, a job that did not require sixteen-hour days or working every weekend. She would be free to have a *life*.

In the meantime, she'd show him a thing or two. He was going to rue the day he lost such a good secretary.

"Slow down, Angie," Garner said from the door of his office. "You're wearing us out watching you."

She put on her most impersonal smile. "I have a lot of energy."

Cliff groaned. "Did you hear that? She has a lot of energy. Would you mind telling me what you eat to get all that energy?"

"I'm like the Ninja Turtles. I eat a lot of pizza." Angie tackled a dust ball behind the leather sofa. "When I can't get pizza, I eat tacos."

"Lord, I'm starving." Cliff headed for the door. "See there, Garner? Pizza is good for you. Carry on, Miss Brownwood. This office needs you."

"Call me Angie," Angie said, smiling.

She liked Cliff. Garner, on the other hand, was now Mr. Holt, and she didn't care what he said. If he wanted his office cleaned and caught up, he'd better go along with her.

She returned to sweeping the moment Cliff left. Opening the door, she swept vast quantities of dirt and dust out, waving as Cliff rode by on his red bicycle.

"He's on an exercise program." Garner joined her. "He decided riding his bike ten blocks rather than driving his car will work off a few more calories."

"Isn't that what exercise is supposed to do?" she asked coolly.

"When you're counting every little calorie, they do eventually add up." Garner studied her a moment while she made a point of ignoring him. "I need to ask a favor of you, by the way."

"Yes?" Angie stopped sweeping and waited.

"Mindy Adams is going to make my life miserable if I don't turn up at her party." He turned his most charming smile on her.

Angie felt the impact of that smile, but her professional demeanor didn't crack. She lifted her brows and said nothing.

Garner frowned, no doubt detecting a distinct chill in the air. "What I had in mind was bringing you. You'll have a chance to meet people, and Mindy will think you're my date. What do you say?"

Angie swiftly drummed up a speech about professionalism and secretarial ethics. The man was out of his mind if he thought she'd pretend to be his date while she was working for him as his secretary.

She opened her mouth to make a speech on high secretarial standards.

"Thank you," she found herself saying instead. "I'd love to go."

Chapter 4

Garner arrived at his office at eight the following morning. He still couldn't believe the sight that met his eyes. Angie Brownwood had spent most of the evening cleaning her own office, then she'd turned her formidable energies toward his.

Cliff followed him inside. "Gawd," he said, in awestruck tones. "I haven't seen the place this clean since the day you moved in. What did you offer her?"

"My body," Garner quipped, and laughed when Cliff turned an indignant glare toward him. "Seriously, Cliff, I don't know what the woman's agenda really is, but I'll tell you one thing. I no longer care."

"You'll give yourself? Just like that?" Cliff's sardonic tones didn't sit well on his smoothly guileless face. "Wait'll I tell Mindy she didn't use the right bait when she went fishing for a husband."

Garner felt abashed. Perhaps Cliff was right. Perhaps his time in Dallas had warped his thinking.

Still, he couldn't think of any secretary he'd ever known who would do the amount of work Angie Brownwood had done last night without demanding something in return beyond her salary. Most of them would have flatly refused to touch a broom and would have told him in lofty tones that cleaning duties were not in their job descriptions. Now that he'd seen the lengths to which Angie would go to impress him, Garner was willing to believe almost anything about her motives.

She had carted every stack of books out of his office, then she'd tackled the floor. After that, she had attacked his desk with the zeal of a Green Beret primed to kill. Once Garner had realized she wasn't going to touch the papers he was working on, he had given her a key and gone home.

That had been at ten o'clock, the hour he usually went to bed. At four that morning he'd received a phone call from a client who had landed himself in jail in the nearby city of El Dorado and needed a lawyer to bail him out. When he drove by his office, he discovered the lights blazing and Angie still hard at work. She was cleaning windows with paper towels and spray cleaner.

When, he'd wondered, did she plan on sleeping?

"You're right, Cliff." He stared down at the shining, hardwood floor. She had actually polished it. "Why would a woman go through this much work just to get me?"

No woman would do that much hard labor just to impress a potential husband, Garner reiterated inwardly. She wanted something else. She had to. But what?

"That's what I'd like to know." Cliff studied the neat stacks of books waiting on the clean floor for their shelves. "It isn't as if you're good-tempered, or rich, or any sort of social asset …"

Garner turned and caught his brother-in-law's grin. "You're right about that. Maybe I'm the key to saving her beloved little brother from prison or something."

"Actually, she's probably just a woman trying to hold a job, and who happens to have a lot of energy." Cliff studied a framed painting of wood ducks nesting in a hollow tree that hung in the outer office. The painting was the only tangible evidence of Garner's former glory as a corporate attorney. "Yesterday this picture had cobwebs and dust an inch thick on the frame. The woman's a treasure. Better give her a big raise before one of those old lawyers in the Pritchard Firm discovers her."

Garner scowled. Any lawyer's office would be happy to have someone like Angie Brownwood sitting at their front desk.

"At four this morning, she was still at it," he said, inspecting the clean, polished floor in his office. "In white linen trousers, no less. What time do you think she'll come dragging in this afternoon?"

"Who cares?" Cliff followed, gazing in awe at Garner's diplomas, newly dusted. "Give the poor girl a break, Garner. She just did the work of six cleaning services."

"I just hope she's here to supervise those shelves," Garner grumbled. "They're supposed to be delivered at nine on the dot, just as Her Highness ordered."

He set his briefcase on the shining hardwood floor beside his desk and followed Cliff across the street to the diner. Naturally, he was thrilled at the state of his office, but the idea that his wonderful new secretary wasn't likely to be on time depressed him. He'd been looking forward to seeing her.

Perhaps he should make an appointment with a good psychiatrist.

On the other hand, who could blame a jaded cynic such as himself for wanting to warm himself at the blazing fire of her innocent enthusiasm for life?

He ordered his usual lean breakfast and the same for Cliff, ignoring the other man's hangdog expression. "Cheer up. You've lost five pounds already."

"Is all this suffering worth a mere five pounds?" Cliff asked Dolly Sims, who was grumpily writing down the order.

"Five pounds?" Dolly glared over the edge of her order book at Cliff's middle. "Can't tell it," she said, and stalked off.

Cliff buried his face in his hands with a heartfelt groan.

"Shut up, Cliff. You have a pretty young wife to enchant. She—" He broke off and stared out the picture window. "Good God. Look who's here."

Cliff turned to look. "Well, I'll be. Didn't you say she was still cleaning at four this morning? She looks mighty chipper to me."

Sure enough, Angelina Brownwood walked briskly toward the diner. She wore a beautifully tailored pink cotton suit with a slim, short skirt, and her blond hair was tucked into a neat chignon that wouldn't dare shed a tendril. High-heeled pumps, a leather briefcase, and the tortoise-shelled glasses added to the impression of big-city efficiency. The elegant, businesslike sight of her stunned the diner occupants into silence.

She sailed inside, blithely unaware of an audience, and headed toward the booths.

"Does she really need those glasses?" Cliff muttered.

"I doubt it."

"She looks much prettier without them," Cliff went on. "And with her hair down."

"The glasses and the hair are part of the outfit." He waited until Angie was beside them. "Hi, Angie. Won't you join us?"

• • •

Angie directed a beaming smile at her new employer, then caught herself. No professional secretary should display this much emotion in public. The truth was, she was responding to his dark good looks and the lurking smile in his silvery eyes. This was what happened when she went a whole day without reviewing her manuals and imbibing the proper secretarial attitude.

She reminded herself this job was a three-month prelude to a better position, probably in nearby El Dorado. "Thanks, but I'll just sit over here so I won't disturb your discussion. You'll be seeing enough of me the rest of the day."

"What discussion?" Cliff asked. "Since you were the subject of our conversation, you might as well sit down and keep us straight."

Angie shook her head. "If you're still dieting, you don't want to watch me eat. I'm having buttered toast and grits."

"Oh, Lord," Cliff said on a groan.

"Sit down, Angie." Garner moved aside, so that Angie had little choice but to sit. "I just want to know one thing. When do you sleep?"

She had slept only three hours, thanks to her excitement about the job and planning her new life, but Garner didn't need to know that. He already had the wrong impression of her. "I don't need much sleep. Besides, I wanted to be early in case those shelves are delivered this morning."

Angie noticed Garner studied her profile closely. When she turned her face toward him, he focused on the dark circles beneath her eyes, which she feared her careful makeup job had failed to cover.

"You need a heck of a lot more sleep than you've been getting," he said roughly.

She blinked. "Who says?"

"I do. Are you bucking for overtime pay or something? You were cleaning windows at four this morning when I drove by on my way home from El Dorado."

"What were you doing in El Dorado at four in the morning?" Angie countered in disbelief.

It was incredible. Usually, her father yelled at her because she took time off from her usual long days at BrownWare occasionally to catch up on her sleep. He'd claimed late nights were a requirement in software development. This was the first time anyone had ever told her she had a right to more sleep than she'd gotten.

"Who's the boss around here?" Garner wanted to know. "I was getting someone out of jail, for your information. It's part of what a small-town lawyer does for a living."

"Anyone getting himself put in jail at that hour deserves to stay in jail until a decent hour the next morning," Angie said with an austere frown. She turned as the sour-faced Dolly Sims slapped a glass of water and a menu before her. "Oh, thank you. The water here is really wonderful. I'll have scrambled eggs and crisp bacon, please, with toast and grits and lots of extra butter."

A sound like a dying bullfrog emanated from Cliff.

"It'll have to wait till the cook can get to it," Dolly said, glaring. "Folks who order chicken dinners first thing in the morning take up all the cook's time."

Angie nodded sympathetically. "I know exactly what you mean."

Dolly snorted and headed back toward the counter. "Five pounds. Humph."

Angie turned a beaming smile on Cliff. "You've already lost five pounds? That's wonderful. You'll be eating grits again before you know it."

The dawning expression of hope on Cliff's face vanished when Garner spoke.

"No, Angie," he said, as if chastising a child. "Cliff will not be eating grits again. Unless, of course, he wants to eat them without butter. I have an obligation to my sister. She wants a live husband, not an early statistic at the coronary unit."

"You have such a way with words," Cliff complained. He eyed the plate Dolly slapped on the table before him with dislike. "What makes you think I'm a potential statistic?"

"The fact that your father and grandfather are no longer alive to view their first grandchild," Garner returned ruthlessly. "Bad genes, son."

"My genes aren't any worse than yours." Cliff picked up his fork, resigned. "According to Laura, your family has a long history of early heart trouble."

"Why do you think I'm such a fanatic on the subject?" Garner grinned. "What Laura needs to do is pitch a fit and ask how you expect her and my incoming niece or nephew to get along without the family breadwinner."

"What nonsense," Angie struck in. "With all the advances they've made in the field of heart disease, why should a man barely thirty years old have to eat shoe leather for breakfast?"

"You're hired," Cliff said. "Whatever he's paying you, I'll triple it."

"You can't afford her," Garner said. "You have a baby on the way. And a big bypass-surgery bill in your future if you listen to her."

A plate of grits, bacon, and scrambled eggs whomped down on the table in front of Angie so hard, the eggs defied gravity and rose up a couple of inches. "Extra buttered toast on the house," Dolly said.

"Extra toast and butter on the house," Cliff repeated, watching Dolly's retreat with a stunned expression. "She's never given me one free extra slice in all the years I've been eating here."

"Mr. Holt probably bribed her," Angie said. "Don't you hate it when people have your best interests at heart?"

Cliff turned his reproachful brown gaze on Garner. "You Benedict Arnold."

Garner's broad shoulders shook with laughter. "I thought Dolly hated everything and everybody. Looks like I was wrong."

Angie registered the brush of Garner's shoulder against hers with an involuntary clenching of her stomach. If she moved slightly to the right, she'd be touching his thigh. She should never have sat down beside him.

Cliff grinned at Angie appreciatively. "Looks like you were. Here, Angie, hand over a slice. Maybe a little toast and butter will make this shoe sole palatable."

Angie obligingly passed Cliff the butter plate and a slice of toast, only to have it intercepted by Garner's long, slim hand.

"Five more pounds," Garner said. "Until then, no buttered toast. And if you want to keep the weight off, you'll eat your grits minus the butter in the future."

"I can't wait to tell Laura." Cliff gazed after the butter dish with longing. "I'll bet Dolly never gave her an extra slice of anything, either."

"Actually, I left her a good tip the last time I ate here," Angie said. "Dolly probably responds to proper appreciation just like everyone else."

She tried not to notice Garner's nearness and concentrated on his hands. His hands were works of art, long and slim, with smooth oval nails and beautifully shaped fingers. She studied the way he held his fork. Surely it was impossible to describe the way a man handled his dining utensils as sexy.

"Is that right?" Garner watched her layer the mound of grits on her plate with enough butter to render them liquid. "Look, that's a ridiculous amount of butter for one person to eat. What are you trying to do? Drop dead in my office?"

"I'm only twenty-si—seven years old," Angie said, amending hastily. "My parents are still alive and well, and so are my maternal grandparents. My paternal grandparents died in an accident years ago. They were in perfect health, by the way. And just look at Great Aunt Loretha."

"Aren't you worried about your heart?" Garner winced when she put more butter atop her scrambled eggs, and spread the remainder on her toast. "You must have added at least two thousand extra calories to that meal."

"I have a fast metabolism." Angie spread strawberry preserves on the buttered toast. "If I don't eat lots of calories, I lose weight and look hollow-eyed."

"If you look hollow-eyed, it's probably because you don't get enough sleep," Garner said.

"Yes, I do." She smiled serenely at him. "Last night was an exception. I wanted to have the place clean and ready to work in by this morning."

"I'll bet you haven't had enough sleep for quite a while now." Garner's eyes narrowed thoughtfully. "You've gotten used to it. You probably wouldn't know how to sleep a full eight hours. No wonder you burn up so many calories. Anyone would if they stayed active twenty hours a day."

"Look out, Angie," Cliff said, brown eyes twinkling. "He's about to take over your life. I think he's one of those high-priced personal trainers at heart."

Angie took her time processing a succulent bite of buttered toast and strawberry jam. "I'm impervious to people with sadistic tendencies. Believe me, I've been stalked by experts at torture."

"What an excellent choice of words," Cliff said, chuckling. "That just about describes him. An expert at torture. Definite sadistic tendencies." He winked. "He jogs every morning at dawn."

"Please. You'll put me off my food. If he wants to torture himself, I have no objections. But I have to draw the line at broiled chicken for breakfast."

"If I'm going to be vilified like this, I may as well be shot for a sheep as for a lamb," Garner said. "Miss Brownwood, consider it entered into your employment contract that I now have supervisory control over your diet and exercise regimen."

"My what?" Angie didn't look up from her plate. "The only way I'd sign a document like that is if you agree to give me control of your office and computer."

"I thought you already had complete control of my office and both my computers. It's obvious enough that I don't." Garner eyed her plate meaningfully. "Enjoy it, because you're now on a new regime. It's going to be my personal mission in life to get rid of those circles under your eyes."

"What circles?" Angie stiffened indignantly. "I don't have any circles under my eyes, but I will have if you start trying to starve me."

"He's right about that," Cliff said. "Nothing can hide the effects of a sleepless night."

"Whose side are you on?" Angie smiled at Cliff. "If you ever want to taste butter again, you'd better help me stand against him."

"I can't," Cliff said mournfully. "He was present when my wife extracted a foolish promise from me. I have to cooperate with his health advice if I want to have a happy home life."

Angie turned to look at Garner in a considering way. "I might have known you had no scruples. Although I've never worked for a lawyer before, I've been warned about their devious ways. Looks like everything I've heard was true."

"I'm afraid so." Garner sounded satisfied. "I want you looking really rested by the time I take you to Mindy's party. Otherwise, everyone will think I've worked you half to death."

Mindy's party. Angie could hardly wait, even though she knew she was breaking every rule in the secretarial books. Attending a party would be a great start to getting a life. She would meet new people and learn how to have fun. She would not think about her escort as anything but a business colleague.

Thoughts of Garner led her to wonder if he thought she was going to bow to his dictates out of respect for Cliff's feelings. If so, he had a lot to learn, especially when she began the process of upgrading his computer system. As she ate her scrambled eggs, she thought about what system would best answer a small-town lawyer's needs.

"I've even been known to take candy out of babies' mouths," Garner said in sinister tones. "Our first step in bringing you up to par, my dear Miss Brownwood, is to put you on a suitable exercise program. My personal research shows that if you're tired from plenty of physical exercise, you'll sleep well at night."

"An exercise program." Angie repeated those words in the same way she'd have said, ⊠Slimy, loathsome snake.' "Are you talking about signing away my life's savings at one of those silly gyms full of space-age machines? No. Absolutely not."

"I don't blame you in the least," Garner said smoothly. "Fortunately for you, Smackover doesn't have a gym like that or I'd sign you up tomorrow. Therefore, we're going to embark on a much simpler program. One that won't cost you much beyond a good pair of jogging shoes."

"*Jogging shoes*! No way," Angie said. "I was the only person in my office who never owned a pair of jogging shoes, and I'm not about to break that record."

"Come on, Angie," Garner said, grinning wickedly. "Even Cliff owns a pair of jogging shoes. He never wears them, except to meetings of the Accountants' Society in Little Rock once a year, but at least he owns them."

Angie felt the impact of his smile all the way to her toes. She bit her lip and focused her attention on her plate. Her professional standards were going to be in deep trouble if she didn't get hold of herself right away.

"A man has to maintain his image, even if it's totally false." Cliff sawed away determinedly at the chicken breast on his plate. "All the big city accountants wear them so they can walk to work."

"Really?" Angie glanced out the window at the sidewalk. "I walked to work this morning with no trouble."

"That's another thing," Garner said. "You don't need to wear high heels to work in my office, for Pete's sake. I'm a small-town lawyer, not a high-rise corporate attorney."

"I, too, have a professional image to maintain," Angie said, with great dignity. "If you want to wear jeans and cowboy boots, that's your prerogative. But kindly don't think you're going to dictate my office attire."

Garner turned his head to stare dangerously into Angie's unconcerned face. "Angie, you will no longer wear high heels to work. Is that clear? You'll ruin your feet."

Angie continued to eat with placid enjoyment. A woman who had faced down Vernon Brownwood's vitriolic rages did not find mere cold stares intimidating at all. "Sorry, Boss. Those orders don't compute. If you don't want me telling you what to wear to court, you'll allow me to dress as I please, so long as I don't violate any professional standards."

Garner looked both nonplussed and annoyed. "Angie, I don't want to see you at work in those high heels. As soon as you're through eating, I'm driving you home so you can change."

"No, you're not. Those shelves are due to arrive, and I'm going to be there when they bring them in," Angie said in blissful unconcern. "Besides, I don't own another pair of shoes that'll match this outfit."

Garner leaned back, looking exasperated. "In that case, I'll buy you a pair of pink jogging shoes. Would you like white and blue pairs as well?"

Angie chuckled appreciatively. "That would be a good start. Fashion considerations are about the only factors that would make me consider buying a pair of jogging shoes."

She scrubbed the remaining butter off her plate with the last scrap of toast and ate it, then dabbed delicately at her mouth with a napkin. With Garner's gaze focused on her mouth, she wiped harder than usual. She kept imagining what it would be like to kiss him and ended up making a mess of her lipstick.

Garner's expression remained undecipherable. "If pink is what it takes, then that's what you'll have. Come on, folks. It's almost nine o'clock, and there comes the delivery truck, right on time."

Angie paid her bill hurriedly, careful to leave Dolly a good tip, and followed Garner across the street to his office. In her briefcase she carried several flash drives that contained programs she'd need to jet-power Garner's computers to something near her standards, and her own small laptop in case the programs failed. As soon as she got his books properly placed on the new shelves, she was tackling that computer.

Cliff went directly to his own office, where a client was already waiting. "See you later, Angie," he said, and added in her ear,

"Don't plan on lunch at the diner unless you like broiled chicken breast."

Angie nodded thoughtfully and thanked him with a smile. She'd thought the diner was perfectly located for her needs, but it looked as though she'd be wise to plan on packing a lunch for a while.

Garner vanished into his office, leaving Angie to dictate the placing of the shelves. That suited Angie perfectly. Accustomed to working under her own direction, she enjoyed arranging the books on the new shelves and happily spent an hour at it before being interrupted.

"Leave that until later." Garner appeared in the door. "I need this letter retyped immediately."

Angie glanced up and focused on the letter in his hand.

"What's wrong with it?" she asked.

"You misread my writing. 'Arbitron' should be 'arbitration,' and 'Seagate' should be 'abate.'"

Chagrined, Angie stared at the offending words. "Very well. I'll have it ready in just a moment, as soon as—"

"Now, Angie."

Angie stiffened and turned her indignant gaze upon him. Fortunately, she remembered her new calling before she could tell him to stuff his letter down his throat.

"I'm terribly sorry," she said. "Next time, try writing a little more carefully, please."

• • •

Garner's mouth opened. He didn't want to fire his wonderful new secretary before she had shelved his law library. Or before she had showed him a thing or two about his computer.

He withdrew into his office until he was certain she was concentrating on the computer then he slipped out and watched as she turned on the computer on her desk. The machine, which had been slow and crotchety when he'd last seen it, booted up swiftly. She'd done something more to it, but he was darned if he could imagine what.

She called up the letter without having to search the entire disk the way he did, swiftly altered the two words he had pointed out, and had another copy printed in the time it would have taken him to get his word processing program called up. Garner confessed himself both awed and baffled, not to mention grateful.

Angie turned, letter in hand, and started slightly when she almost walked into him. "Here's the letter. In the future, maybe you'd better dictate your letters."

Garner slowly read every word in the letter while she waited then signed it and handed it back to her. With great ceremony, she inserted it in the envelope and placed it on her desk for mailing.

"Thank you," Garner said, with real gratitude. "Here's a document I need typed right away, please. There are forms stored on the hard disk. Just pull up the correct one and insert the needed information in the blanks."

Angie studied the document he handed her. It was a lease, and he'd penciled in the words he wanted inserted. Hopefully, she could read his writing this time.

"Very well," she said. "I'll have it ready in no time."

She did, as far as Garner was concerned, even though she had to field several telephone calls from Mindy Adams and several other women. Probably, they each wanted him to escort them to Mindy's party.

He watched Angie from his office door. Because she had her back to him, he could easily see the computer screen, where she flashed through the entire hard drive in record time in search of his legal forms. When she found them, he heard her sigh of exasperation and watched as she executed some sort of command that apparently involved transferring the folder of forms to another spot on the drive more to her liking.

Once she found the proper form, however, she swiftly inserted the necessary information, and printed a copy. Garner slipped back behind his own desk when she sent the document to the printer.

"Thank you," he said, when she carried it in to him, her heels tapping resoundingly on the hardwood floor. "I'll be going out for an hour or so. Would you mind typing an answer to this letter for me? I've penciled in the information beside the pertinent paragraphs. You can draft up a reply."

Angie took the letter and studied it with what was unmistakably an interested expression. Once again, he wondered what her agenda could possibly be. From the way she behaved, he'd swear she could hardly wait to perform any secretarial duty he assigned her. As if—he stared at her, wondering—as if she had never done a secretarial duty in her life and could hardly wait to find out what this one would be like.

It made no sense, but far be it from him to point that out and maybe cause her to stalk out of his office in a huff.

He left and ran several errands, then returned within an hour with a shoebox beneath his arm. "You're already done? Great. Here, try these on while I look over your letter."

Angie glared at the box. "If that's a pair of jogging shoes, I'm not wearing them."

"Yes, you are. They're pink. Do you think I want to be responsible for your broken down arches and bunions?"

Angie looked shocked but said nothing.

Garner perched on the edge of Angie's desk and watched, smiling, while she pried the lid off the box and frowned at the shoes.

"Go ahead," Garner said. "Try them on."

He dropped his gaze to the pristine sheet in his hand.

Dear Mr. McDonald: he read. *The legalities of you're proposed lawsuit are not as you have outlined in you're letter. First, state regulations require corporations. To pay corporate franchise taxes in a timely manner. Second, corporations not paying said taxes in a timely manner are subject to penalties and fines, and ultimately may risk losing their corporate charters.*

Garner read the entire letter three times before he spoke.

"Angie," he said gently.

She looked up. "Yes?"

"You're going to have to redo this letter."

She looked at him, blue eyes blank with disbelief behind those serious-looking tortoiseshell glasses.

Cautiously, he handed the letter back to her. "It says just what I want it to say. In fact, it would be perfect, except for your less-than-perfect usage of English grammar."

Chapter 5

Angie couldn't believe it. Less-than-perfect usage of English grammar? Her?

She drew herself to her full height and faced Garner, drawing upon all the poise she'd acquired during her years with Brown Ware, and reminded herself that a professional secretary did not brain the boss under any circumstances. "Very well. Please show me precisely what the problem is."

Garner regarded her warily and she sought at once to soften her tone.

"It'll be easier if I take a pen and mark a few of the mistakes," he said.

Mistakes. Angie stood there in frozen horror, while Garner's pen moved rapidly down her perfect letter, marking item after item. By the time he was done, she felt like a ninth-grader receiving the red-pencil treatment on her essay. Her cheeks burned with chagrin when she noted a couple of items she thought she recalled from long-ago English classes. She'd thought Peter Van Holden was bad. Garner Holt probably thought she was a lot worse.

Maybe she was. When was the last time she'd had to pay attention to grammar?

Angie took the letter with attempted bravado. Although he'd marked her mistakes, he hadn't penciled in the correct word choice. After studying the letter a moment, any bravado she still felt wilted beneath the uncomfortable conviction Garner was right. Each circle marked a mistake, and she'd have to correct every one of them.

"Thank you," she said. "Obviously, I could use a refresher course after working for Mr. Van Holden."

Garner regarded her curiously. "I'd have thought he'd have trained you better than this if he was working on a grammar checking program."

"Why do you think he decided to write a grammar-checker?" she said, trying for humor. It didn't quite come off. She sounded like a little girl whose feelings were hurt.

He shoved his hands in his pockets and regarded her as if he suspected that what she'd really like to do was bean him with the computer keyboard. "Just read over the thing once or twice before you print it out next time," he suggested.

Angie thought seriously of murder, mayhem, and homicide. Her feelings must have showed on her face because Garner vanished swiftly into his office.

The telephone rang.

"Mr. Holt's office," Angie said. "I'm sorry, Miss Adams. Mr. Holt is unable to take calls right now. He's in conference. Yes, I have your number. I'll give it to him the minute he's free."

She hung up the phone with a hint of a bang and felt a little ashamed of herself. It wasn't the fault of the telephone that she hadn't thought to brush up on her grammar skills. She had thought she knew grammar very well indeed. So much for that belief.

She reached for her briefcase and extracted her little netbook. This was a moment to call for expert help, and a smart woman knew when and of whom to ask for help.

• • •

Garner peeped around his door. Angie was busy at her desk, but he had no idea what she was doing until he saw her plug a flash drive into the desktop computer. She removed it then plugged it into a tiny laptop computer she had set up beside the desktop monitor.

He issued forth, fascinated, when she began typing rapidly. The machine dinged and Angie sat back a moment then sat forward when the machine dinged again and the screen lit up. She remained so intent upon her activities, she wasn't aware when he came up behind her.

Spying on his secretary. Those were the depths he'd descended to, Garner thought, with inward laughter. The small-town lawyer's life that had seemed so predictable barely two days ago now hummed with interesting possibilities. He was having a wonderful time, especially when he realized that Angie was using an instant messenger program he had never seen before to exchange messages with her correspondent.

The person on the other end of the exchange went by the name of *FondaC*, while Angie went by VP1. He wondered absently what that stood for even as he shamelessly read the exchange.

Hello, Ang, FondaC wrote. *Fancy hearing from you on a day like today.*

I need help fast, Angie returned, ignoring the provocative comment. *I'm a lot worse than I thought with grammar, and I've got to get a letter out. Can you correct it for me if I send it to you?*

I'm not believing this, FondaC wrote. *On second thought, maybe I can. Working with Peter must've rubbed off on you. Okay, Ang. Send it over. I'll have it back to you in a couple of minutes.*

Thoroughly entranced, Garner peered over Angie's shoulder. Why, he wondered, was Peter Van Holden writing a grammar program if he couldn't punctuate a simple sentence himself? It made no sense ... unless Van Holden had been writing something other than a grammar-checking program and Angie didn't want him to know what it was. Garner resolved to do a computer search on Peter Van Holden that very day.

Seconds later, a yellow gas gauge appeared on the screen as Angie sent the file to this FondaC person.

Immobile with fascination, he watched as Angie leaned back in her chair and stretched, obviously waiting. Then she took off her pink cotton jacket and checked her watch.

Garner studied her back. She wore a thin white cotton blouse that was so sheer, he could see the outline of her brassiere through it. His fingers itched to pluck the pins out of her hair and let it fall to her shoulders in the blond cloud he remembered from his first glimpse of her in the diner.

Within a few minutes, the gas gauge appeared on the computer screen once more. Since Angie hadn't touched the keyboard, Garner gathered FondaC was sending the letter back to Angie.

Angie quickly typed, *Thanks, Fonda. I appreciate it. I didn't realize I'd gotten so rusty.*

Garner watched closely. Sure enough, Angie shut down the messenger program and called up the word processor. The letter he'd ordered her to retype popped up.

Angie printed out two copies and clipped one to the copy he'd circled. Garner realized without surprise she intended to study the changes this Fonda had made. Then she blanked the computer screen and rose.

Garner hastily backed up. He had almost made it back inside his office before Angie wheeled toward him.

"Oh. I didn't realize you were there." She gave him a firm smile, but from the expression on her face, she probably intended to either change the position of her desk or set a mirror up beside her to monitor his office door. "See if this is any better, please."

Garner took the letter and made a show of reading it. Sure enough, the letter was now perfect. He had been right. Angelina Brownwood had never been a secretary before. The question now was what *had* she been, and what was she up to now?

Perhaps she was a reporter, looking for inside tips on his upcoming case defending a local business owner against a sexual harassment suit filed by three of his female ex-employees. The case had the whole town taking sides, and probably taking bets as to the outcome as well. He resolved to keep any information about that trial out of Angie's hands, just in case.

"Thank you," he said. "Are you ready for lunch? How about joining me at the diner?"

Angie's expressive face reflected an unmistakable desire to say yes. He wondered what objection she had conjured up to his company.

"Thank you, but I brought a sandwich," she said. "I really want to use the time to get these shelves in order."

Garner felt sure she had not packed a sandwich in her briefcase. Perhaps she intended to use the time to contact whoever had sent her. "Angie, you need to take a break. You've been going non-stop all morning. It's wearing me out."

Angie smiled suddenly. "I can't stand disorder. As soon as I've got this office in the kind of shape I like, I'll be happy to take my lunch hour."

Garner folded his arms across his chest and decided he might as well make her think twice about picking his office for her spying and have a little fun as well. "All right. I'll make a deal with you," he said, with a smile of pure enjoyment. "If I agree to cease and desist trying to make you eat a healthy lunch, you'll agree to go home peacefully at five o'clock and put on something suitable for jogging."

"*Jogging*," Angie repeated, wrinkling her nose with distaste. "No, thank you. I'm busy this afternoon."

"Angie," Garner said gently. "You're forgetting something. I'm now concerned about your health. If I let you and your alleged sandwich alone, will you promise to put on your shoes and shorts and join me after work for a little exercise?"

"That's a choice?"

"It's your only choice," he said, grinning. "Well? Where's the sandwich? I'll need to inspect it if you refuse to join me after work."

Angie stepped back and frowned at him. "Keep your health-freak hands off my sandwich."

"Fine." Garner turned toward the door. "I'll be at your front door at five-thirty. Kindly don't keep me waiting."

Before she could deliver a reply, he turned and vanished out the front door, laughing to himself. Either she would be waiting for him on her front porch with a stick, or she would have a very good excuse for being far away from home.

Either way, he could hardly wait for five o'clock, because he fully intended to hunt her down if she wasn't there. He was having way too much fun trying to solve the mystery of Miss Angelina Brownwood.

And if she turned out to be a spy for a newspaper, Lord help her.

• • •

Angie stood glaring after Garner's tall form as he crossed the street to the diner. As she had packed no sandwich, she was not going to get any lunch, and Garner Holt was going to force her to jog after work.

Being a secretary wasn't quite as glamorous as she'd thought it would be. Maybe she should have listened to Fonda.

On the other hand, being a secretary beat working at BrownWare, or any other software company she could name, hands-down. Yesterday notwithstanding, she got off punctually at five; she went in punctually at nine, and the job did not come home with her or keep her up at night.

In short, she could actually have a life.

Since she had never had a so-called life before, she could not have said what the advantage of that was, but Fonda seemed to think it counted for a great deal. According to Fonda, she could go on dates. She could have long conversations with girlfriends over lattes or over the phone. She could even pursue a hobby.

Fonda thought she ought to develop a love life, and upon subjecting the matter to a great deal of thought and fantasy, Angie had to agree. She wanted to develop that love life, but first, she had to find a suitable male.

Garner Holt, in her view, was very suitable, but not if he intended to make her eat shoe leather or take up physical fitness as a hobby.

She spent her lunch hour nibbling an old package of Life Savers she found in her purse, and shelving books. Then she sat down at her desk and proudly set out the brand new plastic Rolodex file Fonda had given her as a going-away present. Every professional secretary, according to Fonda, knew better than to trust computer hard drives for such valuables as often-used phone numbers and addresses. Fonda believed in the power of the Rolodex, and Angie could hardly wait to get hers up to par.

She busied herself for the remainder of the afternoon placing Mindy Adams's address and phone number on one of her Rolodex cards and added more cards for the few other clients of Garner's she had dealt with thus far.

By the time Angie left the office that afternoon, her stomach was in the final stages of rebellion. If she hadn't eaten such a good breakfast that morning, Garner would have been picking her up off the floor by early afternoon. She'd almost given in to the temptation to call a pizza delivery service.

She was crotchety and hungry, and her feet hurt. She hit the front door of her own small house at a semi-run, for once ignoring the beauty of the yard and the beds of moss roses lining the sidewalk. Tossing her briefcase and the shoebox Garner had given her on the sofa, she raced to the kitchen, flung open the freezer door and grabbed a frozen pizza. While it cooked in the microwave, she poured herself a glass of chocolate milk and eased her feet out of the high heeled, pink pumps,

This was more like it. Angie felt so relieved, she almost experienced a wave of nostalgia for BrownWare, where she'd gone to work every day in jeans and a T-shirt or whatever she felt like wearing. No one at BrownWare had cared how she looked so long as she produced.

She sipped the milk and rubbed her scalp. Wearing her hair in a chignon all day was giving her sore spots. She removed her glasses and the hairpins holding her chignon, propped her feet on the table, and leaned back, closing her eyes.

The ding of the microwave coincided with a knock at her front door. Angie started. Chocolate milk splashed onto her crisp, white blouse.

"Angie?" Garner called. "Are you ready?"

Angie almost fell off her chair trying to swing her legs down off the table. She leaped up, flustered, and grabbed for some napkins, then hurried to the front door and frowned out at him.

"Of course I'm not ready." She dabbed vainly at her blouse. "I just got home."

"What's that you've been drinking? Chocolate milk? That's a no-no, Angie. From now on, if you want milk, it'll have to be plain milk. I'd hate to see the insides of your arteries." The expression on his face was one of pure enjoyment.

"No one's asking you to see them." Angie frowned severely at him through the screen door. Funny, but men had never looked this good in California. "And I am not going jogging. I hate jogging."

She tried not to stare. The jogging shorts he wore revealed the long, tanned length of his muscular legs. His short-sleeved white T-shirt accentuated his tan and displayed the breadth of his shoulders and the lean, tapering muscles of his torso in a way that made her mouth go dry.

"How do you know?" Laughter tinged Garner's voice, although his face remained brooding. "Have you ever jogged before?"

"I … tried it one time in a P.E. class in grade school. I'm a lot better at exercising my fingers on a keyboard."

Vernon and Celia Brownwood had demanded their only daughter be excused from Physical Education within the first few weeks of the school year so she could spend more time developing her skills in the exclusive school's computer lab. Angie didn't remember much about the P.E. class, except that she'd been totally inept, thanks to being several years younger than the other girls in her class. At the time, she'd been glad to spend the time in the computer lab doing something she was good at.

"Your education has been sadly neglected," Garner said, as if reading her thoughts. "But don't worry, Angie. We're going to remedy any deficiencies, beginning this afternoon. Go change clothes like a good girl. Otherwise, you'll have all the neighbors asking why I'm trying to beat down your door."

"Look, Mr. Holt—" Angie began.

"It won't work," he said gently. "Go change your clothes. I'm worried about those circles under your eyes. Believe me, I know exactly what they mean and how to treat them." He motioned at the sofa, where she'd dumped her briefcase and the shoebox. "Take the shoes with you and put them on. I'll wait."

Something about his voice persuaded Angie to head toward her bedroom without further argument. He sounded genuinely concerned about her, she decided. That concern was what had gotten to her. She wasn't used to having anyone worry about the circles under her eyes.

In her bedroom, she shucked off her pink suit and pantyhose and wiggled her toes gratefully. Then she searched her drawers for something suitable for jogging.

Finally, she settled on a pair of loose white shorts and a blue T-shirt, similar to Garner's attire.

She slipped on the pink jogging shoes and studied herself in the mirror. Perhaps Garner would think she looked so athletic, he wouldn't ask her to prove herself by jogging.

On her way toward the front door, she caught a tantalizing whiff of pizza. Her stomach filed a demand for instant attention.

But Garner was waiting, and not very patiently if his actions were any indication. He used one of the front porch columns as a stretching post and appeared to be putting himself through some sort of warm-up.

Intrigued, Angie tiptoed to the front door and watched a moment. The muscles in his taut back moved in unison with his well-coordinated movements, and his legs were absolutely sinful to watch. Her mouth went even drier than it had earlier.

"There you are." He looked up and noticed her. "Got a house key? Good. Lock the door behind you. We've got to get that sexy body of yours into motion."

Angie registered the fact that he'd called her body sexy right along with the fact that he wanted her to get it into motion. In her mind, the two ideas were incongruous.

"I am not letting you prod me along like a cow. My time is my own after work. You don't want everyone to say you're romancing your secretary, do you?"

"If I'm prodding you along, I can't be romancing you," Garner said. "Get a move on, Angie. We're late already."

"You're late. I'm not. If you want to make better time, maybe you'd better go ahead without me."

"Move it, Angie. I'm determined to save you, whether you like it or not."

"Save me? From what?" She stood in the middle of the porch and regarded him balefully. "When I want saving, I'll scream for help. In the meantime, kindly assume I'm happy the way I am."

Garner smiled at her and her heart promptly went crazy, which paradoxically increased her irritation.

"I know a serious case of dark circles when I see one," he said. "You look a lot like I did when I left Dallas several years back. You may quit tomorrow, but while I've got you, I'm going to teach you a few things about healthful living if it kills me."

"It might." Angie tried to ignore the warmth spreading through her. No one, not even her mother, had ever expressed this much concern for her health before. It was a novel sensation to say the least. She moved toward him almost without knowing how it happened.

He walked her down the sidewalk, one hand at her back. Angie contrasted his masculine appearance with the moss roses lining the sidewalk and the cushioned wooden rocker on the front porch. The prim little old-maid's house she loved so much looked doubly feminine with Garner around.

"Looks like you're going to have to get the yard mowed," Garner observed. "The grass has really been growing since Miss Culp died."

Angie regarded the overgrown lawn with wonder. Her parents had always lived in apartments on or near college campuses, or in close proximity to BrownWare's corporate office. No one around her had ever worried about green growing things, not even house plants. She had no idea where to begin.

But she would by tomorrow. One thing she knew how to do was scour the internet for needed information.

She looked up to find Garner studying her face.

"You're right," she said quickly. "I'll do it Saturday."

From a wire overhead, the resident mockingbird raised its standard objections to her presence in its yard. Angie stared up at the bird and wondered what its problem was.

"That mocker has a nest in the crepe myrtle bush at the side of the house." Garner pointed toward the rear of the house. "Your great aunt kept a lawn mower in that little tin building. It was in good working order a few weeks ago because I saw it being used."

His hand pressed lightly against her back. Angie registered his touch with a slight rise in her heart rate.

"Thanks for telling me. I've been too busy to go see what's in there. The minute I arrived in town, I started looking for a job."

The truth was she hadn't yet located the key to the little building. But she had built up a box full of keys in the past few days. All she had to do was try them out. No doubt one of them would open the building.

"Okay, Angie. We're on the street." He gave her a slight push. "Start your jog."

"If you push me one more time, I'm going to make sure you never walk again." So much for reading romance in Garner's light touch at her back.

"I'm not pushing you. I'm encouraging you to pick up your feet. The idea of exercise—"

"This isn't my idea," Angie reminded him.

"The key to good aerobic exercise technique is speed," Garner informed her, dropping back. "Jog ahead of me. Faster."

She stopped dead. Garner jogged into her and almost knocked her flat.

"I will not run ahead of you and let you mush me along like a sled dog. If you want to go fast, *you* lead, and I'll try to keep up."

"I've never met anyone so determined to stay out of shape," Garner said. "I'll run beside you. Speed it up, Miss Brownwood."

Angie obligingly sped up since he asked so nicely.

"Hold your arms like this." He showed her. "You have to get into the rhythm of it. Are you breathing hard?"

"I'm just right."

She managed to say it without gasping. It was harder than she thought to disguise her steam-locomotive breathing from Garner while he instructed her in the fine points of jogging.

After jogging a slow three blocks, the only thing that was obvious to Angie was that she was extremely unfit. She struggled along, determined to hold it together for one or two more blocks. Her escape plan depended on it.

Garner turned down another quiet street. Angie began dropping slowly behind him, until she was just in back of his right elbow.

They hustled toward a wide, green alley that passed between the backyards of two rows of houses. Angie dropped a little further back. As Garner shot ahead, she turned swiftly into the alley, casting one regretful glance after Garner's perfectly shaped backside.

That one regretful glance was all she had strength for. She made it to a clump of forsythia bushes and collapsed onto the clover behind them, breathing like a bellows at an iron forge. Honey bees working the clover barely had time to dodge. Angie paid them no heed.

She sprawled out flat. Over her head, the branches of a tall sycamore tree screened out the sky. Honey bees buzzed over her head in search of the clover blossoms she was crushing. Such a warm, peaceful afternoon, and fitness freaks like Garner wanted to waste it by pushing himself, and her, into exhaustion.

The clover smelled sweet and grassy, the afternoon temperature was soothing, and her body felt like lead. Angie closed her eyes and waited for her breathing to steady.

"Wake up, Miss Brownwood," an unwelcome male voice said. "You aren't getting off this easy."

Disoriented, she opened her eyes and saw, not her bedroom ceiling, but a canopy of green leaves and filtered sunlight. A second later, Garner's face hovered above hers. He was standing at her feet, with his hands on his hips.

"If I let you alone, you probably wouldn't wake up until morning," he said.

That didn't sound bad. It sounded wonderful. Angie opened her mouth to tell him so.

"In fact, you look so good, I'm tempted to stretch out beside you and do whatever comes naturally," he went on.

Angie's eyes widened, whether with disbelief or with hope, she was uncertain.

"However, if I did that, you'd remain in deplorable condition."

Angie thought about socking him, but her arms felt like iron bars. She thought about kicking his left kneecap, but her legs felt encased in concrete.

Garner smiled. "Haven't you ever heard that making love is a physical activity? Stamina developed by jogging translates into stamina in the bedroom."

"Too bad," Angie said, using as little breath as possible. "If you wait till I've developed stamina, I'll also be in better shape to kill you."

Garner broke into unabashed laughter. "Since a good coach doesn't distract his trainees with lovemaking, I'll have to leave you unkissed. On your feet, Brownwood."

Brownwood. She knew it. He now fancied himself a coach.

"Do I get to choose between kisses and getting on my feet?"

"No." He stood over her and bent at the waist to grasp her under her arms, lifting her to her feet in one smooth motion. "You haven't finished your afternoon jog, yet."

"I think I have." The moment he let her go, Angie collapsed back onto the clover.

"On your feet, Brownwood," he said. "Believe it or not, you'll thank me for this someday."

If she had the strength, she'd refute that instantly. There was no way she was ever going to thank him for prodding her along like a recalcitrant heifer.

"You don't walk for exercise," he said. "You don't jog. It's pretty obvious you don't do a damned thing. What did you do out there in California?"

"Nothing," she managed, between gasps. "It was wonderful."

"Don't you know you're heading for fifty kinds of health trouble?"

Apparently divining he wasn't going to get her back on her feet anytime soon, Garner settled on the clover beside her. He wasn't even breathing hard, Angie noted, with some resentment.

"Bring it on," she said. "It can't be worse than this."

"That's what you think. What time do you normally go to bed?"

It was a trick question and Angie knew it. "Midnight."

"Liar. You don't get to bed before two or three, do you? I've got news for you, Brownwood. Tonight you're going to bed at nine."

At the moment, nine o'clock sounded like the perfect bedtime. Angie knew she ought to protest, but she said nothing.

Garner studied her closely. He paid special attention to her heaving chest and her face, which felt so hot, she figured her forehead emitted steam.

"All right, Angie. I don't want to over-push you. We'll quit for this afternoon. But tomorrow afternoon, we'll do five blocks instead of four."

Angie made a sound like a small, breathy moan. If she could have moved, she might have managed to get herself arrested for attempted homicide.

Garner watched her carefully and finally said, "That's better. You're extremely out of shape, but you'll be surprised at how fast you recover, and how good you'll feel in a week or two."

Enough energy had returned so that she could achieve an adequate scowl. "How can I feel good if I'm about to die?"

"You'll be amazed. Trust me on that."

The next thing she knew, he took her in his arms, turned her expertly, and stretched out on the grass beside her. Stunned into silence, she made no effort to block him when his lips met hers. He pressed her into the clover, and Angie experienced for the first time a man's weight and body lying almost on her. It felt incredible.

Her lips had parted to speak and Garner took advantage of that to slip his tongue gently into her mouth. She made a small movement of surprise and lay still. Then, sensation after sensation exploded through her body.

A moment before, she thought she'd been too exhausted to ever move again. She discovered she retained enough strength to throw her arms around Garner's neck, and that she had enough energy left to pull him tightly against her.

Angie had never dreamed sensations like these existed. She felt hot and tight all over, as if she was expanding inside her skin. She ached in places that had nothing to do with the exercise she'd just done.

She protested when Garner drew back slightly, lifting his lips from hers. She used all her strength to pull him back down again. Perhaps she hadn't kissed him thoroughly enough. Angie sought to show him she'd been paying close attention by imitating what he'd been doing to her.

So this was what she'd been missing by working day and night at BrownWare. This was what she missed because of attending college at the age of sixteen and spending every available minute in the computer lab or studying in the library.

She had rarely dated in college, and definitely hadn't had time for men at BrownWare. The one time she'd had dinner with a man, her father had made her life miserable for weeks afterward. He said she was frittering away time needed to perfect BrownWare's latest software offering.

Well, here was her chance to experience everything she'd missed. Angie threw her entire body and soul into it.

•••

Garner couldn't believe it. Seconds before, he'd been in control of the kiss, but now, Angie had turned the tables on him. She was kissing him even more vigorously than he'd kissed her, and her hands traveled across his back in a way that sent his control spinning dangerously close to collapse.

For a moment, he let himself be carried along on the rush of Angie's passion. Obviously, he'd been mistaken when he thought her inexperienced.

A few minutes and several kisses later, Garner realized wryly that she *was* inexperienced. He mistook her enthusiasm for expertise.

He might have known, he thought with inward laughter. He should have realized Angie would approach any new experience with her usual fervor. The problem was his body didn't recognize what his head acknowledged.

"Angie," he whispered. "Stop."

Her innocent blue eyes opened halfway. "Why?"

"Because." He tried to push away, but Angie held him too tightly. "If you don't, we'll both wind up with no clothes on right here in Mr. Smith's backyard where anyone can see us."

"Oh." Angie thought a moment. "In that case, why don't we go back to my house?"

Garner decided the time had come for stern measures. No way was he going to screw up his relationship with his new secretary before he had solved all the mystery surrounding her.

"Angie, let go of me. I'm not going to make love to you. I didn't mean to kiss you at all. It was a mistake."

"A mistake?" she echoed, looking stunned. "Are you sure?"

"Of course I'm sure."

Somewhere, in the dim, far reaches of his mind, Garner knew he ought to shut up, but the frustration he felt when he parted contact with Angie's soft body made him cutting when he knew he should be gentle.

Or maybe he was just crazy. On that thought, he opened his mouth when he most definitely should have kept it closed.

"You're too young and too inexperienced," he went on. "Which reminds me. You're going with me to Mindy's party, and the purpose is to introduce you to almost everyone in town, and that's it. You'll meet a lot of people at any party of Mindy's."

Angie froze. He felt the tension in her body almost as if he still touched her.

"In that case, keep your kisses to yourself," she snapped.

"Angie—"

"You started this. I didn't."

Garner winced. "You're right. It won't happen again, *Miss* Brownwood."

For good measure, he added, "And you may as well leave those phony glasses of yours at home. You don't need them, and frankly, they don't go with the rest of you."

Angie looked as if various methods of killing him ran through her mind. She lay back on the clover, with bees buzzing around her head, frowning at the sky and firming her soft lips into a straight, adamant line. He had no doubt that she would have walloped him over the head if a stick had been near to her hand.

Thankfully, he had worn her out enough that she was forced to let him live.

Chapter 6

Angie awakened at her usual early hour and lay very still. For a moment, she didn't know where she was. She stared at the fluffy green and white gingham curtains. They didn't coordinate with the usual austere decor of the brown and tan furnished apartments she had grown accustomed to from her old life because she literally did not have time to decorate an apartment.

She snapped awake. She lay in the old-fashioned bedroom she loved in her own house in Arkansas. She'd slept long and hard. Her body felt pleasantly boneless and extraordinarily relaxed … until she moved.

She gasped with shock when she tried to lift her legs over the edge of the bed. Her calves screamed for mercy. She stood and fell back on the bed with a moan.

The telephone rang. Angie looked at it suspiciously. It was four in the morning in California.

"Good morning, Angie," Garner said. "I was just checking to see if you've made it out of bed yet."

"Of course I've made it out of bed." She forced her body to sit straight and placed her feet on the floor. "Why shouldn't I? I have a lot to do today."

"Your list of things doesn't include buying a shotgun to come after me with, does it?"

Angie stood painfully. Muscles she'd never known existed complained. "As a matter of fact, that was the first item on the list."

"In that case, you'd better take a long, hot shower and eat a good breakfast," Garner said, chuckling. "The second phase of your training begins today."

"It can't." She sat back down on the edge of her bed in disbelief. She was too young to feel like this. "There isn't anything left of me for you to train."

"We're reforming your diet next." He hung up, laughing.

Poor shape or no, she was not about to put up with that. Grumbling, Angie hobbled to the bathroom, where she spent almost an hour soaking in the bathtub, trying not to remember her response to Garner's kiss. He hadn't meant anything by that kiss. Worse, he probably thought she was like Mindy Adams, out to trap him.

By the time she emerged from the bathtub, she could almost walk normally. She left her hair down around her shoulders and put on a turquoise and yellow tailored cotton dress and a pair of high-heeled, yellow pumps. She would put her hair up just before she left the house, and she would remember to put on the glasses. In her opinion, those glasses added a professional look no secretarial wardrobe could do without.

She went to the kitchen and opened the back door, where she observed the yard possessively through the screen. It was hers, overgrown grass and all. With this house and this yard to care for, what did she care what Garner Holt thought about her motives?

"Jay!" the mockingbird shouted from an overhead wire.

Angie looked up. Sure enough, the bird had detected the movement of the door and glared down at her.

"You may have been here before me," she told the bird, "but I have a legal deed to the place."

"Jay!"

She drew back, still surveying the yard happily. She had a whole house and yard—complete with a possessive bird—all to herself. It was a novel and exciting experience to someone unused to caring for yards, flower beds, and territorial mockingbirds.

She was also unused to cooking. Angie glanced regretfully around her tidy little kitchen while she put a couple of toaster pastries in the toaster. She'd looked forward to more scrambled eggs and butter-laden grits, but not with Garner around to countermand her order. As soon as she got her yard straightened out, she was going to make use of her new cooking app and learn to cook her own breakfast.

She opened a cabinet and hid a couple of her favorite packaged pastries in her briefcase. At least, she'd have sustenance in case Garner intended to enforce his ridiculous dictates and place her on some sort of ghastly diet.

"What do you think you're doing?"

Angie gasped, slammed the briefcase shut and spun toward the back door. She'd let the door stand open so she could enjoy the sight of the morning sunlight on the tall, thick grass. Garner stood there, blocking her view and regarding her severely through the screen. He held a sheaf of books and papers under one arm, and he wore a dark blue suit with a red tie.

Angie's heart raced. She'd thought he looked good in his jeans and cowboy boots. In a suit, he was spectacular.

"Throw that junk in the garbage," he instructed. "I knew you'd try to pull something of this sort if I didn't check up on you."

"What are you doing here?" Angie sagged weakly against the cabinet, heart pounding. The man had no right to cause this sort of reaction in an employee. "I have a front door, you know."

"Jay!" the mockingbird shrieked.

"Around here, everyone knows to come to the back door. The kitchen is where all the action is." Garner glanced up. "Let me in, will you. That bird looks like he wants a piece of my hide."

She moved slowly toward the door. The morning sun fell across Garner's head, burnishing his dark head with chestnut. He looked tall and fit, altogether too healthy and vigorous for human consumption.

The moment she opened the door, her pastries sprang out of the toaster. Garner stepped inside, scowling at them. Angie ignored her breakfast in favor of noting that although he'd put on a suit, he still wore cowboy boots.

"You ought to throw those outside to appease your man-eating bird," he said. "No wonder you're in such terrible condition. You don't eat anything but high-fat or high-sugar foods."

Angie laughed, determined to show him she hadn't given another thought to yesterday's kiss. "My last job had irregular hours, so I could never count on having time to cook or to eat regular meals."

"This was your secretarial job with Peter Van Holden?"

She tried to remember her résumé. "Yes, it was. He worked strange hours."

It was that voice of his, she decided. Before she knew it, he might hypnotize her into revealing a life that was far removed from the life she'd presented in her résumé. No professional secretary would have put up with the kind of life Angie had lived.

"I'll bet you made a high salary, working those hours," Garner observed. "Too bad it didn't leave you time to take care of yourself."

"I take very good care of myself." Angie crossed her fingers behind her back. "Just because I don't care to cook early in the morning … "

The telephone rang and Angie jumped. Since Garner stood in her kitchen, that meant the caller wasn't him. That meant it was likely someone from her old life who probably wanted to regale her with something really awful Vernon Brownwood had done.

"Want me to get it?" Garner asked, when she made no move toward the phone.

"Please." Angie brightened. Maybe the caller would think he or she had the wrong number.

"Yes, this is Miss Brownwood's residence," Garner said.

"Who are you?" the caller demanded.

Angie recognized the voice instantly and winced.

"I'm Garner Holt, her employer." He gave Angie a comforting smile.

"Well, I'm her mother, and I demand to speak to my daughter this instant," the caller said. "And if you think you can explain what you're doing in my daughter's house at this hour of the morning, I'll be happy to hear your story."

Angie heard every word of her mother's clear, carrying voice and grimaced. She shook her head at Garner.

"It's eight o'clock here," Garner said in ultra-polite tones, grinning at Angie. "I stopped by to give Miss Brownwood some last minute instructions about the office before I leave town."

"Eight o'clock?" Celia Brownwood sounded mollified. "Oh, yes. I forgot about the time difference. I apologize, young man. Kindly put my daughter on the phone before I jump to any more irrational conclusions."

"I'm not a young man." Garner sounded like he was enjoying himself. "I'm sort of middle-aged. Your delectable young daughter is safe with me."

"Is that right?" Angie noted that her mother did not sound particularly convinced. "Well, I knew this was going to happen the minute Angie got away from here. It's too bad, because she was the only one who could have kept things going. Let me speak to her, please. It's an emergency."

Angie sighed and rubbed her forehead. Everything at BrownWare was an emergency these days.

"Hello, Mom," she said, with a complete lack of enthusiasm. "Yes, he's very nice. No, we are not engaged. I work for him. I just met him a few days ago when I got the job."

If that didn't send Garner running, she didn't know what would. After the way she had responded to his kiss, surely he'd think the worst, that she had taken the job especially to bring herself to his notice.

However, on the whole, Angie thought she'd rather have him think the worst than know the truth.

Garner leaned against the kitchen counter with the look of a man prepared to enjoy himself. Angie wondered why he had really come.

"Angie, sweetie, I hate to say this when you've obviously got something a lot more interesting developing than what's happening at BrownWare, but something has got to be done. Your father—" Celia's voice broke off suddenly. Angie heard sounds of a scuffle. "Vernon, you give me back my phone immediately."

"You viper," Vernon Brownwood hissed into Angie's ear. "I'll see to it that you never work again. Never. Do you hear me? I know what you've been up to."

"I'm glad you do," Angie said, "because I sure don't. Goodbye, Daddy."

"Don't hang up while I'm talking to you," Vernon yelled. "I know you're out to destroy me."

"I don't work there anymore, remember?" Angie said wearily. She'd thought putting a couple of thousand miles between her and her father would ease the situation. It looked as though she'd been mistaken. Vernon sounded as furious and irrational as he'd been the day she walked out of her office for the last time. "Gotta go, Daddy. My new job is waiting."

"New job?" Vernon yelled. "I'll have you blacklisted. You'll never get another job as long as you live."

Angie held the phone away from her ear. When she did, Garner stared in shock at the receiver in her hand, which continued to scream until Angie hung it up.

"That was your father?" Garner asked in disbelief.

"Unfortunately, yes," Angie said, grimacing. "He's the main reason I left California."

"Was he … yelling at you?"

"As a matter of fact, he was."

"Is he all right? I mean, is he well?"

"Who, Daddy? Of course, he's all right. Why shouldn't he be?" Angie said defensively. "It's everyone around him who's worn out."

"Have you done something to make him angry?"

"Only in his mind," Angie said through gritted teeth.

Garner grinned at her. "Well, I won't say any more, since I can see you don't want to talk about it right now." He motioned toward the stack of items he'd brought. The top item was a book which bore the title, *The Business Executive's Low-Fat, Low-Stress Diet.* "Now, Angie, I'll be pleading a case in Little Rock for the next two days. While I'm gone, I want you going to the grocery store and buying some fresh fruits and vegetables. It's time someone taught you how to eat properly."

Angie couldn't believe it. What adult female needed someone to teach her how to eat? "I already know everything I care to."

The telephone rang again. Angie ignored it.

"Are you sure you don't want to answer that?" Garner asked.

"I'm not about to answer it. You say you're going out of town, and you have orders for me?"

The phone kept ringing. Garner glanced at it.

"Angie, that may be your father," he said gently. "Why don't you try talking to him?"

"I have talked to him. It doesn't do any good."

The ringing stopped at last.

"I'm not talking to either of them," Angie said. "Their problems are no longer my problems. Tell me what you want done, please. And you can take that book away with you. I am not going on any low-fat diet. People need fat in their diets."

"Just read it," Garner said. "That's all I'm asking. I have a feeling you'll recognize someone in there."

Angie took the book, moved against her will by the gentle pleading in his tone. "Did the author happen to make a case study of you, by any chance?"

Garner laughed. "Who have you been talking to?"

"No one." She looked at him. "Are you saying you used to be on a high-fat, high-stress diet?"

"Believe it or not, I was in worse shape than you are right now. I slept about four hours a night, if at all, and drank coffee all day long. When I remembered to eat, it was a burger and fries I grabbed at the hamburger joint across the street from my office."

The phone rang again.

Angie opened a cabinet and deliberately rattled plates. If she made enough noise, maybe Garner would ignore the telephone.

"Aren't you worried about him? Your father, I mean," he clarified, when Angie turned a genuinely baffled gaze upon him.

"I worry a lot more about the people in his vicinity than I do about him," Angie said. She suddenly felt exhausted, that same soul-deep weariness she had suffered when she decided to leave California for good.

"Maybe you should call your mother back," Garner suggested gently.

She shrugged and stared out the window at her wonderful back yard. The sight was almost enough to fully restore her newfound joy in living. "Don't worry. She'll call back this evening, when Daddy's at work."

"She might have something urgent or important to tell you."

"I don't want to hear it," Angie said in steely tones. "I moved here so I could be far away from my parents and my former—life." She caught herself before she could say, "my former career."

Garner nodded. "She may need to tell you something important."

"I'll call her after my father has left the apartment."

She wouldn't, but Garner didn't need to know that. She was well aware Celia Brownwood was probably, at this very moment, tapping out a long, descriptive text message about the latest upheaval at BrownWare. Angie would read it later, after she'd fortified herself with a large pizza and a tall cola.

She reached for one of her toaster pastries and took a big bite. Hearing from her old life called for something more serious, like ice cream, but a toaster pastry would do for right now.

"Now, Angie," Garner said. "You don't have to eat that just to show me. You've got time to order a decent breakfast at the diner."

"I do?" She brightened then regarded him suspiciously. "You haven't bribed Dolly into feeding me chicken breast, have you?"

"When has bribing Dolly ever worked?" he asked, laughing. "I don't know what the situation with your father is all about, but I do know that when a person is feeling stressed, the only foods that seem to taste good are sweets."

Great. Now Garner was going to assume she was stressed out over the situation with her father, and she would rather let him think so than tell him the truth. On that thought, she took another bite of the pastry.

"Your father must be an important part of your life," Garner observed.

Angie looked down at the half-eaten pastry in her hand and shrugged. "He *was* an important part of my life. Fortunately, I moved."

• • •

Garner wisely gave up for the time being, in hopes that Angie would take herself off to the diner for a regular breakfast. After giving her the list of items he needed done, he backed his Blazer out of her driveway, wondering how he'd gotten himself into this. For a man who didn't intend to get involved with a woman again for a long time, if ever, he was awfully concerned about Angie Brownwood.

No doubt about it. He was going nuts, and all because he'd been stupid enough to let a pair of innocent blue eyes and a rare enthusiasm for life sucker him in.

To her credit, Angie was behaving as if she hadn't kissed him back yesterday. She had regarded the list of ordinary legal documents he'd given her with intense interest, as if she actually looked forward to the work. He had yet to research her on the computer, hoping she'd tell him the things he wanted to know on her own, but a man could only stand so much suspense.

Angelina Brownwood was a puzzle, all right, and Garner looked forward to solving it with an interest he hadn't felt for anything in a long while.

. . .

The minute Garner's battered Blazer disappeared, Angie hastily grabbed her briefcase, locked the front door, and hurried the few blocks to the diner. She barely had time for a good breakfast before she needed to be in the office.

"Hi, Angie," Cliff called, motioning. A beautiful, dark-haired woman sat beside him. "Join me in misery. Garner was in earlier and left strict orders about your future breakfasts."

Angie's happy smile vanished. "He what?"

"This is my wife, Laura, Garner's sister. She couldn't resist the chance to meet the brave woman who took on Garner's office."

Laura Holt Jones was tall and slender like her brother, and her eyes were the same clear, silver-gray. Her face held none of her brother's cynical charm. Instead, she sparkled with love and happiness and interest in Angie.

"Garner is absolutely fascinated with whatever you did to his computer." Laura shook Angie's hand. "And his *office*. I can't get over it."

"Both just needed a little attention." Angie sat down, liking the other woman immediately. "He's like most people, expecting the computer to keep on working smoothly, without any maintenance."

"He says you ran a lot of maintenance programs on the hard drive," Cliff said. "Can you teach me how to run them?"

Angie realized Garner had seen and understood a lot more of her operations than she'd supposed. "Certainly. Your computer will last a lot longer if you keep the hard drive in good shape."

Dolly Sims stalked over to them. She slapped a plate down on the table before Angie. A glass of milk followed, then a small dish of extra butter.

"That isn't what Garner ordered for her." Cliff regarded the plate hungrily. "What's up, Dolly?"

"I ain't partial to these nasty low-fat diets." Dolly glared at him. "Makin' folks mean is all they're good for."

"Ouch." Cliff pretended to cower. "How are you going to explain this to Garner?"

"I ain't explaining nothin'." There was a hint of triumph in Dolly's voice. "What he orders for himself is his business, but when it comes to orderin' for other folks, what he says don't cut no ice with me."

"Thank you, Dolly," Angie said, with a beaming smile and a heart filled with gratitude. "This is exactly what I was going to order, butter and all."

Dolly nodded proudly. "I knew you was a girl that knew how to eat the day I laid eyes on you." She sailed back to the counter, righteous triumph in every line of her.

Laura and Cliff exchanged glances.

"You see?" Cliff said to Laura. "Old Garner is going to have an uphill battle if he wants to reform this one."

Angie serenely heaped butter on her grits. "The reformee has to want to be reformed. I think I'd rather remain in my current corrupted state. Congratulations on your pregnancy, by the way. I think Garner is as excited as you are."

"Thank you." Laura smothered a chuckle. "No wonder Garner is going around in circles. I knew I was going to like you."

Cliff regarded Angie's plate, then his wife, mournfully. "Why is it that when I express a desire to remain corrupted, you and Garner both gang up on me?"

"Because, darling," Laura said, winking at Angie, "Angie doesn't have another five pounds yet to lose."

• • •

Angie thoroughly enjoyed the week Garner spent out of town. She shelved the rest of his books. She filed all his outdated files. She took apart his computer and printer and cleaned them. She completely rearranged the files on the computer's hard disk then installed a few programs of her own that made it perform like a newer, faster computer.

And she reread all the "Professional Conduct" sections in her secretarial manuals, just to remind herself of the folly of falling for her boss. The activity helped keep her mind off her mother's constant attempts to get her to return to Palo Alto and "do something" about her father.

Don't be afraid to show initiative, her favorite reading matter adjured. *Your boss will appreciate your interest in helping his performance.*

Angie took that advice to heart. She left nothing undone that would serve to prove what an expert, well-trained, professional secretary she was. She also wrote her mother a long e-mail, followed by a text message just in case the e-mail was missed, describing her total lack of interest in ever working in the software industry again, no matter what happened at BrownWare. She was burned out, she said, and needed a complete change. Thanks to Great Aunt Loretha's generosity, she had achieved that.

She also drove to the larger city of El Dorado and signed up for a dictation class and a Business English class. The classes would begin in two months. If she was busy with classes and her yard, she wouldn't have time to care whether or not Garner ever kissed her again.

In the meantime, she skimmed his book and decided to try incorporating a few aspects of the diet, such as more fresh vegetables and fruit, into her regimen. It couldn't hurt, and it might help her dark circles.

She also decided she was never going to let herself be half-killed jogging with him again. She began a careful program of brisk walking every afternoon after work. After a week, she thought she noticed a difference in her already high energy levels.

Garner breezed into the office the following Friday afternoon. Naturally he had not seen fit to call and warn her of his return.

"Hi, Angie." He headed straight toward her desk. "Did you miss me?"

Angie looked up from the book about English grammar she was studying and blinked a couple of times. Then her face broke into a radiant smile of welcome.

"I didn't," she said, "but all your girlfriends did."

Garner halted at her side. "My what? You mean Mindy Adams, I suppose."

"That's right. Her party is tonight, and she wants to be sure you're planning to attend."

"Oh, Lord." Garner circled her desk.

Angie half-rose, puzzled, and glanced around her desk to see what brought him closer in this determined way, other than her glasses, which she hadn't been wearing the way she should. She grabbed for them, but her logical thought processes fell apart when he pulled her into his arms.

Her surroundings whirled. She had planned on holding Garner at arm's length, and here she was back in his arms again, kissing him wildly. She couldn't hold back. So much for her elaborate plans for projecting cool disinterest if he ever made a move to kiss her again. So much for all the rereading she had done of her secretarial manuals and her determination to improve her grammar skills.

Her arms went around his neck before she realized what she was doing. She didn't know how it happened, but somehow her hands wound up inside his suit jacket to rest on the thin cotton of his shirt.

"How long have I known you?" he asked, between kisses.

"About a week and a half." Angie wondered why he wanted to waste time talking.

"That's what I thought."

"Is there a problem with that?" Angie noted the change in atmosphere and tried to force her mind to work again. It wasn't easy when her body still craved more of his kisses.

"The problem, I think, is going to be with you," Garner said quietly. "How many men have you dated?"

It was another trick question, and Angie knew it. She considered her reply a moment. "Are you asking how many men I've dated, or how many men I've slept with?"

"Never mind. Angie—"

The door swung open. Garner stepped back hastily, and Angie quickly turned toward the door in her most professional manner.

"I knew she was lying." A statuesque brunette entered the room like an avalanche. She wore a pair of tight jeans, a fitted yellow gingham blouse, and a pair of gold hoops that dangled from her ears. Her dark hair lay on her shoulders in perfect curls, and she wore high-heeled boots that added to her height. "You've been in town all this time, Garner Holt."

"Hello, Mindy." Garner sounded remarkably unenthusiastic. "I've been in Little Rock the past week, defending Arty Gierow in that embezzlement case—which you'd know if you ever read the *Gazette*. I just walked in five minutes ago."

"Sure, you did." Mindy approached, staring at Angie. "That's your new *secretary*?"

"This is Miss Angelina Brownwood," Garner said. "She moved here from California a couple of weeks ago."

"She's a *secretary*?" Disbelief lay heavy in Mindy's voice.

"What makes you think she isn't?" Garner countered, looking amused.

"Come on, Garner," Mindy wheedled. "She didn't buy that outfit on a secretary's salary. Are you sure you can afford her?"

"Well, Angie?" Garner said, grinning. "Can you explain how and where you got that classy outfit?"

"Clothes are cheaper in California." Angie said with a grin. She stared appreciatively at Mindy. "Those are nice boots. Did you get them in El Dorado?"

Mindy stared back. "Honey, you don't look like the cowgirl type, so what do you care?"

"I've never been a cowgirl before." Angie assessed Mindy's outfit with covetous eyes. "It looks interesting. I'll have to try it."

"Are you for real?" Mindy faced Garner. "I came to remind you that my party's tonight. Since *she* hasn't been giving you my messages, I thought I'd better come tell you, myself."

"She's been reminding me," Garner said drily. "I've had at least five messages a day about that silly party. Now run along, Mindy. I've got work to do."

Mindy turned on her heel. "Sure, you do. More of what I interrupted, no doubt. See you tonight, Garner. Nice meeting you, Miss *Blackwood*."

The door slammed behind her.

Angie busied herself shutting her book and clearing her work papers away.

Garner chuckled. "I can see I haven't been giving you enough work to do, Miss Brownwood."

"I'm a fast typist, Mr. Holt." Angie tossed her head back. "Is there something you need typed?"

"Why don't you come sit on my lap and take a little dictation?"

Astonished, Angie stared at him.

"I feel sure I'll be properly impressed with your speed,' he added, grinning.

The door opened again and Cliff entered with a thick sheaf of papers. "Hi, Garner. Boy, am I glad you're back. These are the papers for that house Laura's so set on buying. Why don't you look them over and see what you can come up with?"

Angie, who had heard all about the house from Laura, smiled sympathetically at Cliff.

"And if you've got a minute,' Cliff went on, "I'll drive you over to have a look at the place."

Garner looked at Angie. "Don't forget, you're taking me to Mindy's party tonight."

"I'm what?" Angie's mouth dropped open.

"You're protecting him from Mindy's advances," Cliff translated.

The two men went out together, laughing. Angie sat back down, smiling wryly at her own stupidity. She might have known Garner's interest in her was directed at something he wanted to achieve, namely, freedom from Mindy Adams.

She might as well get back to her main agenda, which was catching up on all the living she'd missed during all the years she'd been under her father's thumb.

Mindy's party seemed like an excellent place to start.

Chapter 7

"Some dress." Cliff stood beside Garner on the edge of the dance floor in Mindy's apartment. "I've never seen anything like it before around here."

Garner scowled at Angie's short, black dress. "Neither have I. It's going into the Salvation Army donation box tomorrow morning." He ignored the way Cliff bit back a grin and glared at Angie.

On the dance floor, Angie danced energetically with some college kid. It was quite a performance. Everyone thought so. Her blond hair flew out in all directions, and her slender arms and legs were in constant motion.

"You know," Mindy said, appearing suddenly beside him, "I thought I was going to hate her, but I don't. She's a great kid."

Garner frowned again. Mindy and her friends had taken Angie into their circle. They *liked* her, for Pete's sake.

"She's got so much enthusiasm," Mindy went on. "It's contagious."

"We know exactly what you mean," Cliff said, grinning. "I think I'd better take Laura home before she falls asleep on the sofa."

Laura sat on a sofa talking with two of her long-time friends. In spite of her obvious enjoyment of the conversation, she looked sleepy.

"Just think," Cliff added. "Once upon a time, Laura could out-dance Angie. I wonder what Angie will be like when she gets pregnant."

"Don't get any ideas," Garner muttered.

The thought boggled his mind. He turned to stare at Angie. Her fitted black dress was trimmed with glittery fringe that bounced when she moved. Mostly, the fringe stood straight out from her slender body. The dress fitted every luscious curve she had and barely covered her bottom. Garner had been fooled into complacency by the giant scarlet Chinese shawl she'd thrown over the dress when he picked her up.

He decided he'd had enough of watching every male in the room stare at Angie. He cut through the small crowd on the dance floor and whirled her around to face him.

"Party's over, Cinderella," he said.

"It's only ten o'clock." Angie's eyes were brilliantly blue and fairly snapped with excitement. "Are you cutting in?"

"Darned right, I'm cutting in," Garner said. "How many glasses of that punch did you drink?"

"I've only had two glasses. Why? Mindy told me it's her dad's special recipe. It's made with guava juice and—"

"And liberal helpings of Rebel Yell whiskey," Garner finished curtly. He guided her firmly off the dance floor.

"I read in that book you gave me that guava juice is great for your health."

"How much hard liquor do you usually drink?" Garner asked.

"I never drink," Angie said with dignity. "It dulls the mind. I'm really enjoying this music. Come on and dance with me."

"How much dancing have you done in your young life?" he asked.

Angie's innocent blue eyes widened with insult. "Are you saying I'm a lousy dancer?"

He grinned. "Not at all. It's just that you seem to be making up for lost time. If I danced that hard, I'd be crippled for two weeks."

Angie worked this out. "I guess I am making up for lost time. My last job didn't leave much time for fun." She fanned herself with her hand. "Let's get something cool to drink. Dancing sure is thirsty work."

"No doubt," Garner said drily.

Angie clung to his arm. "I've never had so much fun in my life. And Mindy says she'll introduce me to the saleswomen at the boutiques where she buys her clothes. Don't you think I'd make a great cowgirl?"

Garner stared at her and tried to imagine it. "No."

"Well, I think I would." Angie cast a glowing smile at him. "Furthermore, if I'd known guava juice tasted this good, I'd have gotten it years ago. The book said it had lots of antioxidants—"

"And I'll bet that if you believed jogging would give you the stamina to dance all night, you'd have taken it up at the same time." Garner steered her away from the punch bowl in spite of her attempts to veer toward it. "You've had enough punch. Any more, and you'll hate me and everybody else in the morning. Here, have a glass of diet cola."

Angie accepted the drink with a grimace. "Why is it that diet anything doesn't satisfy a person nearly as much as the real thing?"

Garner caught her gazing longingly at the punch bowl while he turned aside a moment to speak to a friend.

"Here, Ang." Mindy proffered a sheet torn from a note pad. "It's my dad's recipe for Peveto's Punch."

Peveto's Punch? Garner recognized it at once as a local legend. Worse, he could tell it made Angie's mouth water. She eyed the punch bowl thirstily.

"Here." Mindy handed her a cup of Peveto's finest. She wore a fringed white western skirt and blouse, complete with fringed white boots and a cowboy hat that had apparently made a big hit with Angie's fashion sense. "I poured this for myself, but you look like you need it more."

"Thanks, Mindy."

Before he could stop her, Angie had downed the punch with a grateful expression that effectively both froze his blood and covered him with guilt. If she didn't kill him tomorrow, she would hate him thoroughly for weeks to come.

"Come here, please, Angie." Garner reached for her hand, well aware that he was probably too late to save her from herself. "I want you to meet a couple of friends of mine."

Angie acknowledged the introductions gracefully and accepted another cup of punch from one of the men.

"You'd better not drink that," Garner warned. "Three cups of that punch of Mindy's have been known to lay out strong men."

Angie scoffed. "I've already had three cups, and I feel perfectly fine." She thought a moment. "Better than fine, actually. And my mind is still perfectly functional."

"I'll bet," Garner said, resigned. She was going to hate him in the morning for sure.

She sipped delicately at the punch. "I'm definitely switching to guava juice for breakfast from now on. Great stuff, this guava juice."

She finished the cup and set it down on a nearby table. It crashed to the floor and shattered. Angie looked down at it in puzzlement.

"What do you think you're doing?" Garner asked, even though he feared he knew. "You just held that cup out and turned it loose."

"I put it on the table." Angie sounded baffled.

"You didn't put it anywhere near the table." He shook his head regretfully. "I told you not to drink that last cup of punch. Come on, Angie. You've had it for tonight."

"I'm not ready to go home," she protested. "I'm having a great time."

"You've had an overdose of good time." He dragged her along by the hand to Mindy's bedroom, where he found her shawl and threw it over her shoulders.

Angie had made so many new friends who wanted to personally tell her goodnight, he had a hard time getting her out the door. He had an even harder time getting her into his Blazer. The punch had finally hit its mark. Angie raised her foot to step up on the running board, missed, and almost fell on her face.

"Angie," he said, struggling to lift her onto the seat. "How many cups of that punch did you drink?"

"I don't know for sure," Angie said dreamily. "Five, I think."

"*Five!*"

"Or four. I really don't remember. Everything seems a little hazy." She laughed exultantly. "I've never had so much fun in my life. Thanks so much for taking me."

"You're welcome." Garner buckled on her seat belt since she made no move to do so herself. "Although this isn't exactly the way the evening was supposed to end."

"It isn't?" Angie blinked. "But the evening isn't over yet, is it? I thought the idea of a party was to have a lot of fun."

"You certainly managed that," Garner agreed. "You're a hostess's dream. Even Mindy loves you."

"I love Mindy." Angie smiled hazily. "She's going to show me all the cowgirl boutiques in Little Rock."

He shut the door and came around. He drove her home in a silence punctuated by Angie's attempts at humming one of the songs she'd been dancing to.

He pulled up in front of her house. Her white compact car was in the drive, or he'd have pulled in closer to the front steps.

"Out you come," he said.

She didn't respond. That last cup of punch must have hit her hard. She didn't even know she was home.

"'*A professional secretary,*'" Angie said in slightly slurred tones, "*never allows herself to be seen with her boss in situations that can be interpreted as social.*'"

Garner unsnapped her seat belt and lifted her down. "Did they teach you that in secretarial school?"

"More or less." Angie looked a little startled. "I don't know why I suddenly remembered it."

"Neither do I." Garner held her, enjoying the way she automatically slipped her arms around his neck. Her body felt like warm silk against his. "After all, tonight was definitely a working situation."

"It was?" Angie's voice brightened. "In that case, everything's okay."

"That's for sure."

Garner escorted her up the sidewalk between the two lines of moss roses. If he hadn't kept a good grip on her, she'd have meandered into one of the flower beds.

At her front door, he propped her against the jamb. "Where's your key?"

"It's somewhere in here. I think." She frowned. "'*Professional secretaries are always organized.*'"

She gave him her little clutch purse and waited in contemplative silence while he fished around inside it for her keys. When he opened the door and lifted her bodily across the threshold, she showed an alarming tendency to sink to the floor.

"I don't feel so well," she said, looking up at him in an owlish fashion. "Do you mind if I go lie down for a few minutes?"

"That would be an excellent idea. Let me help you to the bedroom."

He got her down the little hall to her back bedroom, grinning at the contrast between Angie's ultra-modern little black dress and the old-fashioned, white chenille bedspread. The moment she lay down, her eyes closed and she was effectively dead to the world.

Garner slipped off her shoes and let his hands linger on her fine, slender ankles. She never stirred. He thought better of removing any more of her clothing. She'd probably be mad enough at him in the morning.

He'd been an idiot to let her drink that punch. Angie was a lot more innocent than he'd thought. In a way, she was as naive as the sixteen-year-old girl he'd first thought her. She had behaved like a woman released from prison tonight, one who sought to make up for lost time. He shouldn't have let her out of his sight for a minute.

"What kind of slave-driver did you work for in Palo Alto?" he asked aloud, staring down at her.

He no longer thought she might be a reporter on the lookout for a story, but he still didn't know what she had done in Palo Alto. She had so much knowledge of computers, he felt sure it had been something to do with them.

He glanced around the little bedroom. There was little in it he could pinpoint as belonging to Angie. The only items that obviously belonged to her were the dozen or so secretarial manuals lined up neatly on top of the chest-of-drawers.

He plucked one up and scanned it. Paper clips and markers filled the pages so thickly, the book seemed twice its size. Moreover, the books were all older tomes, which struck him as odd in itself. He'd have picked Angie as someone likely to own the newest smart phone or e-reader and who had never owned an actual book.

"Talk about well-thumbed books," he observed aloud.

He let the pages fall open as they would. She'd studied filing, letter formatting, message-taking, and telephone-answering techniques, he discovered, in the manner of a research scientist who parsed every word. After reading some of the material, Garner suddenly realized she had trained herself to be a secretary by studying those books rather than attending an actual school.

But why? He had no idea, unless he'd been right when he told Cliff she had an agenda of her own. Angie was an enigma, all right, and he needed some answers before he did something really stupid.

He looked at Angie wistfully. He'd like nothing better than to lie down beside her, but she was probably going to hate him enough already. If she remembered anything at all about the evening, he thought wryly.

He laid her keys and her purse on her dresser where she would see them immediately and closed the door softly behind him. He supposed he'd better call her about ten o'clock the next morning. Perhaps by then she'd feel a little better.

Strangely exhilarated, Garner headed for the front door. He wasn't sure how or when it had happened, but he felt like a man who had just come back to life after a long, miserable hibernation. In less than two weeks, since he'd met Angie Brownwood, he suddenly realized he was completely healed from his Dallas experience.

It was a reversal, he thought, grinning. The kiss of the beautiful princess had brought the sleeping prince—or was it the frog?—back to life.

His hand was on the front door knob when he heard a peculiar sound coming from the front bedroom. He peered inside. Five tiny red lights blinked and danced. Entranced, Garner flicked on the light and stepped inside.

He bit back a gasp. Angie didn't have just one little net-book computer. She also had two desk models, and they were the newest, most advanced machines available. Garner knew that much just from looking at them.

She also had another laptop, a larger model with a sleek red metal casing and little red LED lights across the front below the screen. It was a gaming computer, he realized abruptly. He'd never have guessed Angie enjoyed computer gaming.

Garner watched the blinking lights a moment then studied the room. Angie had turned it into an office of sorts. One computer occupied the dresser top. The other desktop computer and the laptop sat atop the chest-of-drawers, and the dresser stool had been pulled up beside them.

A printer sat on the dresser stool. Garner gazed at it with longing. It was a new and expensive color laser model.

Several cardboard boxes had been stacked in a corner out of the way. Garner walked over and bent to peer into one. It held several dozen computer books, fat and thin. He scanned a few of the titles. They were so specialized he didn't even know what part of the computer's operation they referred to.

He touched the space key on the keyboard of the laptop computer lightly. The screen lit up. He found himself looking at an elaborate mythical world, one that combined the beauty of a tropical jungle with a handsome black man and an equally lovely black woman. The pair apparently lived in a paradise full of lurking dangers, because a few moments of studying the screen revealed stealthy movements in various areas of the greenery, not to mention other hints like a reptilian tail, a gleaming sword, and a clawed foot.

Fascinated, he knelt on the floor and watched the screen. It was obviously a game, one that tempted him to reach for the joysticks beside the computer. He had never seen a game with such gloriously rendered animation before. It looked like an actual jungle, and the two characters inhabiting it looked almost like real people.

Suddenly he noticed a small pad of paper lying on the floor beside the chest-of-drawers. He picked it up and studied the rambling list of titles and sketches that decorated it.

Ra-thor and Lenora: On The Run, he read, and frowned. He wasn't sure, but he thought he had heard of Ra-thor and Lenora before.

A second title on the list read, *Ra-thor and Lenora: Tulip Mania*. Beside it Angie had sketched a tiny forest of what looked like man-eating tulips and two little stick figures fleeing.

The third title read, *Ra-thor and Lenora: The Venus-Flytrap Forest*. The two tiny stick figures stood in the center of some crudely sketched Venus Flytrap plants that had aimed their pod-like appendages at them.

He grinned. So Angie had something to do with designing computer gaming programs. That would explain a lot.

He studied the on-screen jungle once more, admiring the realism of the two characters and their background. If he'd known anything at all about computer gaming, he might have dared try his hand at it, but for all he knew, he'd blow up the machine or something equally awful.

He checked on Angie once more. She slept peacefully, her breathing deep and even, so he closed her bedroom door and let himself out of her house, careful to lock the door behind him. It was high time he found out who Angelina Brownwood really was, and why she now called herself a professional secretary.

He drove to his office and sat down at his computer. When he turned it on, he noted that it booted rapidly, without any error messages or other notifications, and displayed his startup screen without a single hitch. Happily, he went to his internet browser and called up a search program. Obviously, Angie knew her computers, even outdated devices like his. Garner decided to start his search by typing in: Angelina Brownwood, Palo Alto, CA. The search engine responded swiftly, with a veritable list of hits. He scanned them swiftly. There was even a Wikipedia entry that described an Angelina Brownwood who worked as head of project development at BrownWare, the major software company. She was the daughter of Vernon Brownwood, one of the company's founders.

BrownWare? Garner almost laughed aloud. Everybody who used a database program probably used VP-Base, BrownWare's major program. Offhand, he couldn't recall any other programs the company put out.

He clicked on the top link. The headline explained almost everything that had been puzzling him.

Major Upheaval: BrownWare Head Fires Daughter

Garner skimmed the article. It stunned him so much, he wound up printing it out for a more leisurely perusal. According to the reporter, Vernon Brownwood had literally gone to war against his cofounder, Peter Van Holden, and his daughter, Angelina over a list of grievances that made so little sense to the reporter, he only discussed the major grievance, namely an update to VP-Base. He fired his daughter and filed a lawsuit against his old friend, and since then business at BrownWare had come to a halt. When contacted, Angelina Brownwood had said she wasn't fired. She had quit. Peter Van Holden claimed he was filing a countersuit against Vernon Brownwood and was asking for half the company's assets.

He whistled. In his relatively short career as a corporate attorney in Dallas he had seen a few of these company feuds. They could get really nasty, and it looked to him as though things at BrownWare had gotten nasty.

He scrolled through a few more articles about the upheaval at BrownWare. One woman, a secretary named Fonda Clancy, stated that she knew nothing. Furthermore, her job description did not entail taking sides in company disagreements and any reporters wanting comments should contact someone in management. Garner almost laughed out loud at the boatload of attitude that came through so clearly in the woman's words.

Angelina Brownwood declined all requests for interviews and said she was leaving the area permanently to explore "new opportunities."

One of those new opportunities, speculated one computer magazine columnist, might be the Ra-thor and Lenora computer game, developed jointly by Angelina Brownwood and Peter Van Holden, which had gone over unexpectedly big with young gamers. In his opinion, there was an entire series of Ra-thor and Lenora games just crying to be developed.

Garner found the whole scenario almost unbelievable. Everyone had heard of Vernon Brownwood and VP-Base, but who expected to run into Vernon Brownwood's daughter in Smackover, Arkansas, of all places?

The most recent article said that product development at BrownWare was reputed to be at a standstill, and Peter Van Holden had filed a countersuit against Vernon Brownwood. Worse, the company's government contract was supposedly in jeopardy, thanks to Vernon's disinterest in taking care of business.

Angelina Brownwood had vanished. Obviously, she had gone on to bigger and better things.

As his secretary? Garner's mind boggled, but he kept reading. By the time he'd finished, he realized two things. One was that Angie had genuinely lost all interest in the problems at BrownWare. The other was that the people at BrownWare appeared to think Angie was the only person who could save their jobs and the company.

He logged off then went to his file cabinet and searched out Angie's résumé and Peter Van Holden's telephone number. It was time he found out the truth about Angie's situation. He called the number and introduced himself.

"You're who?" Peter said suspiciously.

"Look," Garner said. "Angie Brownwood is working for me as my secretary, but you know as well as I do she's no secretary. Suppose you tell me the truth about what's going on here?"

"Not me," Peter sputtered. "Ang made me memorize a spiel I'm supposed to give all prospective employers, and that's what I'm sticking to. Want me to read it to you?"

Garner somehow managed not to laugh. "Not particularly. Besides, I'm not a prospective employer any longer. I'm her boyfriend."

"*Boyfriend!*" Peter exploded. "Angie? Our little Angie? Hold it just a minute here. Who the hell is this?"

"I'm Garner Holt, and I want to know why a beautiful young woman like Angie moves here and behaves like she just got out of a dungeon."

"Are you talking about Dungeons and Dragons? That's old stuff, man. Ra-thor and Lenora is the game of the future. And I'm not saying that because I helped write it."

"What is it about working with grammar-checking programs that turns a person into a complete idiot?" Garner broke in. "Or did you ever have anything to do with a grammar-checking program?"

"Not me," Peter said. "Never fooled with the stuff myself. Look here. Angie's like my own daughter. If you're messing around with her…"

Garner gave up. "Maybe you'd better go ahead and read me Angie's spiel."

Peter read off a piece about Angie's previous employment with "Van Holden Software" that detailed numerous secretarial duties and contributions to the mythical company. When he'd done so, he apparently felt he'd done his duty.

"Don't know where Angie came up with the idea for being a secretary," he confided. "She was one of those child geniuses, you know. Never did anything but fool with computers from the day she was born. Vern thought she was going to set the world on fire, but between you and me, Ang didn't have what it takes. She just didn't *care* about programming."

"She seems…very knowledgeable about computers."

Peter made a sound indicating there were some things more important than computer knowledge. "She burned out long before they gave her a Master's at Cal Tech and sent her home. It was sort of a consolation prize, you know. She wasn't Ph.D. material."

"She has a Master's from Cal Tech?" Garner repeated. "Sounds pretty impressive to me. But what do I know?"

"They don't give Master's degrees at Cal Tech," Peter explained. "The only people who get them are the ones who can't cut it in the Ph.D. program."

"I see." He didn't, but he vaguely remembered a friend who had gone to MIT telling him something along the same lines. "Still she must have been pretty smart to get any degree at all from Cal Tech."

"Ang left Cal Tech when she was twenty-one and went to work at BrownWare," Peter said. "Poor kid never had a normal life. I told Vern she'd go off the deep end one of these days if he didn't let her get on with something she liked instead of trying to make her follow in his path."

"How old is Angie?"

"She'd be twenty-five or so now, I think," Peter said. "It's one hell of a thing. Ang turned out to have a talent for game development. She came up with a great scenario, so I helped her program it. When it took off and made us a lot of money, it got Vern on our case. He's so busy living in the past, he doesn't realize there's more to programming these days than databases and business software."

"Why is her father mad about that?" So, Angie and Peter Van Holden had created the Ra-thor and Lenora game. About the only thing he knew about the game was that it had been a huge hit around last Christmas.

There was much more, all delivered in the chatty tones of a man who had been sitting in front of a computer screen for the past two weeks and needed someone to talk to. Garner hung up at last and sat staring at the wall where his law degree hung.

He remembered how he'd felt when he'd left Dallas and wondered if Angie had felt anything like he had when she'd driven into Smackover. He had considered his professional life over and figured everything he did next would be a comedown.

He recalled the beautiful young blond who regarded everything as a new and wonderful experience. Angie had been like a person getting out of jail. To her, everything was new and exciting.

It was all in how you looked at it, Garner realized, smiling ruefully. He, too, had more or less gotten out of jail when he left the demands of corporate practice and his equally demanding, disastrous marriage. Life would have been a lot more fun back then if he'd looked at leaving his life in Dallas the way Angie obviously looked at leaving her life in Palo Alto.

Angie had chosen to believe herself liberated. No wonder she was having such a good time being a secretary.

They had a lot in common, Garner realized. One of the major things they had in common was something she'd already let him know she wasn't interested in discussing—her father.

Chapter 8

Garner waited until ten o'clock the next morning before calling Angie. When no one answered the telephone, he realized he had miscalculated. He drove into town and parked his Blazer in Angie's driveway behind her white car. Sure enough, Angie was in her back yard. She appeared to be wrestling a large lawn mower.

He studied her slender form appreciatively as she struggled to lug the mower around. She wore white shorts and a pastel madras blouse, and her blond hair was pulled back into a ponytail.

A movement in the crepe myrtle bush by the side of the house caught his eye and made him smile. Angie's resident mockingbird watched the drama from a high branch, ready to sail forth and defend its territory.

She must have an iron constitution. Either that or an iron will. Garner thought it was most likely the latter. From everything he'd learned about Angelina Brownwood last night, she wasn't a woman who would let too much Peveto's Punch get her down. She had probably arisen at her usual hour.

He watched her bend over the mower, apparently studying its parts. She walked around it a couple of times and bent over it once more. Then, she pushed the starter button.

The lawn mower won the match. The moment Angie started the motor, it took off on its own and tumbled Angie to the ground.

The mockingbird took the opportunity to dart out and scream, "Jay!" Angie flinched.

"Hey!" Garner leaped out of his Blazer and ran toward her. "What do you think you're doing? You're going to get your foot chopped off."

Angie lay in a heap on the ground and peered up at him. "How can I hold on to a mower that wants to take off and mow the yard by itself?" She struggled to her knees, shaking a fist at the bird. "What's wrong with this stupid machine?"

"Are you thinking this lawn mower is supposed to know how to mow the yard by itself?" he asked. He lifted her and set her on her feet, conscious of the feel of her softness in his hands.

"Isn't it?" Angie regarded the mockingbird cautiously and brushed off her backside.

He stared into her face. She looked remarkably recovered, but the dark circles were still there. He was surprised they weren't worse, considering her state the night before.

"Come on, Angie. Surely you don't believe those TV commercials," he chided.

She did. He almost laughed when the telltale color swept into her cheeks.

"According to the commercials," she said, with dignity, "the lawn mower waits while you start it, then it leads you gently around the yard. What I want to know is what's wrong with this one?"

"I don't think anything is wrong, unless you've got more mower there than you can handle. Miss Culp bought that mower especially for her hired man to use. I'd suggest you rehire him and let him use it."

"I don't want a hired man," Angie said stubbornly. "I want to mow this yard myself."

"Jay," the mockingbird commented, then sang out the trill of a sparrow.

Angie glared at the bird. "Without your help."

He ought to offer to take over the job, but Garner could no more resist watching Angie learn how to mow a yard than he could resist watching her method of achieving a correctly punctuated letter.

"First, you get a good grip on the handle," he said, showing her. "Then, you press the starter button." He demonstrated, and the mower roared into life.

"I got that far," Angie shouted, over the roar of the machine. "But when I put it into gear, it takes off without me."

Garner pushed the gear lever that engaged the self-propelling device. The mower strained against his hold. No wonder she was having trouble. The mower had been built for a man accustomed to mowing yards—lots of yards.

He shut it off. "Angie, if you're so determined to mow your own yard, I'd advise you to trade this mower in for a smaller one. This one is too much for a woman to handle." He saw the mulish set of her jaw and realized he'd made a bad choice of words. "I mean, this mower was built for someone who mows yards for a living."

Darn the woman. Did she think she could work on the mower and reprogram it the way she'd done his computer?

That was exactly what she thought, he realized. It was there in her sky-blue gaze as she considered the lawn mower once more. She probably thought all she had to do was reprogram the gears or something. Garner bit back admiring laughter.

"I'll consider it." She reached for the mower handle. "Hadn't you better get going? I understand you spend Saturdays working your own land."

Garner felt ridiculously heartened. She hadn't wasted the time she'd spent making friends with Mindy and company last night. They'd evidently discussed him.

"I have a little free time today, thank you," he said. "If you're determined to mow the yard today, I'd better stand by with tourniquets and bandages."

Angie acknowledged his grin with a reluctant smile of her own, then turned her back on him and bent over the mower. She gripped the handle, pressed the starter button and braced herself. The powerful grumble of the engine drowned out Garner's warning to hold on. Cautiously, she reached around the handle and pushed the lever that engaged the front-wheel drive system.

The mower jerked forward, pulling Angie with it. She held on, leaning back with all her strength and digging in her heels.

It was no use. The machine took the bit between its teeth and set off at a fast trot. It shot across the yard, dragging Angie behind. The mockingbird followed, darting at Angie's golden head every few feet.

The mower approached the back fence at a hard gallop. Garner watched, wincing, as Angie tried to leap forward ahead of the machine so she could push against the handle and turn it. She succeeded in partially turning the mower. Only the left front wheel tried to climb the fence.

She pulled back desperately, but the mower refused to respond to her shouted commands. It managed to get its right front wheel into the act and began digging a pit on the theory that if it couldn't climb the fence, it might as well burrow beneath it.

When Angie made no move to simply let go of the handle and kill the motor, Garner judged it was time for him to help out. He ran over and jerked her hands off the handle. The motor shut off instantly.

"Well? Are you convinced?" he asked.

Once more, he'd chosen the wrong words. Angie wasn't a woman who gave up when she ran into problems.

"No, I am not convinced. There has got to be a way to handle this machine, and I am going to find it."

"Your best bet would be to trade this monster in," Garner reiterated. "In the meantime, how about letting me finish the job?"

Angie glanced at the swath she'd cut through the tall grass. "Thank you, but I'd rather do it myself. I have a few other things to try."

"After I've gone away, right?" Garner laughed. "Sorry, Angie. I've come to spend the day. There are a few things I need to talk to you about."

Angie frowned. "Does this have anything to do with the events of last night?"

Garner backed off, laughing. It struck him that he hadn't laughed this much in years. "Are you saying you remember any of them?"

The mockingbird strafed Angie's head again. "Jay!"

"All right." Angie backed off, gesturing at the mower. "It's all yours. I can handle the mower, but this bird is just too darned much."

. . .

Thoroughly disgruntled, Angie sat on the back steps and watched Garner handle the big mower easily. Adding to her failed lawn mowing experiment was the fact that the mockingbird didn't strafe Garner. Instead, it darted down and snatched grasshoppers off the newly mowed grass. The two of them were cooperating to make her feel like a fool.

She should have listened to the advice in her secretarial manuals about socializing with the boss. She'd let her attraction to Garner override professional conduct. Her face burned with embarrassment every time she thought about the way she must have passed out last night. Talk about unprofessional.

She fanned her hot cheeks. He probably intended to fire her after mowing her lawn, probably as a kind of severance pay.

Garner wore his favorite cowboy boots with a pair of old jeans that looked molded to his long legs and a blue work shirt. He had no right to look so good and so vigorous while she felt like something better suited for a cemetery. It was unfair.

The telephone rang. Angie struggled to her feet and went inside to answer it in spite of her better judgment.

"Hello, Daddy." This was all she needed to complete a horrendous weekend. Angie held the phone away from her ear. "Isn't it a beautiful morning?"

The phone erupted. From arm's length, Angie heard Vernon's opinion of her perfidious behavior in siding with Peter Van Holden against her own father in the squabble over the updates for VP-Base.

"Does Peter know I've sided with him on using a new algorithm for VP-Base?" Angie asked, when the tirade faded. She wondered vaguely what had brought this on. "I'm not involved any longer in your fight with Peter. If that's all you have to say … "

The receiver levitated from her hands. Angie whirled. Garner had come in so quietly, she hadn't heard him.

"Hello, Mr. Brownwood," he said. "I'm Angie's new employer, Garner Holt." He listened a moment and grinned. "No, I don't manufacture computer chips. I'm a lawyer." He held the phone away from his ear a moment, frowning. "And I happen to believe family stands for something. So I'd suggest you cease and desist making those comments. Good day, sir." He replaced the receiver and turned to Angie. "How long has he been like this?"

Angie had turned away, unable to face Garner any longer. This wasn't the question, or the action, she'd expected.

"How long?" The question baffled her. "Forever, I guess."

"Angie." Garner grasped her shoulders gently and turned her to face him. "Think, darling. What was he like when you were a little girl? What was he like five years ago?"

Darling? Angie stared up at him, unable to think.

Garner stared back. His eyes were the gray of an overcast sky backlit by the sun. He framed her face with his work-roughened hands. The scents of sunlight and newly mown grass surrounded him.

The faintly scratchy, warm feel of his hands on her smooth skin electrified her. Angie trembled and knew he felt it. She lifted her face naturally. Everything she had reviewed in her secretarial manuals that very morning about professional conduct evaporated from her memory.

Garner's lips touched hers gently then brushed lightly across her mouth. Angie parted her lips for him. Instantly, his arms went around her, locking her against him. She sighed with pleasure and put her arms around his neck. For this, she'd brave a dozen mean mockingbirds and maverick lawnmowers.

She kissed him back enthusiastically. BrownWare and her own embarrassment faded into the far distance of her mind. She was a woman, and Garner was the only man who had ever made her so keenly aware of that fact.

"This is what I looked forward to and didn't get last night," he said in her ear. He smoothed his hands across her back, making her quiver with feeling then moved them around to cup her breasts. "You owe me, woman."

Angie couldn't believe the sensations rioting through her while his warm hands palmed her breasts. "I do? Then please let me pay up immediately."

She quivered with pleasure. Nothing in her life had ever felt like this. Not that she would know, given the fact that Vernon kept her working such long hours, she had barely even dated, much less had the time for extensive kissing.

Not that she had ever met anyone she wanted to hold extended kissing sessions with in the first place. One had to date in order to find a suitable partner.

According to Fonda Clancy, dating meant a woman had a life. Angie registered a thought that for the first time in her life, she had a life. Right now, she stood in her own kitchen getting kissed within an inch of her life. Could life get any more exciting than this?

A few minutes and a few kisses more, she realized it could. Garner kissed her eyelids, her ear, her neck, and returned to her mouth again, while his hands moved over her body, spreading fire in their wake.

Angie had never felt anything like it. She moaned when he nipped at her earlobe and at the same time rubbed his thumbs over the sensitive tips of her breasts. Swamped by sensation and unsteady on her feet, she leaned back to give him better access to her body.

He accepted her invitation by lifting her in his arms and using his foot to shove the back door closed. Disoriented, she rode in his arms to her bedroom, unaware of where she was until they arrived and not particularly interested so long as Garner kept kissing her. A kaleidoscope of light and color passed before her blurred vision when he placed her in the center of the bed. Then he came down beside her and she closed her eyes.

How had she managed to live so long without ever experiencing these feelings? If she'd had the faintest idea she could feel like this, she would have rebelled against the regime at BrownWare years ago. She tried to wrap herself around Garner's body but he trapped her hands and held them gently above her head while he hovered above her.

"Angie, open your eyes, darling," Garner said softly.

She opened her eyes and looked into his intent gaze.

"How many men have you been with in your life?" he asked.

"How many?" She frowned. "Why do you want to know? There's my father, and Peter, and a bunch of guys in management and on the development team who come and go, but—"

Garner looked as if he was choking on laughter, but he managed to say, "That is not what I meant. I'm asking how many men have you made love to?"

"Oh. Well." Angie thought a moment. "That's different."

"I'll say it is." Garner laughed openly now. "Just answer the question."

Angie wondered what the best policy was in a case like this. If she said none, he was liable to stop what he was doing on the grounds that she was an innocent.

Never let it be said that she had wasted her time at Cal Tech.

"Work the answer out for yourself," she said, lowering her eyelashes in what she hoped was a seductive manner and rattled off a mathematical equation involving velocity-squared, the speed-of-light-squared, and the square root of the entire bunch of squared items.

As she had hoped, Garner looked as if he had no idea that she had just given him a version of the Lorentz Transform. He stared down at her in thoughtful silence.

"I have a feeling the answer to that equation is going to boil down to the square root of zero," he said at last. "And the answer is, of course, zero."

Angie winced. Who would have thought lawyers knew anything about physics?

"Which is about what I figured," he went on.

"Assuming that's true, is there something wrong with that?" Angie tried to keep the defensiveness out of her voice. "There's a first time for everybody, you know."

"I know." He smiled tenderly. "The question is, are you ready for this?"

"Garner, a couple of things ought to be obvious by now. One, I'm twenty-si—seven years old and more than capable of handling the natural progression of events between us, and two, you're about to destroy the mood."

"Peter Van Holden says you're twenty-five," Garner said.

"Actually, I'm twenty-six." Looking into his face, with its high forehead and sensitive, bracketed mouth, Angie thought again of a sunrise after a stormy night. That expression made it difficult for her to put her mind on the issue at hand. "You talked to Peter? When?"

If Garner talked to Peter, there was no telling what he'd found out. Peter was the world's worst about forgetting what he was supposed to say when he was in the middle of a programming fit.

"Don't worry." Garner laughed. "He was very careful to read me the sheet you gave him about your previous job experience with 'Van Holden Software.'"

"Garner—"

"It's more than obvious, Miss Brownwood, that your capabilities know no bounds. Therefore, I think it's best to continue with the task at hand."

Angie let out her breath. "Why didn't you say so in the first place? Now is not a good time to bring up Peter or anything else going on back in Palo Alto."

He released her hands and kissed her again with due attention to reestablishing the mood. Angie found his efforts so satisfactory, she locked her hands behind his neck and sought to bring him closer still.

Now that Garner had decided on a plan of action, Angie found herself in total agreement with it. She signified her pleasure with every means at her disposal and never thought once about what the professional secretary ought to do when her boss lay beside her on a bed and began removing her clothing, item by item.

The midday sunlight filtered through her bedroom curtains. Angie discovered that making love with a man in broad daylight was extremely exciting. She could see everything they did together, and that fact increased her desire.

She had never been naked with a man before and found it a novel sensation. Nor had she ever had a man look at her as if she was something he wanted to immortalize in marble or devour in one gulp. In fact, she had never seen such a look on a man's face before, and she rejoiced that the look was for her alone.

He had enormous patience, she realized through the haze of desire that swamped her mind. Every touch, every kiss brought her to higher and higher peaks of excitement, until she knew she couldn't stand much more.

At that moment, he withdrew his incendiary touch for a moment while he stripped off his own clothing. Angie stared at him, entranced, and reached out to touch him experimentally.

Garner groaned. "Maybe you'd better not try that until later."

Before she could ask what he meant, he kissed her again and touched her intimately. Angie bowed up, shaking all over. If he stopped now, she would surely die.

Fortunately, Garner did not stop. He touched her in new and even more exciting ways, and when he finally joined his body with hers, she could only be thankful for her ability to feel his hair-roughened skin against her own smooth body.

The pleasure drew to a tiny point that suddenly exploded into a thousand shards of brilliantly colored light interspersed with stars and exclamation points. Angie had never felt anything like it in her life. That, she decided later, was probably why her brain almost totally shut down, until she felt, saw, and heard nothing unconnected to Garner Holt and the feel of him inside her.

When it was over, she lay very still, panting for breath and contemplating the decisions that had brought her to this time and this place. She really, really owed Fonda a huge birthday present. Or Christmas present. Whichever came first, she decided lethargically.

As if he read her mind, Garner held her, spooning his body around hers, and kissed her temple. "I'd really like to know what gave you the idea of becoming a secretary. It's been driving me crazy."

She smiled, drifting on a sea of warmth and pleasure that was unprecedented in her life until now. "It's very simple, really. Out of all the people I came into contact with at BrownWare, the only one who had a life that looked like any fun at all was Fonda Clancy, my father's secretary."

"That bad?" Garner feathered his fingertips over her forehead. "One of these days, you'll have to tell me about life at BrownWare. But first, I've got to find out why you seem to be having such a good time being a secretary."

"Fonda ruled the roost at BrownWare," Angie said. "Not even my father dared to cross her. She knew everything, and what she didn't know, she had in her files or her little desktop Rolodex. When five o'clock came, Fonda went home. Nobody dared tell her she had to stay after hours to finish a software update, or ditch her plans to travel to Los Angeles on a weekend so she could meet with some industry executive on Monday."

"I suppose I can see the attraction." Garner sounded as if he was smothering laughter. "Go on, please."

"I had begun to realize I was going to have to leave BrownWare, but I didn't know what to do because software development is all I've ever done." Angie sighed and let herself float on the cloud of warm contentment that surrounded her. "From all I could see, going to work for another software company wouldn't have been any improvement, plus I really didn't want to stay in the field any longer."

"Not even after Ra-thor and Lenora hit the big time?"

"You know about that?" Angie considered this with supreme disinterest. "The Ra-thor and Lenora game is what really sent Daddy off the deep end. For some reason he thinks Peter and I are conspiring to take over BrownWare, and it really frosted him when the game started selling."

"Because BrownWare wasn't selling it?" Garner asked.

"You've got it." Angie sighed again. "So he tried to tell us the company owned the game because we created it while employed by BrownWare. But since Peter owns half the company, he told Daddy to go fly a kite on the freeway. Not to mention that we never worked on the game at Brown Ware. It was just an idea I had that I did some programming on in my spare time, and Peter put the finishing touches on it in his own spare time."

"I think I see a lawsuit approaching," Garner said.

"And you don't even need a telescope to see it coming," Angie agreed. "Anyway, things got worse and worse, and no matter what we said, Daddy stayed on the warpath." She drew in a deep breath and snuggled against him. "So I started doing some research into job openings, even though I knew Daddy would make getting one anywhere in California almost impossible. Then Great Aunt Loretha died and left me her house. I researched Smackover and realized there were no openings anywhere around here for someone with my particular skill set."

"So you talked it over with someone," Garner said. "Someone who told you that good secretaries were needed almost everywhere."

"Fonda said it was too bad I hadn't learned how to type letters and set up filing systems, because then I could hire out as a computer-savvy secretary. And the more I thought about it, the more I knew I could do it."

"That's amazing. You actually learned to do secretarial work out of a book."

"Fonda showed me what to study." Angie felt a twinge of defensiveness and banished it. After all, Garner had told her she was the best secretary he'd ever had.

"You didn't want to move here and become a lady of leisure?" he asked.

She felt Garner's lips on her shoulder and smiled. "Where's the fun in that?" She turned back to face him. "The best way to become an accepted member of a new community is to get a good job where you can meet people."

Garner drew her closer. "I'd say you've achieved that. Mindy's crowd loves you, and Dolly at the diner has officially adopted you.

She actually told me to keep my filthy paws off your breakfast plates or she'd have my head."

"I think you're absolutely right." Angie smiled and reached out to touch his face with her fingertips. "And the best part about it is that I can now truthfully say I've got a life."

Chapter 9

In the midst of a peaceful doze, Angie heard the telephone in the kitchen ringing and automatically started to slide from Garner's embrace. Then she remembered where she was and relaxed once more.

"Are you going to just let it ring?" Garner asked. "Don't you have an answering machine?"

"Not on the house phone," Angie grumbled. "I haven't wanted to buy one yet. The peace when I come home has been wonderful."

"You'd better answer it. It might be important."

"I doubt it." She threw on her robe and hurried to the kitchen.

"Angie, darling, you have to come home," Celia Brownwood said, without ceremony. "This can't go on any longer."

"I'm not coming home, Mom. This is my home now." Angie sought for patience. "I don't ever care to work in software development again."

"It's that man." Celia sounded resigned. "I knew something like this would happen if you ever got out of Vernon's sight." She sighed. "I'm sorry, Angelina. I should have realized what was happening at BrownWare, but with all my responsibilities at Stanford, I'm afraid I didn't keep an eye on things the way I should have. Vernon is going to lose the company if he doesn't—"

Angie heard her mother's gasp of outrage and the sounds of a struggle, then her father's voice came on. The moment she heard his voice, she hung up the phone. "Someone you don't want to talk to?" Garner stood in the door, clad only in his jeans.

"It's my parents again." She came toward him and slipped her arms around his neck. "I'm not answering if it rings again. Let's go back to the bedroom."

He smiled against her hair then moved his hands to her waist to set her gently away. "Sit down, Angie. There's something I have to talk to you about."

Angie remained standing with her arms around his neck a moment, hoping he'd kiss her again. Maybe she could entice him back into the bedroom so he could continue helping her develop a life.

"We need to discuss where you go from here," he said.

She frowned. "What do you mean? I'm not going anywhere from here."

He went on, as if she hadn't spoken. "Even if I hadn't looked you up online, I'd have eventually called Van Holden. It was easy enough to see you weren't an ordinary secretary."

This was it, Angie thought. He was about to fire her for conduct unbecoming a professional secretary. Or was it because she had never attended a single day at a real secretarial school?

Maybe he had scruples about sleeping with his secretary, and the only way he could continue to do so was fire her.

On that thought she pulled out a kitchen chair and sat down, folding her arms across her chest. "Go ahead. I may as well be sitting when you fire me."

"Fire you? You've got to be kidding. You're the best secretary I've ever had."

Angie watched him suspiciously. He looked nothing like the man she remembered from barely two weeks ago—the one who looked as though he'd eaten something that disagreed with him. It was amazing how a mere change in expression could change every line in his face. The man pulling out a chair across the table from her looked happy to be alive.

Garner's face grew serious. He studied the ceramic hen and rooster salt and pepper shakers in the center of the table before he spoke.

"Since I found out the truth about you, it's only fair that I should tell you the truth about myself," he said at last.

Angie's eyes widened. "You're not really a lawyer?"

He laughed. "Now that you mention it, I'll bet you could hang out a shingle as a lawyer. A lot of the legal work out there consists of forms someone like you can find on the internet with the greatest of ease."

"Provided I could also find out what to do with them." Angie stilled suddenly and shot a horrified glance at him. "You're not about to tell me you're married, are you?"

"No way." He smiled somewhat grimly. "I'm about to tell you what everyone in Smackover would like to know." He looked up and met her gaze. "Two years ago, I came back home after spending several years as a corporate attorney in Dallas. I was in pretty bad shape, both mentally and physically."

"What was wrong with you?" Angie admired his tanned face and broad, athletic shoulders. Mindy had said Garner's immediate past was mysterious, but Angie had written off the comment. After all, from everything she had pieced together, Garner had grown up in Smackover. Everybody in town knew him.

"I worked as one of several corporate attorneys for a big chemical company in Dallas. It's a kind of life you're probably very familiar with."

Angie gazed at him uncertainly. She had no idea how to compare her life to anyone else's except the other programmers in the software development lab at BrownWare—and Fonda Clancy's.

Garner smiled at her with understanding. "You get up early every morning and arrive at the office before anyone else. You're still there long after everyone else has gone home. By the time you do get home, you're so jittery you can't sleep and can hardly eat. You get up the next morning and drink an entire pot of coffee so you can make it to the office and start all over again."

Angie nodded slowly. That did sound like a version of the life she'd been leading.

"After a couple of years of that, I had advanced enough in the company to consider myself a huge success. So I married the first woman who came on to me, chiefly because her opinion of me seemed to equal my own. Glenda was one of the leading saleswomen for Coralon Cosmetics and just about the most beautiful woman this small-town boy had ever seen," Garner went on. "Barely three weeks after the wedding, we had a huge fight about why I couldn't come home early one night and attend a business party with her.

"That was when I first realized she had married me because she thought I would be a big boon to her business where everything was built on image. Needless to say, my image of myself did a big crash-and-burn, because I also discovered that I didn't like the woman behind her image, or the man behind mine."

She regarded him with sympathy.

Garner leaned forward earnestly. "One day soon afterward I woke up and realized I was destroying myself, body and soul, by trying to lead a life I hated in order to live up to a mistaken idea I had of how life ought to be. But the worst was defending actions I was totally opposed to for the sake of keeping my job."

"That must have been the day you realized there was a better life somewhere out there," Angie said. "I know the feeling."

"You're one of the very few who really does." Garner's silver gaze rested on her face as if he found pleasure in just looking at her. "Rather than simply bow out and leave the way you did, I decided to make a stand and point out the error of the company's ways in terms of actions that affected the environment and federal law. The company retaliated by firing me and trying to have me disbarred. It took everything I'd saved to fight the charges and keep my credentials as a lawyer."

Angie gulped. Garner's story did resemble her own in certain respects, although Vernon Brownwood's attempts to blacklist her in the software industry hardly ranked with disbarment.

"The day I got the papers from the State Bar, it occurred to me to wonder how I'd come to that point," Garner said, watching her. "And the answer was simple—I'd been trying to live up to the image I thought my father demanded."

Angie clasped her hands in her lap and stared at the tabletop. She didn't know what to say. Hadn't she done the same thing for way too many years?

Garner rubbed his forehead. "The change in Dad had been so gradual, it never occurred to me the things he wanted me to do weren't the fair-dealing actions he'd taught me as a boy. When I graduated from law school he said he wanted me at the top of the ladder no matter what I had to do along the way."

"Even illegal things?" she asked.

Angie watched the play of emotion across his face. It was incredible. She'd thought Garner cynical and reserved, but he wasn't. He'd been wearing a veneer to cover enormous hurt and disillusionment. She longed to hold him and comfort away his hurt, but he wasn't looking for comfort. He was trying to tell her something—something Angie feared she didn't want to hear after all the trouble she'd gone through to get away from Palo Alto.

"That job represents the worst three years of my life," Garner said. "I worked from sunup until sundown, gulping coffee and trying to figure out how to stab someone in the back, whether it was the community or another lawyer."

"Did you try to quit?" She thought of all the times she'd tried to quit, even going so far as to interview with a couple of other companies, neither of which would touch her, thanks to Vernon Brownwood.

"Every time I mentioned quitting, Glenda pitched a fit," Garner said. "The day she dragged Dad into our arguments, I finally woke up to what had happened to me and to my old man."

"But you got away, didn't you?" Angie pointed out. "And you've made a success of your solo practice."

"All's well that ends well?" Garner gave her an understanding half-smile. "Angie, don't you see? Your little career and lifestyle change aren't going to be any easier than mine, although I have to admit you've done a far better job than I did." He reached for her hand. "What you don't seem to realize is that you've left a lot of loose ends behind. I don't want you to have the kind of regrets I've had."

Angie couldn't imagine having any regrets at all, but she forbore saying so. "Maybe you didn't move far enough away," she suggested. "Unless Daddy comes all the way here, he can't bother me anymore."

"That's what you think," Garner said gently.

"I can always hang up on him when he calls." Angie smiled at him. "If necessary, I can sic my lawyer on him."

•••

Garner smiled back and marveled at how easy it had been to tell Angie the things he'd never told anyone else, not even his sister Laura. Maybe it was because he knew Angie had been through much of the same thing. Or maybe it was because Angie accepted what he told her without judging his actions or telling him what he should have done.

But he could also see that getting her to understand what he was really trying to tell her would not be nearly so easy.

"Angie, the things I heard your father saying earlier weren't … " he hesitated, "quite sane."

She regarded him curiously. Garner bit his lip, wondering how to say the rest. In the end, he remembered she'd had a lot of scientific training. He decided to give her the straight truth as he saw it.

"Your father's reaction isn't normal," he said. "I think there's something radically wrong with him."

"With Daddy?" Angie looked puzzled. "I can't imagine what it could be."

"Think, Angie." Garner realized she was so used to Vernon's behavior, she saw nothing unusual about it. "What was he like when you first went to work at BrownWare?"

"He was exactly the same," Angie said, with emphasis. She thought a moment. "Well, maybe he wasn't quite as rabid, but this is an unusual situation. He and Peter grew up together, went to school together, opened BrownWare together, and developed VP-Base together. It's even named after them. But I don't have the faintest idea where he got the idea that Peter and I were conspiring against him. After all, it isn't as if either one of us is interested in taking Daddy's place at BrownWare."

"And now, your dad and Peter are no longer partners," Garner said, recalling some of the things Peter Van Holden had said.

"They were fighting over an update for VP-Base before all this happened." Angie shrugged. "Daddy wanted to use the same algorithm—the one that was his idea ten years ago—and do a minor update of some of the features. Peter wanted to do a major revision of the way the program works." She heaved a deep, weary sigh. "The problem then was that every time we talked about it, Daddy would swear we were conspiring to ease him out of the company because we wanted to scrap his algorithm. Once he discovered that Peter and I had had co-written the Ra-thor and Lenora game, he really hit the ceiling. He thought it was some sort of mutual declaration on our part as to our intent."

"Is Peter still a partner?"

Angie rubbed her eyes. "I think so. They've filed so many ridiculous lawsuits against each other these past few months, they may be fighting over the company's assets for the next fifty years. Peter says he doesn't care because he's discovered a new way to make a living, but he's still not letting Daddy get away with anything on principle."

Garner smiled at that, although he didn't like the tired, defeated look Angie had suddenly developed. It told him more clearly than anything she could have said what her life had been like at BrownWare.

"BrownWare sounds like a lawyer's paradise right now," he said. "One of these days, when you're able to look back on it and laugh, you can tell me all about it. In the meantime—"

The telephone rang. Garner couldn't blame Angie for letting it ring, but he also thought she needed to take some sort of action in regard to her father. He rose, lifted the receiver and handed it to her in spite of her pained wince.

"Hello, Daddy," she said, with a complete lack of her usual enthusiasm.

She immediately moved the phone several inches from her ear. Garner could hear every word of the ensuing tirade.

"You've betrayed me!" Vernon yelled. "How dare you tell that fly-by-night computer chip company you're working for that BrownWare is going belly-up?"

Angie had evidently grown so accustomed to Vernon's accusations, it took her a moment to realize this was an example of what Garner meant when he said Vernon's speech was not quite sane.

Garner took the phone from Angie's limp hand once he decided she wasn't going to reply. "Hello, Mr. Brownwood. Angie isn't working for a computer chip company. She's working for me. May I speak to your wife?"

"You can't fool me," Vernon shouted. "You're the lawyer for Verilynn Chip Makers. You're using my daughter's reputation to build your penny-ante business."

"Actually, I'm your daughter's lawyer. Let me speak to your wife, please."

Vernon slammed down the phone.

Garner looked at Angie. She stared at the phone with a stunned look in her blue eyes that told him his words had hit home.

Now was not the time to say anything more about Vernon's behavior. Angie would have to decide on her own what to do. Garner stood and walked around the table to lift her to her feet.

"Where is your mother?" he asked, holding her. "Maybe you could let her know you're concerned."

Angie snuggled against him, comforted by his presence. "At this hour on a Saturday, she's usually supervising some of her graduate students at Stanford, but she's the one who called just now."

"What do you say we vacate the premises a while?" he asked, smiling tenderly at her.

Enthusiasm lightened her expression. "I'd love to. Let's go have a pizza someplace."

"Now, Angie, you've probably eaten way too many pizzas in your life." He laughed. "I know a place that does tacos with baked shells and a really good cheese filling. Let's grab a couple of those and go fishing. Have you ever been fishing? I didn't think so. It's the best thing in the world for stress relief."

Moments later, Angie rode beside him in his beat-up, green Blazer, munching a reasonably healthy taco and gazing happily out the window. Smackover had once been an oil boom-town. The stilled rocking-horse remains of old oil wells dotted the landscape, cropping up in the middle of trees and fields. Every here and there among the rolling tree-covered hills, a well arm still pumped busily, working to extract any oil remaining in the limestone reservoir below.

Angie gazed around happily. "I love this scenery. Sometimes I feel as if I've spent my entire life in computer labs and offices." She thought for a moment and added, "I suppose I have."

The highway was closely lined with trees, and when they turned off the highway onto a gravel road, the trees moved closer. Leafy branches brushed the Blazer. Garner watched Angie's fascinated face from the corner of his vision.

He wondered what she'd say when she saw his cabin, and what she'd think when she discovered she was the first woman he'd ever brought to it.

They burst out of the trees and into a clearing that fronted a small, tree-lined lake, although it might be better considered a large pond.

"Oh," Angie breathed, clearly enchanted. "Did you know this was here?"

"Now, Angie, do I look like the sort of man who'd drag you out into the wilderness without knowing where we were going?"

Angie sat forward eagerly. "There's a rowboat. Do you think they'll let us rent it?"

"Are you saying you want to row out on the lake?"

"Can we? I've never been on a lake in a boat before."

"Then we'll do it." Privately, he marveled. What kind of life had Angie led, that she could be so fascinated by a tiny lake most fishermen would have considered beneath them? "What do you think of the cabin?"

He wasn't even aware that he was holding his breath until she focused on the cabin.

"It's the most beautiful cabin I've ever seen in my life," she said, with sincerity. "It's perfect."

"I'm glad you think so, because the lake and the cabin are ours for the day." He swung his Blazer beneath a shed at the side of the cabin.

Angie hardly waited for Garner to come around and release her. She sprang out the moment he opened the door and breathed the fresh woods air deeply. She never took her eyes off the lake in spite of the noon sun that reflected off it in blinding sheets of white light.

Garner watched her, as captivated by her as she was by the lake. The sun turned her blond hair into a golden-white blaze of light. Her translucent skin, still with the telltale dark circles beneath her eyes, looked like fine porcelain.

She looked eagerly around in all directions, enchanted even by his old beagle, Dixie. "What a beautiful dog."

Dixie roused herself from her sunny slumber on the front porch of the cabin and uttered a bay or two typical of her breed. Then she lost interest and lay back down, tail thumping rhythmically.

"Some watch dog." Garner's tone unintentionally roughened to cover his emotion. "You could steal every silver spoon in the place and she'd wish you God-speed."

He had a tough time coaxing Angie inside the cabin to help him put together a picnic lunch. She behaved like a little girl, running to admire a passing butterfly or a big, colorful grasshopper. He hoped she never lost that ability to find everything around her interesting—especially now that she'd given that same ability back to him.

Inside the cabin, she called his interior decorating a triumph of naturalism. As Garner had made no effort to decorate at all, other than to hang white curtains over the windows, he declared her a person of rare good taste as well as beauty. After all, what did a man need to be comfortable, other than a good television set and a comfortable sofa and some stuffed chairs?

"So this is your place in the woods," Angie said, when he guided her back outside. "Mindy said you had one, but no one knew where it was, including Laura and Cliff. She said you were a real hermit."

Garner urged her toward the rowboat, grinning. "Cliff hates to hurt anyone's feelings. Rather than refuse to tell Mindy how to get here, he opted to say he didn't know where it was. He and Laura spend many a weekend fishing here."

They carried fishing rods, a bait bucket full of crickets, and a basket packed with the sandwiches Garner made with Angie's haphazard assistance. Angie peered into the bait bucket, almost beside herself with excitement.

"I suppose he's right," she said. "Mindy's cowgirl look wouldn't fit in here." She clutched his hand and climbed into the rocking boat. It was a plain aluminum dinghy with no motor and few amenities other than thick cushions on the seats. "A country-girl look might be a lot better. I'll have to ask Mindy how one achieves that."

"Angie," Garner said gently. "Don't. You look perfect. A little pale, perhaps, but a few days of fishing ought to remedy that."

She chuckled appreciatively and collapsed on the forward seat. "You'd better not let me get too much sun or you'll be doctoring me for heat stroke."

"I know." Garner flashed a swift smile at her. "Don't worry. I'll time your exposure."

He shoved off from the bank expertly and settled on the rear seat with one oar. "Sit still and let me do the work. If you aren't careful, you'll tip us over."

Angie obligingly sat still. "This is supposed to be relaxing?" She dipped her hand into the sun-heated water.

"You're just excited." He dipped the oars into the water and shot the little boat forward. "You'll relax as soon as we find a quiet place."

"Is this whole lake yours?" Angie clearly thought it incredible, perhaps on the order of owning an entire Pacific island. "The entire lake looks quiet to me."

"This piece of land was the last thing left of my father's estate by the time he died," Garner said. "It belongs to Laura and me."

The momentary silence was broken only by the sounds of birds, the scratching of the crickets in the bait bucket, and the chuckle of the water as Garner's oars cut through it. Angie looked up. "Your father lost most of his holdings before he died?"

"What he didn't lose through unwise investments went to pay his hospital bills when they discovered he had cancer. You can imagine how I felt when I found out most of the changes in the way he thought and acted were due to a series of ministrokes he'd had some time before the cancer was discovered."

Angie stared out over the shining water. "Daddy had a medical checkup two weeks before I left. The doctor said he was in great shape for a fifty-year-old man."

"Angie, you know as well as I do your father's actions aren't normal." He guided the boat toward a tiny cove shaded by two tall, spreading pines. "From what I was able to piece together from the Internet, Vernon Brownwood has always been considered a quiet man who prefers his computer to human society."

"Daddy's always been eccentric. Once he actually hid under his desk with his keyboard so he could avoid meeting with government officials negotiating for the rights to use VP-Base." She gave him a wry smile. "I had to meet with them."

He guided the boat into the cove and tethered it to a low branch. Angie was starting to grasp what he wanted to tell her. Now he would let her think. "Want to learn how to bait a hook?"

"What's wrong with plastic crickets?" She covered her face while Garner baited a hook with a live cricket and tossed it into the water.

"The fish are about as fooled as you would be by a plastic pizza." He baited another hook and tossed it into the water, washed his hands in the lake, then settled down into the shell of the boat, using the seat cushion as a pillow. "Here's where you learn the true art of fishing. Come on over and join me."

Angie rose carefully and settled on the boat cushion beside him. He put an arm around her and encouraged her to rest her head on his shoulder.

"What was it like for you, attending college at the age of sixteen?" he asked, kissing her ear gently.

She tilted her head back. "What do you think it was like?"

"You tell me," he invited, and kissed her neck.

He felt sure Angie had never told anyone about her childhood. She probably didn't know it had been different.

"It was horrible," she said at last. "My parents loved me dearly, so they gave me everything *they* would have enjoyed. Computers, books, trips to technological exhibits." She swallowed. "I wanted the doll Great Aunt Loretha sent me, and a tree to climb and a grassy lawn to play on and some friends my own age."

"You were a normal little girl forced to act out the role of a budding computer genius," Garner said, understanding instantly.

She nodded and closed her eyes. "People expected me to be a genius because both my parents were so smart, but they didn't know how hard I had to work. Then when I couldn't do it anymore, they said I'd burned out." She buried her face against his shoulder. "The truth was I was never that brilliant to begin with, not like my parents." She paused then added, "My parents enhanced my intelligence with clever teaching and early childhood games that made me look like a child prodigy."

Garner strained to hear the softly spoken confession. He felt sure she'd never told anyone this.

She looked at the branch over their heads. "The truth is I've been burned out from the day I turned twelve and realized life was going to be one long, hard study session, and that no knight in shining armor was likely to come along and rescue me."

"In the end, you have to rescue yourself," Garner said gently, turning her to face him.

Angie gazed at him as if surprised he wasn't condemning her. "We both rescued ourselves," she said. "Goodbye, Dallas and Palo Alto."

They stared into each other's eyes a moment. Only the lapping of the water and soughing of the branches in the breeze broke the heavy noon stillness.

Garner drew her deeper into his embrace. No woman had ever fit in his arms the way Angie did, and no other woman had ever touched all the tender places inside his heart. He wanted to cherish her, to protect her dreams, and to guard that endearing, childlike enthusiasm of hers until she was in her nineties and beyond.

She parted her lips willingly for his kiss, wrapping her arms around him. Her short, perfect nails scored his neck and forked through his hair, leaving his scalp tingling with sexy rivulets of feeling.

"One thing you do have in spades is tremendous learning potential," he said. "In fact, I'd have to say you're very close to the genius-level when it comes to kissing."

Angie's soft laughter brushed his neck. She found his ribs and tickled him. "Don't you dare call me a genius."

He reacted by laughing and holding her off. "You'd rather be called a dumb blond?"

Angie dug her fingers into his ribs. Her blond hair tumbled in a fluffy mass over her shoulders. "How about calling me a student of great potential?"

She touched his face with both hands as if learning the contours of his sun-warmed skin with her fingertips, feeling the texture of his jaw where his beard gave the skin a slight roughness.

"Does that make me a great teacher?" His voice was deep and slow, and his eyes half-closed with the pleasure of her touch.

"Obviously," Angie said. "Look at the way I'm lying around on this lake kissing a good-looking man when I should be home studying grammar and filing."

He slowly eased her to her side and rose above her, staring down into her face. "This lake and this day would be wasted without a man and a woman present to enjoy it. Kiss me again."

Chapter 10

Garner rowed toward the shore and leaped out, splashing through the shallow water to pull the small boat ashore. He turned and looked at Angie. With the afternoon sun reflecting off her pale hair, she looked like a happy angel.

"A few months back, when I realized Daddy was going to make it impossible for me to work in the software industry, I started looking around for a new career," she said, "something that would utilize the skills I already had. The answer soon occurred to me—I could get a job like Fonda's almost anywhere, and at the same time, I could get a life."

"From what Van Holden said, you were essentially running BrownWare," Garner said. "You could have gotten a similar job at another software company, probably one that pays a lot bigger salary than what you could earn as a secretary." He stretched out his hand to help her ashore. "But I suppose I can see the attraction of doing something entirely different."

"Money isn't everything," Angie agreed. "Besides, the Ra-thor and Lenora game is still bringing in lots of royalties."

Garner laughed and lifted her to shore. "So you really don't have to work. Tell me about Fonda."

"Fonda is one of my dearest friends." She walked beside him toward the cabin, gazing happily about as though the scenery still fascinated her. "She has dates and goes to parties all the time. She gets off every day at five and comes in every morning at exactly nine o'clock. No one dares interfere with her, including Daddy."

He couldn't resist a grin. "In other words, Fonda had a life and commanded respect, and you didn't?"

"Got it in one," Angie said. "Fonda's my idol. She's the only person at BrownWare Daddy fears. I decided my new goal in life was to strike that kind of fear into people's hearts. I'm telling you, Garner, the truth is there's only one real boss in a company, and that's the secretary. She's the only one who knows where anything is, where all the phone numbers are, where all the contracts are, why you want to talk to so-and-so instead of whomever you think you ought to call." Angie laughed happily. "That just goes to show how much attention Peter paid to the business. I might have run the development lab, but Fonda actually ran the company."

Garner chuckled and tucked her against him so that his stride matched hers. "So you decided to become a second Fonda. No wonder you had me so terrorized."

She gave him a playful shove.

He ushered Angie inside and shut and locked the door. A boss planning an assignation with his secretary, he told himself, should always take steps against interruptions.

Angie noted his action and smiled innocently. "Is this where I get to sit on the boss's lap and take dictation?"

"Only if I'm lucky." Garner laughed and went toward her.

• • •

Angie thought she had never been so happy in her life. At last she had a life. Even Fonda, who had gone above and beyond the call of friendship in advising her on job hunting and duties, would be proud.

However, Fonda had also advised against dating her boss or any other superior in whatever company she landed in. In fact, Fonda thought a wise secretary would avoid dating anyone in the company she worked for. It would, she said, save the secretary a lot of unneeded misery.

But Fonda had always worked for companies, Angie reminded herself. She had never worked in a one-man office before. Angie fully intended to advise her friend of the benefits of a one-man office, especially if the man happened to be young and single.

She spent the entire weekend with Garner, fishing and rowing on his lake, lying beneath a tree on a blanket and watching the sky, walking down wooded trails, listening to birds and watching turtles sunning themselves on the banks of the lake. No one made any demands on her, and by Sunday afternoon, Angie actually felt a knot of tension deep inside her begin to loosen.

How odd, she thought, that she hadn't even realized the tension was still there, even after several weeks away from BrownWare and all that it represented. It just went to show. Getting a life did a lot more for a woman than anyone, especially Angie, had ever dreamed.

She lay beside Garner Sunday night, tucked against him while he slept, and gazed happily around at what she could see of her surroundings in the friendly darkness. As a denizen of sterile apartments, she fully appreciated the country character of Garner's spare décor, so different from Great Aunt Loretha's old-fashioned little house, which she also loved.

Maybe she ought to look into home decoration. Now that she had a home of her own, she ought to give it her own touches. The only problem with doing that was the fact that she had no clue what a "touch" consisted of, and she'd hate to make mistakes on something so obviously important. She fell asleep listing the magazines and books she needed to collect that would create the equivalent of a home decorating course and dreamed of a flower-filled home shared with Garner Holt.

Garner's cell phone awakened them both early on Monday morning. He stirred, mumbling something uncomplimentary about clients who called at the crack of dawn, and reached for the bedside table where he'd laid it.

His brother-in-law's voice carried well to Angie's ears. "Garner, for God's sake, pick up the phone. There's a weird guy outside your office, one of those long-haired dudes, and he looks like he's literally camped out on your doorstep."

Angie watched, interested, as Garner assimilated this and asked, "Did you ask him what he wants?"

"Are you kidding? Between us, he's a weird one and I don't need any trouble. I came down early to get a start on the quarterly reports, but when I spotted him I turned in at the diner. Thanks, Dolly. You're a lifesaver."

"It's probably a druggie who needs his girlfriend sprung from the slammer," Garner said, resigned. "Well, these days, a client is a client. We'll join you at the diner shortly so we can get a look at him."

"And eat a good breakfast," Angie added, when Garner clicked off his phone. "You might need some fortification if this is the way the week is going to start off. Seriously, you have no idea who this client is?"

"No. No long-haired dudes in my case files just now." Garner lay back down and looked at her with pleasure. "Of course it could turn out to be one of my childhood friends who went off and joined a rock band. Who knows?"

Angie smiled at him. "Look at it this way. It isn't every lawyer who's so much in demand, clients camp out on his doorstep."

"He would pick this morning of all mornings." Garner put out his hand to stroke her hair back from her face. "I had hoped for … a much slower start to the day."

Angie found she was all for a slower start to the day, if it involved making love to Garner and sharing the shower with him afterward.

On the drive back to Smackover, Angie happily watched the passing trees and shrubbery while assessing the turn her new life had taken. Definitely, becoming a professional secretary was the best career change she could possibly have made.

"If you'll drop me off at my place, I can get changed and meet you at the diner for breakfast," she said, when they drove into the outskirts of town.

"And leave a potential client sitting on my front doorstep?" he asked, grinning. "We'd better go by the office first. I can at least let him inside while I run you home."

But when they arrived at Garner's office and turned into the drive, and the man on the front doorstep unfolded himself to his full height and stuck the tablet computer he had been working on into his waistband, Angie wondered if the sky had just fallen in on her wonderful new life.

"It's Peter," she announced in tragic tones. "I might have known."

"Peter Van Holden? What do you think he wants?" Garner opened his door and stepped down. "Sit still, Angie. Let me talk to him first."

Peter loped up, peering at Garner through rimless glasses that were meant to be used only when he sat at his computer terminal. "You're the fellow Angie is working for? Good. Fantastic. Where's Angie? We've got to get started right away."

Garner indicated Angie, still seated in his Blazer. "What can I do for you, Mr. Van Holden? Are you wanting to sue BrownWare?"

Peter squinted then appeared to realize he was wearing his glasses. He took them off and stuck them haphazardly in his pocket.

"To hell with BrownWare," Peter said succinctly. "Vern has gotten so fuddy-duddy, he wouldn't know a game from an app." He reared back and peered at Garner. "This is your place, right? You can rent me some space in your office, for starters." He waved his arms for emphasis. "I've just signed a contract for a second Ra-thor and Lenora game. Angie's got to set me up with a scenario so I can get to work."

"What?" Angie fairly shrieked in dismay. "You went and signed a contract before talking to me?"

"Well, sure," Peter said, clearly surprised. "You said they were going to want another one, and that you had some ideas already in mind."

"That was six weeks ago."

Angie heaved a deep sigh and imagined Garner trying to conduct a legal practice in any building occupied by Peter Van Holden. No one could say she did not know her duty. She unfastened her seat belt with reluctant fingers and forced herself to climb down. Somehow, Peter's arrival had changed everything in her sparkling new life.

She also knew that there was no easy way to get rid of Peter. He was simply impervious to all hints that he might be in the way, and he would not budge until he had completed his preliminary programming to his own satisfaction.

"You'd better come to my house, Peter," she said. "This is a legal practice, and you would drive Mr. Holt crazy."

"Me?" Peter looked vaguely surprised. "I wouldn't be a bother. Never am. But Ang, we've got to get cracking. You were right when you said the Ra-thor and Lenora game would need a sequel. The fans are already calling for it. And you know I can't even get started until we have a scenario." He gazed hopefully at her. "You said you were fleshing out some ideas. How about giving me the outline for one?"

Angie looked down at the tablet Peter plucked from his waistband and held out to her. "Sure, Peter. I have it at home. I'll show you where you can access everything you need so you can get on it right away. Where's your car?"

"Car?" Peter looked around in search of his vehicle. "I don't have one. No, wait. I think I left it at your place. Somebody next door told me how to get here, so I walked over and decided to wait. It says the office opens at nine."

"Climb in." Garner, to Angie's relief, took the development in stride. "I was about to run Angie by her house anyway. You might as well ride with us."

Peter brightened in his vague way. "Thanks. You're the computer chip manufacturer Angie is working for, right? I thought so. Angie said you were a lawyer, but Vern swears it's a front." He glanced back at the house that sheltered Garner's office. "I really would like to rent some space for a while. I don't do well by myself, and—"

"You'll do just fine at my place," Angie nipped in swiftly. "You can't be wandering in and out of a lawyer's office while he's seeing clients, Peter. It would be an invasion of privacy."

"Privacy?" Peter repeated. "No such thing. I wouldn't think of disturbing a private conference. But I do like being able to walk around and see what everyone else is doing. Stimulates the creative juices, so to speak."

He lapsed into silence, gazing out the window in his usual absent fashion. Angie watched him cautiously a moment then glanced at Garner. She reminded herself again that Garner had no idea what went on in a software development lab. She just hoped he followed her lead in refusing to rent Peter any office space.

"Are you sure he'll be okay at your place?" Garner asked. "He wouldn't be in the way—"

"Trust me, Garner, he'd be in the way." Angie sought for the steely tones Fonda Clancy used in laying down the law to one of her employers when he departed from the bounds of sanity. "Client privacy would be totally out the window."

"I don't need privacy," Peter said from the back seat. "I just need a desk and a couple of computers."

"I've got everything you need at my place." Angie began to fear she was fighting a losing battle, but she struggled on. "You'll be able to work in perfect peace."

Peter thought a moment. "I don't like perfect peace. You know that, Ang. I work better when I can take a look around at what everyone else is doing."

"That's what I'm afraid of," Angie said. "The problem is that a legal practice is different from software development, and legal clients expect privacy."

"Cliff has an unused room—" Garner began.

"Cliff is using every bit of his office space," Angie nipped in. "Believe me, Garner, if you want family harmony, don't volunteer Cliff's space. Peter will do very well at my house. For one thing, I have the right computers he needs for his work."

Garner glanced at her, clearly amused but said no more. He turned into Angie's driveway, which now held two cars, Angie's little compact car and the rented car Peter had driven from the airport.

"I didn't know you could drive," she said, turning to Peter. "You've never even owned a car since I've known you."

Peter looked up from the tablet balanced on his knee. "Never needed one before. My apartment is right on the bus line. But I learned how to drive when I was a teenager, just like everybody else." He returned to frowning at the tablet. "Cars are a lot fancier now. Liked 'em better when they didn't try to put computers in them. And they've got them sealed off so you can't program them the way you want them."

Angie felt a twinge of sympathy upon remembering her fight with the lawn mower. "We're here, Peter. Come on inside. I'll get you set up so you can start work."

"Good." Peter brightened. "You can drill me on the scenario while I eat. Is there any coffee?"

"I'll make you some." Angie led the way down the flower-lined sidewalk to her front door. "Then I've got to—"

"Jay!" the resident mockingbird shrieked as it dove at Angie's head. Angie bit back a scream and ducked.

"Good grief," Peter said, mildly surprised. "I didn't know you had a pet bird, Ang. What's his name?"

"He's not a pet. He's a menace." Angie gave him a look of disbelief. "He thinks he owns this yard and he objects to my presence and nobody else's." She unlocked the door. "Sit down while I get some coffee going and change clothes."

Peter stood on the porch a moment and stared at the slim gray bird. It shot him back a beady-eyed, suspicious glare.

"Maybe we should name him Vern," he said at last.

"Now that's an idea." She bit back laughter and pulled Peter inside. "Now that I think about it, he does remind me a lot of Daddy."

The things Garner had pointed out to her the day before arose in her mind and created a sinking feeling of fear in her heart. Banishing it resolutely, she marched Peter inside. Later, she would call her mother and urge her to haul Vernon Brownwood to a doctor, whether he liked it or not. That was all she could do while Vernon remained hostile to her and Peter.

She swiftly put coffee on to percolate then fled the bright little kitchen for her bedroom, where she changed into a severely tailored navy suit and pinned her hair into a smooth French twist. This was a day when she needed to look her professional best. She could see catastrophe approaching but didn't know what form it would take.

The feeling grew when she returned to the kitchen and found Garner and Peter engaged in conversation about the situation at BrownWare. It was obvious Peter felt no remorse at abandoning BrownWare temporarily while he programmed his new game.

"Vern will be glad enough to see me when I get back," he predicted. "He hates the routine programming you have to do in order to get to the good stuff, whereas I don't mind it a bit. Gives me a chance to think and get it right the first time."

Angie felt sure she had been right about impending catastrophe when she ushered Peter into the second bedroom where she had set up her desktop computers. When she spread out the scenario she had worked out for a new Ra-thor and Lenora game, he looked the whole setup over with a critical eye then cast his experienced gaze over her outline.

"I don't know, Ang," he said vaguely. "I'll have to have some coffee and think about this for a while. You're calling for a whole new approach here, and there are probably two or three ways we can achieve it."

Angie's heart sank further. "Why don't you rest up from the trip and think about it a while? I'll call you a little later and see what you've come up with."

"Is there anything to eat?" Peter asked in plaintive tones.

She hardened her heart. "You can eat anything you find in the fridge or in the cabinets. I've got sandwich makings and fresh fruit, and there's a frozen pizza in the freezer and toaster pastries in the cabinet."

Peter wandered over to the refrigerator, opened it and stood staring at the contents, still clutching the notebook Angie had given him.

"Maybe we should eat here," Garner suggested.

Angie gave up trying to get Garner out of the house before he could do something crazy, like invite Peter to visit his office. She toasted bread and buttered it lavishly, then toasted some of her toaster pastries and put the frozen pizza on to bake. Maybe Peter would decide he needed a nap after he ate a good breakfast.

Instead, he ate whatever Angie set before him while studying the game notebook and writing cryptic notes to himself in the margins with a pencil. Garner watched in obvious fascination but refrained from comment. He ate the toast but eschewed the pastries and pizza.

It was almost nine o'clock before she managed to escape, with Garner in tow. Peter had wandered into the living room and settled on the sofa to study the notebook and connect to his office computer on his tablet. He barely noticed when she left.

"It won't last long," she told Garner. "Once he finishes his preliminary work, he'll start wandering around the house. If he decides he wants company, he'll go looking, first around the house, then in ever-expanding circles until, somehow or other, he ends up at your office."

Garner looked back regretfully as Angie hurried him toward his car. "That's one interesting guy. Did you know he knew Steve Jobs and—"

"They all knew each other," Angie cut in. "Peter knew everybody in the computer business back in the nineties and probably has wandered around their offices. Or their garages, depending. Come on, Garner. You have appointments this morning, and one thing you don't need is Peter wandering in and out while you're consulting with a client."

"Would he really?"

Garner didn't add that he would like to see that, but Angie could hear it in his voice. He was fascinated by Peter, and unbeknownst to him, he was likely to get all too many chances to indulge his fascination.

Peter observed no limits or borders when he was in a programming frenzy and wandered everywhere, day or night, in search of conversation, inspiration, or nourishment. Not even Cliff, in a completely separate section of the building, would be safe, nor would the denizens of the New South Diner across the street. Peter liked his coffee while he worked, and lots of it.

Garner held the Blazer door open for her and frowned. "Why are you putting your hair up again? I thought we agreed that it looks better down."

"Believe me, Garner, this is a day when I need to maintain my professional image." She frowned back and indicated her upswept blond hair. "You have no idea what we're in for. I need all the help I can get to keep Peter intimidated."

Garner laughed. "Oh? Do you think he'll even notice that he's being intimidated?"

"Probably not." Angie let out her breath in a deflated way. "But I owe it to my boss to try."

Garner appeared to find this exquisitely funny.

When they arrived at Garner's office, Cliff awaited them on the front doorstep.

"I gather you two know the weird dude," he said reproachfully. "Why didn't you bring him over and introduce him? I didn't see that tablet in his hands until he got up, and it looks like one of those brand new Trypster tablets. I sure would have liked to see it up close."

"You'll probably get a good chance later today," Angie said. "But not if I can head him off."

"He's one of Angie's old business colleagues, Peter Van Holden," Garner explained. "He's a computer programmer, and he thinks Angie needs to provide him with the specs for his next programming project. I'll explain all this to you later. But he's an interesting sort."

"Peter Van Holden? VP-Base? No kidding. I'd sure like to meet him. And get a look at that tablet of his," Cliff said. "Bring him over if he comes back down."

"He doesn't know what he's asking for," Angie told Garner, when Cliff returned to his own office.

She went to work assiduously typing up a legal form while Garner met with a prospective client. While she typed, she prayed Peter would get bogged down in some knotty programming problem for the rest of the day.

She was really beginning to get the hang of being a professional secretary, she thought, proudly studying the printout of her work. Anyone could benefit from a good review of grammar and punctuation, and no one could deny she knew how to make a printed page look pretty.

Her laptop instant messenger program pinged, and a message from Fonda Clancy appeared.

How's it going, Ang? You-know-who is on the warpath. There was a notice about a new Ra-thor and Lenora game in the 'Programmer's Daily' today. Why didn't you tell me, you little sneak?

Angie winced and swiftly typed back.

Peter went and signed a contract without a word to me, so you probably knew before I did. Now he's here. Any ideas on how to get him to go back home?

She could almost picture Fonda reared back in her chair laughing.

LOL. So that's where he went. I might have known. But don't worry. I know how to keep my mouth shut.

I know you do, Angie returned. *Too bad I can't say the same for Peter. I'm sure Daddy will call my house and Peter answers.*

ROF and LOL, Fonda wrote. *I'd love to hear that conversation. On second thought, forget it. I think I'll take a long lunch break today so I can stay out of the line of fire. Talk to you later. I've got to get him to sign some letters before I can escape the front lines. I'm telling you, Ang, the atmosphere here is pretty grim. If he fires the entire development lab like he's threatening, he won't have a company.*

For a brief moment, Angie's swift fingers halted and she stared at the words Fonda had written. If Vernon fired all the best programmers, his new iteration of VP-Base would never see the light of day. What on earth was wrong with him?

Let's hope he doesn't go that far, she typed.

Yeah. I'm not in the mood right now to hunt for another job, Fonda returned.

Fonda signed off. Of all the people she knew, Fonda was the one least likely to worry about Vernon Brownwood's temper tantrums. If Vernon fired Fonda, the world would truly have come to an end.

At lunch, she crossed the street alone because Garner had to drive to the nearby town of El Dorado and file a case. Before he left, he bent over her chair and kissed her thoroughly.

"Stay out of trouble," he said, laughing down at her. "For some reason, trouble seems to have followed you here, all the way from California."

"It isn't funny," Angie grumbled. "Just when my new life has really gotten on track, here comes all the old trouble, right to my doorstep."

"And how." Garner laughed harder than ever. "I've never seen anybody like that guy, Peter. Did you work with a whole platoon of people just like him?"

"Not many are like Peter. But he's unusually good at what he does, so maybe that's why he's always been what's euphemistically termed 'eccentric.'"

Garner went out, laughing, and Angie looked wistfully down at her little black Rolodex. She knew very well that her wonderful new job might be about to end, no matter how much Garner enjoyed the situation at present. He might have to fire her in order to preserve his own sanity. Literally.

Angie shook off her mood and marched across the street to the New South Diner, where the grits were always well-buttered and the bacon always crisp. Cliff joined her, still expressing great interest in Peter's Trypster tablet.

"Dolly is allowing me two slabs of butter for my toast every morning," he told Angie happily. "Laura came in here and bribed her properly, I'll bet."

"Who cares, so long as you get butter?" Angie asked reasonably. "You can't possibly eat a slice of toast with no butter on it."

"My feelings exactly." Cliff looked over her shoulder. "Say, Angie, your friend is coming up, and he's still got that tablet. Do you think he'd let me take a look at it?"

Angie managed not to groan aloud. "I don't see why not. But you'll probably get to see more than you want to without ever touching it, if I know Peter."

Peter had spotted her through the window, it appeared, because he wasted no time in hastening to her side with his loping amble. "Say, Ang, you've got the first sequence featuring a field of carnivorous plants. But it might be better if we have them escape a flowing lava field. What do you think? I can do a great job with rivers of lava and fire all over the place."

Angie looked at the tablet he held out to her. "I don't know, Peter. It's hard to scare kids these days. How about a swarm of evil carnivorous bats?"

Cliff's eyes focused in a longing way on Peter's tablet computer. "I've always been terrified of hypodermic needles, myself. If you're interested in a kid's worst fear."

"That's an idea," Peter said, almost to himself. "A bunch of blood-sucking bats with mouths like hypodermic needles. That'll scare the little buggers."

He settled in the booth beside Angie and tapped on the screen. "Okay. Blood-sucking bats for the first scene. Now this second scene ..."

He trailed off into silence, staring in fixed concentration, as Dolly approached with glasses of water and banged them down on the table.

"I'll have the chicken-fried steak," Angie announced, "with lots of gravy. Peter, do you want any lunch?"

"Lunch?" Peter looked up. "Oh, sure. Get me whatever you get, Ang. What do you think about having Ra-thor save Lenora from the bats?"

"It's Lenora's turn to save Ra-thor." Angie rolled her eyes. "Two chicken-fried steak dinners, Dolly. With lots of gravy, please."

Dolly glared at the notations on Peter's tablet. "He has to put away the game. I don't serve gamers in here."

"He will," Angie promised and hoped she could keep the promise. "And a glass of milk for me. Mr. Holt has finally convinced me that it's good for my bones."

"Humph," Dolly said. "There's them as says milk is for baby cows, too. But I ain't got nothing against a good cold glass of milk."

"Milk?" Peter looked up, interested. "That's an idea, Ang. How about some killer cows in the fourth scene?"

"Killer cows?" Dolly stared at Peter in clear outrage. "There ain't no killer cows around here, mister."

"Not around here," Peter explained. "In here." He tapped his tablet screen.

Dolly glared at it. "That ain't nothing but hire-o-glifics. This guy's crazy as they come, folks. I wouldn't listen to nothing he says."

She scribbled something on her pad and marched off, muttering.

Angie and Cliff exchanged glances and struggled to keep from laughing.

Peter cast a temporarily focused glance after her and looked back down at his tablet. "On second thought, maybe an evil tribe of females with giant water glasses on trays to sic the cows on our heroes."

"I don't know, Peter." Angie decided she might as well laugh now, since she probably would have no reason to later. "But I do know that if you want any lunch, you'd better put away the tablet and keep your mouth shut."

Chapter 11

Garner returned to his office about mid-afternoon and found his secretary typing busily away at the forms he had left with her. He still professed amazement that a woman with absolutely no secretarial training had managed to turn herself into quite a credible secretary via books and computer knowledge, and he professed himself overjoyed that she had chosen his office to practice her new skills. He had definitely come out ahead on this deal.

He stepped inside, fully intending to kiss her thoroughly, until he spotted Peter Van Holden ensconced on one of the chairs near Angie's desk.

Peter almost lay in the chair. Another six inches in a downward direction, and he would be on the floor. Above his head he held his tablet computer while he frowned at something on the screen.

"Good afternoon, Mr. Holt," Angie said professionally. "You have two calls to return, and Mr. Denberg phoned about the drunk-driving case. I've put the numbers on your desk."

Garner adapted himself to the new reality and admitted that Angie might have a point. Peter Van Holden definitely detracted from the professional atmosphere Angie had brought to his office.

"Good afternoon, Angie," he said, taking his cue from her. "I see we have a visitor."

She gave him a speaking look. "No lunch for poor Peter. He didn't put away his tablet fast enough, and Dolly refused serve him." She glanced at Peter. "Not that he noticed."

"I see. How long has he been here?"

"Since lunch. He showed up at the diner just after Cliff and I got there." She smiled in a deprecating way. "I thought it might be better if I kept him here instead of letting him wander next door to visit Cliff."

"You probably know best. Get your notebook and come on in my office. I've got some instructions to give you."

He held open the door to his office and shut it the moment Angie had stepped inside. When she turned to see why, he took her in his arms and kissed her with all the joy and passion he felt just in looking at her.

"Now don't tell me this is unprofessional behavior," he said. "Because I intend to do a lot more of it in the upcoming days."

"So long as you close the doors," Angie said, quite demure. "Especially when Peter is around. Sometimes he acts like he thinks he's my father."

As if to lend credence to her words, the door opened and Peter wandered in, frowning at the tablet in his hand. "I need a computer. I've got to check something on my office desktop." He looked up and frowned. "Why are you hugging up to Angie? Who are you, anyway?"

"He's giving me some instructions he wants carried out." Angie stepped out of Garner's arms with what dignity she could assume. "Where are your manners, Peter? Don't you know better than to go walking into offices that have closed doors?"

"Never bothered anybody before." Peter peered at Garner. "Does Vern know you're kissing Angie?"

"You'll have to be sure and tell him," Garner said. "In the meantime, why don't you try using the computer on Angie's desk? She's got it about as fine-tuned as possible."

"Doubt if I'll be able to tell him anything," Peter muttered. "He was screaming about the game contract this morning. Couldn't get a word in edgewise."

"Daddy called this morning?" Angie asked. "Why didn't you tell me?"

"He didn't ask to talk to you. He was too busy yelling at me." Peter lapsed back into his fog of concentration and turned back to the door. "I've got to check the specs from the last game. Otherwise, it's back to writing a whole new block of code."

He excited and closed the door behind him.

"Is he really as spacey as he acts?" Garner asked, staring after him.

"Yes, especially when he's in a programming fit." She headed toward the door. "I'd better try and get him to go back to my place. Otherwise, we're going to be minus a computer."

"Minus a computer?" Garner followed on her heels. "You can use mine."

"I mean really minus a computer. As in, there will be pieces of it lying all over the office."

She hurried out to her desk, where Peter sat frowning at the computer screen and tapping experimentally at the keys.

"Say, Ang, there's no way this thing can handle a download of the size I'm going to need. Do you think I could—?"

"I've told you, the computers at my place can handle anything you want. You need to get back there, Peter. These are older computers designed strictly for office work, and there isn't much you can do to improve their performance for the kind of work you do."

"Maybe so," Peter said doubtfully. "Well, I'll do what I can."

He went to work and within minutes became so absorbed, Angie doubted whether he would have noticed if Bonnie and Clyde stopped by to empty his pockets.

"He'll be busy for another hour, I hope," Angie said, resigned.

"Maybe you should move your home computers down here for him." Garner slid his arm around her waist and drew her back inside his office. "You could keep an eye on him a lot easier. He's really an interesting guy. I'd like to watch him work."

"That's what I'm trying to avoid." She came readily, much to his delight. "You haven't seen chaos until you see Peter when he really gets into a programming job."

"How about creating a little chaos in my system?" he asked. "I could use a good shaking up."

"Poor man. You must have had a rough afternoon at the courthouse." She slipped her arms around his neck. "What can I do to make it up to you?"

"You can take up where you left off when Van Holden came in," he said and breathed in the unique lemony scent that clung to her hair and skin. "I was calming down nicely until then."

Angie obligingly took up where she left off, and Garner soon found himself forgetting all about the visitor in his front office.

• • •

Overall, Angie thought the day could have been worse. True, Peter ensconced himself at her desk and took over her computer, working between it and his tablet, but he stayed quiet and remained in place. That was really all she asked. Since Garner kept her in his office the rest of the day, she had no complaints.

When she told Peter it was time to leave for the day, he shut down readily and followed them out.

"I was getting hungry anyway," he confided. "Is there a pizza place around? I'd better gas up if I'm going to get any work done tonight."

"I'll order one in for you," she said. "Come on, Peter. You'll be able to work at my place. I'll put a card table up in the bedroom for you."

"And some coffee," he said. "Is there a Starbucks around? I sure could use one of their double espressos."

"I'll make you some strong stuff," Angie promised, remembering the days when she had leaned heavily on powerful caffeinated beverages herself. "But what you really need to do is go back to your office in Palo Alto. You've got all the things you need on your office computers, and there's a Starbucks and a pizza place across the street."

"I don't know, Angie." Peter settled on the back seat of Garner's Blazer. "I'm finding everything I need just fine, and between you and me, it's a heck of a lot quieter here. Maybe I'll open a programming office here. That accounting fellow says I'm welcome to use his spare office."

Angie registered a mental note to warn Cliff. "You'll miss all your programming buddies in Palo Alto."

"Haven't missed 'em yet." Peter settled back and glanced around at the blooming flowerbeds and neatly trimmed lawns. "This is a nice place. Besides, you're here, and you understand Ra-thor and Lenora better than anyone else."

Garner grinned at her. "See? You can run, but you can't hide. Palo Alto found you."

Angie smothered a groan. "So long as it's just Peter who found me, we may come out okay."

"It won't be just Peter for long," Garner said, smiling tenderly.

"You mean Daddy will have an apoplexy when he discovers Peter is here?" Angie asked, curious. "Peter said something about Daddy calling the house this morning and really getting ticked when Peter answered the phone."

"I figured as much." Garner sounded satisfied. "We'll soon see if I'm right about Palo Alto following you here."

Angie felt cold all over at the thought. She had high hopes about her new relationship with Garner, not to mention her new life, and she did not need anything or anyone else from Palo Alto following her to Arkansas and ruining everything.

Besides, now that Garner had called her attention to the possibility, she had begun worrying that Vernon might indeed have something seriously wrong with him.

She needed to have a long talk with her mother, at a time when Vernon was nowhere nearby. That meant catching Celia before she left the Stanford campus, which meant allowing for the two-hour time difference.

"Say, Ang," Peter said suddenly from the back seat. "What do you say we pull an all-nighter on this thing. We'll be a lot further along, and—"

Angie could hardly repress a shudder of horror. "Not me, Peter. I've gotten too old for all-nighters. But I'll make sure you have a big pot of strong coffee."

And after this one, Angie thought she might get out of the game-writing business for good. In her opinion, it resembled the business-software field a little too closely.

. . .

It was almost ten o'clock by the time Angie managed to get Peter settled in the bedroom-office she had created for him. He sat before one of the big computer screens, studying the screen and sipping coffee so strong, Garner was certain a spoon stuck in it would dissolve.

She came toward him, uncertainty in her blue gaze, and he realized she wasn't certain he wanted her to come home with him. He enfolded her in his arms, shaken at the tender feelings she evoked in him, and wondered how she could doubt how much he wanted her.

"Let's go to the cabin," he said gently. "You need to get away from here for a while."

"Thank you," she said. "I suppose I do. So long as I'm here, Peter will feel free to come in and ask questions, even if I'm in bed sound asleep."

He waited while she packed a few items into a small suitcase and took it from her. "Are you going to tell Peter goodbye?"

"I'll call him from your place," she said, grinning. "Let's not take any unnecessary chances."

He drove to his cabin, amazed at his own joy and eagerness to be there with Angie. After he had carried her suitcase inside, he came back to the porch where she sat on the glider with Dixie at her feet, facing the peaceful water and talking to her mother. Fireflies blinked in the air and bushes all around, but Angie did not appear to notice them for once.

He sat down beside her and handed her a glass of iced tea. Then he put his arm across her shoulders and listened in, unabashed.

"You're going to have to get him to a doctor, Mom," she was saying. "Something's really wrong. I just didn't realize it until … someone pointed it out to me. He's not acting like himself at all. Remember how he used to hide under his desk so he could avoid business discussions?"

Thanks to the vagaries of cell phones, Garner could hear Celia's side of the conversation almost as clearly as he could hear Angie's.

"You've got to help me, Angelina," Celia said. "I can't deal with him at all. He won't listen to reason. It's as if he's possessed. Now that's a word I never thought I'd use, but that's the closest I can come to this attitude of his. I have no idea what could have gotten into him."

"Mom, if there's something wrong inside his head, or if his brain chemistry is deranged, he may as well be possessed. He won't be able to think logically at all. You have to get him to a doctor and find out what's wrong."

"He was in for his physical not long ago," Celia reminded her. "Everything was perfect." There was a brief pause. "Or so Vernon said." Another pause. "I'll bet he didn't even go for that physical. He hates going to the doctor." Garner could almost feel her gathering outrage. "I'll bet he just told me he went, and that everything was fine."

"You mean he probably didn't get a physical?" Angie put a hand to her forehead. "Mom, you'd better call that doctor tonight just to make sure. Daddy has never behaved like this before. Or, if he went and something was wrong, he may be hiding it. But even if he went and everything was perfect, there's something major wrong with him now."

Garner listened while Angie and her mother talked over the problem Vernon Brownwood presented and what to do about it. Angie thought Celia ought to make an appointment with a neurologist, while Celia leaned toward a psychiatrist.

"You'll never get Daddy inside any office that says 'psychiatrist,'" Angie said. "Find a good neurologist and warn him of the problem. If he thinks it's psychiatric, he can make a referral, and you can haul Daddy right straight over there, no matter what he says."

"I'll get things started tonight," Celia said. "I taught several people who became neurologists, and I know just the one who can help me with Vernon."

Now that Celia had decided upon a course of action, Garner noted that her voice took on added vigor. He had no doubt Angie's father would soon be under the care of a doctor. But he had plenty of doubts as to whether Angie realized what that would mean in terms of her own plans.

Angie clicked off the call and leaned back, resting her head on his shoulder. "That's done. Mom is on the warpath now, and she'll haul him to a doctor no matter what he says. And if he lied to her about having his physical, God help him."

Garner buried his hand in her golden hair and massaged her scalp gently. "Your mom sounds like she can be terrifying."

"Daddy's going to think so." Angie sighed and added, "I just hope there's nothing wrong with him that can't be cured by a couple of prescriptions."

"Let's hope there's nothing wrong with him at all, other than a bad temper. From what I've read, he's eccentric, but he's never been known as an unreasonable man."

"He wasn't when I was a child." Angie sipped some tea. "I'd almost forgotten, but you're right. He didn't change until I went to work at BrownWare, and it was so gradual, I guess I just got used to it and thought he had always been that way." She gazed at the bushes near the porch, where several fireflies blinked their phosphorescent lights at regular intervals. "I've never seen lightning bugs before. This place is so beautiful."

Garner glanced over the lake, which reflected a long silver streak of moonlight down the middle and firefly-studded bushes around the edges. It had taken him a good two years to arrive at the stage of appreciation Angie had already entered.

He ignored her change of subject and told himself it was for her own good. "Angie, if there is something wrong with your father, you may have to go back to Palo Alto for a while."

"If he goes in for surgery or something, I'll go back so I can sit with Mom during the surgery," she agreed. "But I won't be staying in Palo Alto. I live here now, and I'm not leaving."

Garner laid his lips against her temple and felt the warmth of her soft skin. "In that case, maybe we'd better go to bed. You'll want to be up early enough to stop by your place and see what Peter is up to."

"Actually, I was thinking of leaving him alone. He'll make his way to your office all too soon, believe me." Angie rose with him and slipped her arm around his waist, much to his delight. "Mom will let me know what happens when she gets Daddy to the neurologist. In the meantime, I'm not going to worry about it anymore."

"I know several ways to make you forget your troubles," he said, leading the way inside. "They all involve taking off your clothes."

Angie laughed. "They do? What happens when the clothes are off?"

"That's when things really get interesting." Garner let Dixie amble inside then shut and locked the door before sweeping Angie up into his arms. "But let's go someplace private in order to discuss that."

Angie laughed happily. The sound wrung his heart, even though he fully intended to enjoy the night with her to the fullest. Clearly, Angie had no idea what lay ahead and didn't intend to speculate on the subject.

Garner admitted that he didn't either, but he figured he had a better vantage point on what might lie ahead, thanks to his past experiences.

But he would wait as long as he could before he insisted that Angie give more thought to her next actions. Now that he had found her, he did not want to lose her. In fact, he felt downright selfish enough to look for ways to keep her with him, no matter what.

He wanted that, even though he knew that for Angie's sake, he might have to let her go.

•••

The next afternoon, Garner watched as Angie and Peter huddled over Peter's tablet computer and several sheets of paper. Peter rearranged the sheets of paper and gesticulated emphatically. Angie studied them a moment, then nodded and switched out a couple of sheets.

Peter glared down at the sheets, frowning then his face lightened. He gathered the sheets carefully and numbered them with a pencil. Then he sat down in Angie's chair, completely oblivious to the fact that he had taken over her desk.

Angie looked up, saw Garner watching and smiled in a resigned way. He beckoned to her and she came, adopting that businesslike persona she considered appropriate in a professional secretary. For some reason, that look of hers turned him on.

"Maybe I should charge him rent," he said, gazing into Angie's eyes.

"Maybe you should." She gazed back as if she liked looking at him. "He can certainly afford it, and he's definitely disrupting your official business."

"Maybe we can shift him over to Cliff's office if a client comes in," he began, but before he could continue, the front door opened and a man—a very angry man—surged inside.

The man was shorter than Peter and had thick, rumpled blond hair. His irate blue gaze fell upon Peter, who remained hunched over his precious sheets of paper in fierce concentration. He slapped the door shut and charged across the floor like an enraged bull.

"So this is what you're up to, you Quisling! You Benedict Arnold!" he yelled.

Peter looked up in mild surprise. "Oh, it's you, Vern. What are you howling about now?"

Garner drew in his breath and wondered if he was about to watch a murder. Vernon Brownwood's face reddened even more, if possible.

Angie sighed. "It's Daddy. I might have known this would happen if Peter answered the phone at my house."

"Do you think they're going to come to blows?" Garner started forward. "Maybe I'd better—"

"I doubt it. Peter isn't interested, and Daddy is mostly hot air and wild accusations."

Vernon caught Garner's movement and whirled. His gaze focused at once on his daughter. "So. This is where you've holed up. You're not content with destroying everything I've worked for, I see."

"I don't know what you're talking about, Daddy," Angie said, with what Garner now recognized as enormous control. "I have a whole new life. I'm not even working in the software industry any longer. I've had it with development labs and production deadlines and the whole nine yards. I come to work at nine A.M. and I go home at five P.M. I have weekends and holidays off. In short, I now have a life. So go back to California and try that on Fonda."

"Fonda's just a secretary," Vernon shot at her. "You're a top level software engineer, and you ought to know what kind of hours that requires—"

"I'm now *just* a secretary, too," Angie shot back. "And I love it. And I'm never going to be a software engineer again. Never. And I'm not going back to California, either. I own property in Arkansas now, and this is where I'm going to stay."

"You think I don't know what you're talking about," Vernon shouted. His face reddened in a way that made Garner think he might be bordering on a stroke. "You're lying. You're all lying. But you aren't getting away with it."

"Come on, Vern," Peter said, barely taking his attention off his papers and tablet. "What can anybody possibly be getting away with that has anything to do with you?"

"The two of you are conspiring to steal VP-Base and completely rewrite it. Did you really think you could keep me from finding out?"

Angie's mouth dropped open. She shut it, studied her father a moment then looked at Garner with a wide-eyed expression of astonishment.

Peter glanced up at his old friend, shook his head and went back to his papers. "You've finally lost it, Vern. Why would I want to steal VP-Base and get into a whole mess of legal trouble when I can just program this game of Angie's and make a bundle? And it's a heck of a lot more fun for me than the programming for VP-Base, whether we go with a new algorithm or the old one."

When Vernon's face grew even redder, Garner decided to step forward. "Mr. Brownwood, I'm a lawyer. Why don't you step inside my office so we can discuss your lawsuit?"

At this, Vernon swung around and glared toward Garner. "You're a lawyer? Why didn't you say so? I want these two thieves put out of business. I want them stopped. I want a restraining order."

"Then step right this way." Garner stepped back and gestured. "Sit down and let's discuss the matter. Most of the ills in the world can be resolved by means of a good lawsuit. If you sue for enough money, people have a tendency to take you seriously."

Vernon stalked toward him. "That's it in a nutshell. They aren't taking me seriously, and VP-Base was my idea in the first place. They have no right to steal it."

Garner seated the irate man with all due courtesy and shut his office door after exchanging a long glance with Angie. He hoped she received the message and got herself and Peter Van Holden out of the office and back to her home.

It appeared she did. He heard sounds indicative of movement, and a moment later he heard the front door open and close. But a few minutes later he caught a glimpse of a blond head at the front door again. A moment of thought, while he slowly and carefully outlined aloud the costs and probable progress of filing a lawsuit, told him that Angie had likely taken Peter next door to Cliff's office.

"I'm ready," Vernon announced, when Garner had finished his spiel. "How soon can we file?"

Garner groaned inwardly. The last thing he intended to do was file a lawsuit against Angie, but someone had to give her time to come up with a plan to deal with her father. The longer Garner talked to him, the more he felt certain that Vernon Brownwood had something badly wrong inside his head.

"Then we will get started right now," he said, and pulled out a fresh yellow legal pad. "I just need to ask you a few questions."

With any luck, the question-and-answer session would last a good hour. He had the usual set of questions ready, plus he fully intended to investigate Vernon's history all the way back to his grandparents. That should take a good while.

His phone rang, and he glanced at the caller ID. It was Angie, calling from her cell phone.

"Garner Holt," he said in his crispest tones.

"My mother is on her way," Angie said. "The doctor told her Daddy never showed for his physical. As soon as she found out he'd gone to the airport, she booked a flight right behind him. She just landed in Little Rock and rented a car. She'll be here as soon as she can."

Garner calculated. "That ought to take a good two hours. Don't worry. We have plenty to occupy us."

"Thanks for talking to me about him," Angie said. "I had gotten so used to him, I didn't realize how crazy he was sounding. By the way, Peter is next door with your brother-in-law."

"Excellent idea." He glanced at Vernon, who was studying the standard legal contract Garner had laid before him. "By the way, it might be a good idea if you pay a long visit to Dolly." He hoped she understood that he wanted her out of the office.

"And leave your front office unattended?"

"It won't be anything I can't deal with," he said drily. "And if you could have some coffee delivered here, it would be much appreciated."

By this he hoped she understood that she was not to deliver the coffee herself. The longer Vernon went without catching sight of his daughter or Peter, the calmer he would become. By the time Angie's mother arrived, Garner hoped Vernon would be normal enough to go peacefully with his wife.

He sincerely hoped Mrs. Brownwood took Vernon directly to a hospital or a good neurologist's office. The man looked and sounded normal enough, but the things he said spoke of a mind that was being affected by something, and Garner did not consider himself anywhere near qualified to make a guess as to what it was.

•••

Angie walked across the street to the New South Diner and took a seat in a booth. Now that she realized something was badly wrong with her father, she found herself on fire to do something about it. The time until her mother arrived seemed endless, and she wondered how Garner could possibly keep Vernon occupied until then. She wondered if she should locate a neurologist nearby, then decided against it. Her best option was to allow her mother to handle things.

The small diner was empty except for Dolly, who sat behind the counter reading the daily newspaper. She smiled at Dolly and asked for coffee in Styrofoam cups to go, and had just accepted her order when the front door flew open and Cliff dashed in.

"Angie, you've got to help me," he cried. "That guy has my computer in pieces all over my desk. I need that computer. It has all my clients' information in it."

"Peter?" Angie asked, blinking. "Why on earth did he take your computer apart?"

"It's my own fault," Cliff said, groaning. "I mentioned in passing that it was freezing up on me every time I tried to access the state tax filing system. He said he knew how to fix it, and like a fool, I believed him."

Angie put on her most comforting expression. "Chances are he does know how to fix it. Peter's the best there is when it comes to tweaking computer systems. That's why he's such a good programmer."

"Is that the long-haired gaming guy?" Dolly asked. "He's a computer programmer too?"

"He's half of BrownWare, the big database company," Cliff said in a distracted way. "The 'P' in VP-Base. You'd think he knows what he's doing. You'd *pray* he knows what he's doing. But you don't *know* he knows what he's doing when it's your computer, not to mention your *life*."

"He knows what he's doing," Angie said. "Peter was building computers before I was born. Come on, Cliff. If you'll carry this coffee in to Garner's office, I'll go see what he's up to."

"He can take apart anybody's computer but mine," Cliff said on a moaning note. "Here, Dolly. Let me carry that coffee. Maybe when I get back to the office, Angie will have it all put back together."

Angie, trailed by Cliff, hurried back across the street. Cliff carried the coffee toward Garner's half of the duplex while Angie headed to Cliff's office.

She opened the door to Cliff's neatly furnished outer office and immediately focused on the inner office, where Cliff's equally neat desk now held an intimidating array of computer parts.

"Angie, thank goodness you're here." Laura Jones appeared and rushed toward her. "Where's Cliff? I came down to bring him some copies he needed, and Mr. Van Holden says he doesn't know where he went." She reached Angie and grasped her arm. "Angie, what's he doing in there? What on earth is going on?"

Angie patted Laura's hand. "Cliff is taking Garner some coffee. I'm here to make sure Peter puts that computer back the way it was."

"Oh, hi, Ang." Peter looked up in his vague way. "Come get a look at this motherboard. It's one of those Jaxxo models with that weird way of attaching the video card. Ought to be outlawed if you ask me."

Angie grimaced. "You're probably right, Peter." She caught Laura's pleading look and added, "But Mr. Jones needs that computer to finish his work today, so put it back together for him, please."

"If you insist," Peter said regretfully. "But this arrangement really needs to be redone, or it'll never work right."

"So long as it works," Laura said.

Chapter 12

Angie watched as Peter held up the motherboard and cast a considering glance at it. Peter tended to be extremely focused, and his attention had now been claimed by the insides of Cliff's computer.

"Oh, it'll work." Peter bent over the motherboard. "But if I change a few of the jumper settings and alter the cable attachments—"

"It might be better if you look into setting him up with a new computer," Angie hastened to advise. "You've got a contract for a game, remember. You don't have time to tinker with someone else's computer."

Peter lowered the motherboard and gazed on it. "I'd like to see if those settings work. It ought not be freezing up like he says it's been doing."

"I know, but you don't have time anymore to play with computer parts. Your job is to write programs to run on them."

"You have to understand the parts if you want to write a good program." Peter looked around at the various parts scattered over Cliff's desk. "When Vern and I started out, we first had to build the thing before we could write a program for it."

"It doesn't look to me as if it'll ever be the same again." Laura did not hesitate to show her obvious bafflement.

"It'll be much better." Peter set the motherboard in place with an expert hand and used a tiny screwdriver to attach it. "Half the time, they don't even put the parts together properly, or plug in the boards all the way, and that's where a lot of trouble comes from."

The front door opened and Vernon Brownwood charged inside, followed by Cliff and Garner. Garner caught Angie's eye and gave her a wry grimace.

"I knew it. You've gone into manufacturing." Vernon came to a halt and glared down at the parts scattered over the desk. "You'll never make it with desktop PCs these days. Everyone wants a tablet."

"Oh, it's you again, Vern." Peter unscrewed the motherboard, detached it and held it out. "Take a look at the way Jaxxo attaches the video card. I'm thinking that if I change the jumpers here," he indicated an area of the electronic board, "and alter some of the plug-ins, I can change the way the interface behaves. What do you think?"

"My computer," Cliff moaned in the background.

Vernon glared at his old friend then frowned at the motherboard. "If that's a Jaxxo video card, it ought to be changed out for something decent. They get them from some fly-by-night outfit in Malaysia that doesn't know what it's doing when it comes to anything electronic."

To Angie's astonishment, her father approached the desk, accepted the motherboard and studied it critically.

"They've also got a funny way with the memory modules." Peter indicated the offending lines of computer chips. "In my opinion, they ought to be taken out and rearranged. I'll bet this configuration costs a lot of speed when it comes to loading web pages or multitasking."

"But—" Cliff objected.

"I'd be surprised if it managed to load a single webpage," Vernon agreed. "There's only one way to find out. Let's try it."

Angie backed away slowly until she reached Cliff's side and spoke in his ear. "Don't worry. If they don't get it back together, I will. But chances are, when they're done, you won't even recognize the way it runs. They're both experts, you know."

Laura put her arm around her husband's waist. "Let's watch, darling. I've never seen the insides of a computer before."

"Neither have I, to tell you the truth," Cliff admitted. "When they put it back together, will it even run?"

"Better than ever," Angie promised, with an encouraging look at Cliff. "I'll bet you'll never have a problem with it freezing up on you again."

"Just so long as they don't touch anything on my hard drive." Cliff covered his eyes with one hand. "I don't know if I can watch."

Angie backed slowly out of the room and Garner joined her in the big anteroom.

"Sorry about the invasion," Garner said. "When Cliff brought in the coffee, he said you were going to get Peter to put his computer back together again. Your father heard that and came charging over to put a stop to your 'illegal manufacturing actions.'"

"He and Peter will be busy on that computer for another hour or so, I hope." She went into his arms gratefully. "By that time, my mother ought to be here. She said she'd call when she drove into town."

She stood in Garner's arms and absorbed the warmth and comfort he offered. She hadn't even realized how anxious she felt until she rested her head on his shoulder and felt his big palm stroking gently down her back.

"When your mom arrives, will she be able to get him to see a doctor?" Garner asked.

"Heavens, Garner, I don't know." Angie thought a moment. "Generally, they each take care of their own responsibilities, because their professions are so different. We were never a stereotypical family."

Garner chuckled softly against her hair. "Well, this will be a learning experience for both of them. Do you want to go back in and watch them work on Cliff's computer?"

"Not me." Angie shook her head. "I've seen them work on plenty of computers."

"Then let's go back to the office. There's something I need to talk to you about."

Angie walked ahead of him into the office and felt astonished at the amount of comfort she derived from seeing her own desk and her little black Rolodex sitting on it. She had never felt that way upon walking into her office at BrownWare. She actually looked forward to typing up another legal brief, or filling in a legal form … anything that had nothing whatsoever to do with the programming of computer software.

Garner's hand at her back guided her gently into his office, and he shut the door before turning her to face him.

"Angie, you need to think seriously about what's going to happen in the next few days and weeks," he said.

Something about his face warned her that he intended to say things she did not want to hear.

"Nothing is going to happen that my mother can't deal with." She willed him to believe her. "If there's anything wrong with my father, she'll make sure he gets the proper treatment. It has nothing to do with me."

"I'm talking about BrownWare," he said, with exaggerated patience. "What's going to happen at BrownWare if your father is out of commission for a while? Who's running the company in his absence?"

Angie turned and walked toward the window that looked out over the flower beds and the quiet street she loved so much. "I don't know. Daddy and Peter were the official managers, and I used to do the day-to-day tasks, like prodding the development lab and meeting with people from companies where we hoped to license VP-Base." She shrugged and focused on the profusion of colorful moss roses. "It no longer has anything to do with me. For all I know, he's promoted somebody."

"Was there anybody he could have promoted?" Garner came to stand behind her and clasped her shoulders lightly. "Somebody who knew the company's business as well as you did?"

It was yet another trick question, she realized. Garner seemed to specialize in them. She said nothing.

"Angie, if your father has to go to a hospital or something, somebody is going to have to run the company." He tried to turn her to face him, but Angie resisted. "Correct me if I'm wrong, but Peter doesn't strike me as the type who can deal with the day-to-day decisions involved in running a company like BrownWare."

"If Daddy had to go for treatment, Peter would have to take over," Angie stated.

"Angie—"

"I don't work there anymore," she interrupted. She clenched her fists and felt the old helpless tension invade her body. "I don't live there anymore. I'm out of the loop, and I intend to stay out."

Garner remained silent.

Angie's disquiet mounted. "If you're suggesting that I'm the one who should run the company, I won't. I can't go back there, Garner."

"Sure you can," Garner said, in comforting tones. "You can do anything if you have to." He squeezed her shoulders lightly then let her go. "But you may not have to. For all we know, your father may be physically fine. He may just have some sort of grudge against you and Peter."

But Angie knew, even as his hands fell from her shoulders, that Garner thought she ought to start making plans to fly back to California.

"Let's hope so," she said, striving for lightness. "Is there anything you need me to do, now that the office is free of distractions?"

Garner drew in a deep breath. "Angie, I've been thinking things over, and it turns out that I'm not going to be needing a secretary much longer."

Angie froze, unable to believe her ears. "What?"

"You heard me. You've been here long enough to realize that business isn't exactly booming here in a small-town practice like mine. My biggest problem was getting so far behind in filing. Now that you've gotten everything caught up ..."

He trailed off, and Angie turned to stare at him. His gaze rested on a stack of files on his desk, and he did not raise his head to look at her.

"So you're firing me?" she asked, unable to believe it.

"That's right. And if you're wise, you'll wait until your father's situation is settled before you go looking for another secretarial job."

Angie glared at him but he refused to meet her gaze. "You're firing me so I'll have to go back to BrownWare? Is that it? You think I'll just go meekly back to Palo Alto and not even make an attempt at finding another job here?"

"You can't do that, Angie," he said. "Not while your father might need you. Now clear your desk, so you'll be ready when your mother arrives. She's probably going to need your help."

An irrational fury flashed through her. If Garner thought he could force her to go back to BrownWare, he was about to find out differently.

Then despair clutched her heart as she realized there was only one possible reason why he wanted her to leave—he no longer wanted her, and he now had an excellent excuse to ease her out of his office and his life without a nasty showdown.

It made sense, she decided, and turned her back to him. In fact, it was the only explanation that made sense. Never mind that she had just spent another wonderful night in his arms, and that he had held her and offered her comfort of a kind she had never received before in her life. Never mind that barely an hour ago, he had made no mention of any doubts about their relationship.

She had read about this sort of thing, where the woman never saw it coming until the man told her he thought she ought to see some other men.

At least he hadn't said anything about seeing other men. If he had, she might have brained him with his own computer keyboard.

"Sure," she managed to say before turning to head back to her desk. "It's not like I needed the money."

Once there, she packed her Rolodex into her tote, along with her netbook and a few other belongings. Then she marched out of Garner Holt's law office for the last time and went next door to watch her father and Peter argue over the best placement of the jumpers on Cliff's computer motherboard.

• • •

Garner found he had no chance to have another private moment with Angie. Not that she showed any signs of wanting one. She had taken a few personal items off her desk and stowed them in her briefcase before walking out the door without so much as a goodbye.

He told himself it was for the best, at least for now. Angie had no idea what awaited her until her father was under the care of a good doctor, and he didn't have to be a genius to see that Angie did not want to leave Smackover and go back to Palo Alto.

He ignored an overwhelming desire to rush next door where she had taken refuge and beg her to stay with him. Surely, Angie didn't think he was sending her off because he no longer wanted her. Then he reminded himself that Angie probably wouldn't go unless he did send her off, and nobody knew better than he did what guilt would assail her if she wasn't beside her father during the next few days or weeks.

Somehow, he managed to remain in his own office, even though he badly wanted to rush next door and tell Angie he didn't mean it, that her job was safe and so was the place she had made in his life.

But he couldn't concentrate on his work, and he wasn't even sure how he'd make it through the next few days if Angie left town.

Garner turned his chair and stared out the window at the flower beds Laura tended so assiduously. He felt almost like he had when he left Dallas, as if all the pleasure in his life had ended. As if he would never experience joy and happiness again.

Definitely, he was not looking forward to the next few days.

He sat staring out the front window, unmoving, until he saw a nondescript silver car glide to a halt in front of the window. A slender blond woman emerged, stared critically toward the office then down at a piece of paper in her hand. She nodded, tucked the paper into the leather shoulder bag she carried and marched toward his door with a swift, decisive step.

Garner rose and moved toward his front office. He would have known Celia Brownwood anywhere.

"Mrs. Brownwood, I presume," he said, upon opening the door for her. "Your husband and daughter are next door, working on my brother-in-law's computer."

"Is that right?" Celia stepped back and surveyed him through her glasses, then plucked the glasses off her nose. "Damned things. They're for distance vision, and I keep forgetting. So you're the lawyer my daughter says she's working for."

"That's right." Garner figured the less he said, the better.

"Well." Celia studied him a moment, and Garner regarded her in equal silence. "I knew this would happen one of these days. The minute Angie got away from Vern, in fact, and anyone can see I was right." Celia had nothing more to add about his relationship with her daughter and reverted to her current mission. "The sooner I can get Vern back to Palo Alto, the sooner I can get this mess straightened out. Where did you say he was?"

"Next door," Garner said. "Your daughter and Peter Van Holden are both with him."

"*Peter.*" Celia shook her head. "What on earth is Peter doing here? On second thought, don't tell me. I probably don't want to know. I have Vern's doctor on notice in Palo Alto and a plane waiting in Little Rock, so the sooner I can get him into the car, the better. He's not going to get away with telling me his physical was perfect, when he didn't even bother to show."

Celia seemed far more steamed over her husband's lie than the fact that her daughter might have acquired a lover. Garner wasn't sure whether or not that was a good thing in the long run, since he realized that, as a scientist, Celia respected and expected the truth, hence her annoyance with her husband. But he knew that as soon as Celia had straightened out that complication, she would turn her formidable energies toward her daughter's affairs.

"Yes, ma'am," he said blandly, and added nothing else.

His first concern was to get Angie's father on the road to treatment for whatever ailed him. Then he could turn his attention to making Angie understand that he was not ending their relationship. He was merely postponing it. She had to realize that her father's welfare came first.

When he opened the door to Cliff's office and escorted Celia Brownwood inside, Angie looked anywhere but at him. Catching sight of her mother gave her the perfect excuse to ignore him.

"Vernon Brownwood, you have a lot of nerve telling me Dr. Foster said you were in excellent physical condition," Celia announced. "He says you never showed for your appointment."

Vernon almost dropped the screwdriver in his hand. He turned jerkily to face his wife with as guilty a countenance as Garner had ever seen. "Celia? What are you doing here?"

"You may well ask," Celia said in a voice of doom. "But the answer should be obvious, even to a space-pilot like you. I'm here to haul you back to Dr. Foster's office, of course, where you would have proceeded on your own if you'd had a lick of common sense."

"I'll see Foster later." Vernon turned back to Cliff's computer, which Garner saw almost looked whole again. "I had a lot of important things going on the day of that appointment. I'll make another when I get home. Besides, there's nothing wrong with me."

"I'll be the judge of that." Celia marched up to him and took his arm. "Grab his left arm, Angie. If he gives us any trouble, I'm prepared to put a sleeping pill in his coffee."

"Celia, can't you see I'm working?" Vernon held the screwdriver above his head. "It isn't every day I get to take apart one of these Jaxxos."

"Doping his coffee is a little drastic, don't you think?" Angie said, looking everywhere but at Garner. "Take off your glasses, Mom. You'll run into something."

"Celia, this is uncalled for," Vernon insisted.

"You should have thought of that before you lied to me," Celia said flatly. "Put that screwdriver down this minute."

Vernon tried to cover his guilt with belligerence. "I will not. I don't come to your classroom at Stanford in the middle of one of your lectures—"

"Can he please finish with my computer?" Cliff chimed in meekly.

Celia cast a cursory glance over the computer. "It looks finished to me. Peter is perfectly capable of finishing anything that needs doing on any computer that I ever saw." She plucked the screwdriver from Vernon's hand and laid it on the desk.

Peter looked up and pinpointed Cliff. "We're all done here. As soon as I put this last screw in, you can boot it up and try it out."

"Thank God," Cliff said, on a gusty sigh of relief.

"Let go, Celia," Vernon said. "I want to see how it performs, now that we've switched the chips and—"

"Peter, you can help us get Vernon into the car if it becomes necessary," Celia announced. "You might as well make yourself useful."

"Hello to you, too, Celia," Peter said, undisturbed. "It's high time you paid attention to something other than those radiation counters you're so fond of." He looked up at Vernon and gestured with the long, bent-nosed pliers he held. "I'm not so sure one of your little radiation experiments didn't go awry here."

Celia drew herself up. Garner found it educational to see how a woman who was barely average height could suddenly make herself look six-feet tall.

"Peter Van Holden, you will get up this minute and take my husband's other arm, or I will personally devise a laser beam-of-death and direct it toward the bedroom of your apartment."

Garner's eyes widened and he regarded Celia with considerably more caution. Angie stepped forward. "Let Peter finish putting this computer back together, Mom. I'll help you get Daddy out to the car."

"Hey, wait a minute, Ang," Peter said. "You aren't leaving, are you? We've got this game—"

"I knew it," Vernon yelled, face reddening. "You're both in collusion against BrownWare. I'll—"

"Shut up, Vernon Brownwood." Celia's tone brooked no nonsense. "You are in very deep trouble here. With me, your wife. You no longer have time to carry out some ridiculous vendetta against Peter and Angie. You are about to become very, very busy trying to keep me from skinning you alive. Do you understand that?"

"Now, Celia . . . " Vernon began.

"How dare you lie to me?"

Garner had to admit that if Celia Brownwood spoke to him in that tone, he would very likely wither up in the same way Vernon did.

"It wasn't a lie," Vernon said in a small voice. "Not exactly. I was going to see Foster in another week or two."

"I'll bet," Celia said grimly. "Well, let me tell you something, Vernon. You are going to see George Foster tonight. I don't care if it's midnight. Then you are going to do whatever he tells you, depending on what he finds upon examination."

"There's nothing to find, Celia." Vernon's tone of mild exasperation lost most of its impetus when he encountered his wife's fiery blue gaze.

"You'd better hope there isn't," Celia said.

In the meanwhile, Cliff quietly took his chair at his desk and stared at his computer monitor with an awed gaze. Behind him, Peter watched the screen critically.

"Go ahead," Peter said, and placed the last screw. "Try it out."

Cliff punched the power button on his computer with apprehension. Then he sat back with a look of dawning hope that was replaced by burgeoning awe.

"Look at this, Garner," he exclaimed. "I've never seen a computer boot up this fast before."

Laura peered over his shoulder. "Try one of your spreadsheet programs, darling. Try the one that was so slow to load."

Cliff tapped at his keyboard. "Wow," he breathed. "It just popped open. I'll bet it'll even multi-task the way they claimed it would when I bought it."

Laura and Peter gathered behind Cliff to issue suggestions and commentary on the turbo-charged computer, and Garner remained where he was, still trying to catch Angie's eye. Just as assiduously, she avoided his gaze.

"It was nice to meet you, young man," Celia said. "Sorry about the misunderstanding over the phone last week." She examined Garner's face with her slightly far-sighted gaze. "Not that it was a misunderstanding at all, by what I can see."

"Yes, ma'am," Garner said. Apparently Celia knew exactly what his relationship with her daughter was, but whether or not she approved, he remained uncertain.

"Come along, Vernon. We have a plane to catch in Little Rock." Celia marched toward the door, towing her husband along with her.

Angie, on Vernon's other side, gave him her best professional secretary's smile without meeting his eyes and accompanied her parents out Cliff's front door.

Vernon deflated like an old balloon and allowed himself to be hustled out to Celia's rented car and placed in the front seat beside her. Angie quietly climbed into the back seat and cast him a glittering little smile.

Garner had remained standing on the curb looking after her.

...

Angie made it through the first two weeks after her departure from Arkansas like a robot. Only by carefully refusing to think about her time in Smackover and pretending she had never left Palo Alto could she make it through the comic catastrophe that ensued.

Celia dragged Vernon onto a departing flight the moment they arrived at the airport outside Little Rock. In Denver, after a wait made almost unbearable by Vernon's alternate pleading and cursing, they boarded a direct flight to California, and by six o'clock the following morning, they escorted Vernon into Dr. Foster's office.

By then, Angie felt like the walking dead, and she didn't much care how she looked, especially when Dr. Foster ordered an ambulance to transport Vernon to a hospital, where he was scheduled for a list of tests and scans.

After two days of intensive tests and assessments by numerous specialists, Vernon was scheduled for surgery to remove a growth inside his brain that might or might not be cancerous. The doctor said most of his erratic behavior, and definitely the pain in his head was caused by the growth.

"I've never had a headache in my life," Vernon said. "How was I supposed to know that's what was going on?"

"If it's your head, and it hurts, then it's a headache," Celia said. "Common sense. Something you're sadly lacking in, Vernon."

Angie didn't know whether to feel relieved or angry, and she felt so tired, she could feel neither. Nor would she allow herself to think about Garner. The only way she could keep going was to not think about him, to pretend the brief time she had spent in Arkansas was a dream.

When Vernon's surgery was completed and the tumor successfully removed, she stood beside Celia to receive the doctor's report and Vernon's prognosis, then could not recall a word of it five minutes later.

"Well, thank God," Celia said, in her brisk way. "Now things can get back to normal, and you can come back to work without his constant harassment. But you might want to call that young man you were working for and let him know the outcome. From all I can gather, he's the one who alerted us to the fact that something was wrong with Vernon."

Angie said nothing at the time, but as soon as she was alone at her parents' home that night, she called Garner's office, hoping he would not be working late that night.

He was not there, and she left a succinct message, "Thank you for alerting us to my father's illness. He had surgery for a nonmalignant brain tumor this morning and is expected to make a full recovery."

The moment she clicked off the phone, the tension of the past few days released in a bout of tears that left her drained and exhausted.

At least, she thought, after spending a good half an hour in a hot shower and drinking two glasses of milk, she ought to sleep really well.

Chapter 13

Angie sat at her father's desk at BrownWare and frowned at the list of things she had to see to that day. Matters at BrownWare had deteriorated so badly, she had spent the first two weeks of her father's recovery trying to re-gather the reins of the company and find out the true state of affairs.

It had taken her an entire six weeks to simply get the company back on track again. The only thing that made her exhaustion worthwhile was the fact that Vernon would soon return, hopefully as his old self, the father she remembered and loved.

"Hey, girl," Fonda Clancy said from the door. "You look beat down. What's the trouble today?"

Angie looked up and absorbed Fonda's classy little red linen suit, with its short skirt and lacy white blouse. It set off Fonda's chocolate complexion and crimson tipped black hair beautifully. She thought wistfully for a moment about those cowgirl boutiques Mindy Adams had promised to introduce her to, then told herself firmly that the cowgirl look wouldn't go over nearly as well in Palo Alto.

"Just tired, I suppose. Mom says Daddy is itching to get back to work." She sighed and stretched. "It can't happen too soon for me."

Fonda came inside and took the chair beside the desk. "So. Have you thought about what you're going to do?"

"Sure." Like she didn't do anything but think about what she was going to do. "I'm going back to my house in Arkansas and look for another job."

"You don't think your old job is still available?" Fonda's large brown eyes narrowed as she studied her friend. "Why not? From what you said, that lawyer hadn't been able to keep a secretary."

Angie hadn't told anyone the truth about her relationship with Garner Holt, not even Fonda. The hurt of leaving still felt too raw, and Angie didn't want to burst into tears in front of anyone. Plus, if she didn't think about it, she couldn't obsess endlessly about what he might be doing right now with one of the many women in Smackover and the surrounding cities who would like to date him.

She rubbed her forehead. "Well, the truth is, we had a thing going, and—"

"You *what*?" Fonda shot to her high-heeled feet. "And you didn't tell me? Angie, Angie. What am I going to do with you? I knew something was going on, but I had no idea you were such a fast worker." She paced the office, shaking her head. "You should have called me. You know I'm loaded with good advice when it comes to 'things.'" She stopped before the desk, hands on hips. "So what kind of 'thing' are we talking about here? Kissie-kissie or the full hoochie-koochie?"

Angie figured her face must be a shade of crimson rivaling Fonda's suit. "It was an affair, okay. We slept together."

"Hoochie-koochie," Fonda agreed, with a knowing smile. "So why do you think he was glad to see you go?"

"He's the one who told me I needed to come back to Palo Alto if Daddy had to go in the hospital for treatment. There's only one reason I can see that he would suggest that. He didn't care enough about me."

"*What?*" Fonda clapped her hands to her head.

Angie began to feel slightly foolish in spite of the fact that she knew Garner hadn't cared about her. After all, he hadn't called her once, not even to reply to her message. He hadn't even sent her an e-mail. And she had too much dignity to call him. Never mind that she paced the floor in the guest bedroom of her parents' apartment every night in an effort to keep herself from calling him again.

Fonda made a great show of pulling out her own hair. "It couldn't have been because he cared about you, could it?" She raised her hands to the ceiling. "Nope. Not possible. Couldn't happen." She lowered her hands and propped them on Angie's desk so she could lean over it until her face was about six inches from Angie's. "Sit back, Angelina. It's time you and I had a long discussion about men. *After* you tell me every single detail of everything that happened."

"That could take a while." In spite of herself, Angie began to feel better.

"Don't worry. It's time for lunch." Fonda glanced at the big, gold bangle watch on her slender wrist. "Besides, I have a feeling this relationship of yours is a lot further from over than you think. *If* you handle things right." Fonda plopped back onto her chair and took out her cell phone. "I'll order in Chinese food. You seem to have been on some kind of health kick lately, and they say Chinese food is healthy. Right?"

Angie grinned and agreed, even though she had no idea whether Chinese food qualified as healthy. Still, it had to be healthier than the pizza or hamburgers she and Fonda had shared in the old days.

Fonda placed an order for a number of exotic-sounding dishes, then clicked off her phone and leaned forward. "Now talk. And don't leave out anything."

Angie complied and found herself astonished at the relief that ensued. Fonda was right again, as usual. Bottling things up never solved anything, whereas talking it over with your best friend would likely turn up unexpected solutions. Hope arose in her heart. When she had finished, ending her tale with the short phone message she had left on Garner's answering machine the day of Vernon's surgery, Fonda pursed her full lips and sat back. She stared at the ceiling with her hands linked behind her head.

Finally, she said, "Angie, you should have talked to me first. Then you could have left him a message that would have had him out here in a flash. You don't seem to realize that he does care about you, or he wouldn't have made sure you were free to come back here. Correct me if I'm wrong, but I don't think you would have set foot in Palo Alto again."

Angie said nothing but her face probably revealed the answer clearly. Her heart leaped. Could Fonda be right?

Fonda nodded. "The situation is still salvageable, but you're going to have to do things carefully."

Angie's heart promptly fell to the floor.

"But don't worry," Fonda said. "You've got me on your side. We're going to get your affair going again, or my name isn't Fonda Clancy."

Angie felt a moment of trepidation, but she was able to quickly banish it. Fonda knew what she was doing when it came to men. There had never been a weekend when three or four different men hadn't been hounding Fonda for a date.

"The first thing you've got to do," Fonda said, with the expression of a woman on a mission, "is get things straightened out here. Then you can get back to your own life."

Her own life. Angie savored those words because she knew they were true. She now had a life. At long last, she had a life, and it was up to her to preserve it.

• • •

Garner spent most of his time either brooding in his office or brooding on the front porch of his lakeside cabin. In each spot, he found himself constantly glancing up in hopes of catching a glimpse of Angie. Then he would remember she wasn't there, and his mood would take a nosedive.

He wished he hadn't fired her. Then she might have been calling him with updates on her father's condition and making sure he wasn't hiring another secretary. In short, she would have been letting him know she was coming back as soon as the crisis was over.

Garner's thoughts ran in constant circles, in search of ways he could have gotten Angie to go back to help the people who needed her without going so far as firing her. That, he decided, with the benefit of hindsight, might have been a mistake. What if Angie thought that he had fired her because he didn't want her around anymore, now that she had gotten his office into shape?

He thought and thought, but came to no conclusions as to how he could have handled the matter differently. Besides, there probably wasn't another way. No one knew better than he what it was like to live with the knowledge that one had failed to come to the aid of his loved ones, and he wasn't about to let that happen to Angie.

Angie had a lot of determination, and she was determined never to set foot in the door at BrownWare again. Probably nothing less than firing her would have succeeded in getting her to leave Smackover, and he couldn't have lived with himself if Angie had evaded her responsibility to her family in order to remain with him.

But he still wished he could have kept her with him. He needed her. She'd given him back his hope and belief in life. She had brought him back to life.

Although Angie clearly thought she'd been a failure at BrownWare, Garner knew that wasn't the case. Angie had been a major power at BrownWare, and everyone had known it but Angie and Vernon Brownwood. He had been right to let her go. He just wished she would call him and tell him she was coming back. Or not coming back.

He'd just like to know something.

On that thought, he spotted Cliff crossing the street to the New South Diner and hurried to join his brother-in-law. Eating lunch alone really palled on him these days.

They settled in their usual booth, but before they could even think about the menu, Dolly slapped a plate down before him.

Garner glared at the plate and said through his teeth, "I did not order this."

Dolly ignored him. "You're getting' what I'm servin', or you ain't gettin'. Take it or leave it."

The plate held Angie's favorite breakfast of bacon, eggs, grits, and toast. Garner had to admit, it both looked and smelled enticing.

"Extra toast on the house," Dolly said, and banged it down beside the plate.

Cliff, who had been sitting very quietly across from him, whistled softly.

"I don't want extra toast," Garner growled.

"Yes, he does," Cliff said hastily. "Thanks, Dolly. I'll have the same."

"That's more like it," Dolly said approvingly.

"Whose side are you on?" Garner demanded.

"Dolly's right. Low-fat diets do make people mean," Cliff said, meeting Garner's silver gaze. "You've been behaving like a sore-tailed cat for weeks. Now, you either eat that, or you'll wear it out of here."

Garner regarded his usually mild-mannered brother-in-law cautiously. "Are you saying I've been … a trifle testy lately?"

Who could blame him? It had been eleven weeks and three days since the day Angie had called him and left that terse little message that Vernon had emerged from a successful surgery and was expected to make a full recovery.

"A bear with buckshot in his bottom would be a better lunch partner," Cliff said.

Garner rested his forehead on his palms. "Peter Van Holden has just been named president of BrownWare. It was in yesterday's technology news."

He hadn't even looked at today's technology news. What if the company's interim chief executive said she had accepted a position as head of some other company?

Oddly enough, Cliff understood this *non sequitur*. "That's something, isn't it? The guiding light of BrownWare was right here in Smackover, running your office. She seems such a young thing to have all that experience."

The technology news sites had duly reported Vernon Brownwood's successful surgery and recovery, just as they'd reported the actions Vernon's daughter had taken to cease hostilities with Peter Van Holden and bring him back into the BrownWare fold. Peter had been placed in charge of the long-awaited update to VP-Base, which was expected to restore BrownWare to its former glory. The programmers were working twenty-four hours a day. Garner had figured Angie would remain as head of BrownWare several more weeks, until her father was back at work.

"She started college at sixteen," Garner said, in what he knew were hollow tones. "She got her Master's from Cal Tech and has worked at BrownWare ever since."

After glaring at his plate another minute, Garner finally gave in to the succulent odors and scooped up a big bite of buttered grits. Unexpected warmth filtered through him and he studied the yellow pool of butter. Maybe Angie was right when she said a person needed some saturated fat in their diet.

This was it, Garner decided, on a forkful of egg with its thickly liquid yolk. Angie needed him. The world needed him, because without Angie's wide-eyed appreciation of life and everything it involved, the world would be a poorer place. His job was to preserve all that joy. He frowned at the butter plate and absently spread a pat across his toast. Angie was the light of his life, and he'd done nothing to make her want to come back to him. He had expected her to call him, and now he was upset because, other than relaying the news about her father, she hadn't.

"She was supposed to be some sort of child genius who burned out early," Cliff agreed placidly.

Garner frowned across the table. "She didn't burn out. She loved her parents and didn't want them to know she wasn't as driven as they thought she was. That she wasn't like them, in other words."

Cliff nodded wisely. "I'm not surprised. In spite of all that steel in her spine, she had a tremendous desire to please. Here, Garner. Have some more butter on those grits. Real butter has a way of making you feel better."

Nothing would make him feel better. Angie wasn't here, and it was his own fault.

He scowled down at Cliff's hands. The other man busily added butter slices to the steaming mound of grits on Garner's plate.

"Eat," Cliff said. "Dolly and I are testing a new scientific theory."

Such was the state of Garner's mind, he obediently ate a forkful of buttery grits. He rolled them around in his mouth absently and thought about Angie.

Straightening out the mess Vernon Brownwood had made at BrownWare wouldn't leave her much time to develop her personal life. But a woman as determined as Angie would manage the time. If she wanted to. If she found someone she wanted to be with.

Garner gritted his teeth and flung down his fork. How was he supposed to digest his food thinking about Angie finding someone else?

"Looks like our theory was wrong, Dolly," Cliff said, deadpan.

"What theory?" Garner snapped.

"We thought getting a little real butter inside you might oil your disposition," Cliff said, brown eyes twinkling.

Garner managed a reluctant smile. "Sorry, Cliff. I'm not fit for human company these days."

"You sure aren't," Cliff agreed. "Why don't you take the day off and go fishing or something? You aren't doing your fellow humans any good around here."

Garner agreed with that. He was going to have to do something about Angie. If he just let her go without making an effort to get her back, he'd lose every bit of peace of mind he'd so painfully rebuilt the past few years. He'd also lose the heaven-sent chance to build a deep and lasting love with a woman who made his bones feel like water and his heart behave like a jumping bean.

Garner shot to his feet. He'd do it. He was flying to Palo Alto tonight. To hell with his pride. He needed Angie. He paid his bill and crossed the street to his own office, where he grabbed the mail from his box, carried it inside and dumped the stack on his desk. Locating the phone book from beneath a stack of files on his untidy desk, he called the airport in Little Rock about an evening flight to Palo Alto.

Then, after walking restlessly out to look at Angie's vacant desk, he wandered back into his own office, propped his feet on the desk and thumbed through the stack of mail. It was barely six in the morning in Palo Alto, too early to start calling Angie. He would pass a little time then call her. If necessary, he would fly out this evening.

Not a single envelope enticed him to reach for the letter opener he kept handy, until he reached a single envelope made of high quality paper and bearing a local address he recognized. He grabbed the letter opener and slit it open haphazardly. It was a résumé for Miss Angelina Brownwood, experienced legal secretary.

Garner flung the document into the air, oblivious to the way it kited through the air on its way to the floor. He was already out the front door by the time the page landed.

• • •

Angie watched through the curtains of her living room and pressed a hand over her heart, which was threatening to pound its way out of her chest. So much for her worry that Garner might pick today to ignore the mail. He leaped out of his vehicle and charged up the sidewalk. His entire body sizzled with fury. She hadn't expected Garner's reaction to be anger.

Now that the time had come, she wasn't sure she could carry off the scenario she had planned so carefully. She even wore one of her secretarial suits, complete with glasses, as if she was sitting around awaiting phone calls from employers.

And now she was about to find out if he still wanted her. If he'd ever wanted her. At the moment, she couldn't tell.

But he had cared enough to open her résumé and come over at once. Surely, that meant something.

Angie winced as the front door shuddered beneath his knock. He was supposed to be curious, interested and perhaps even mildly annoyed. He wasn't supposed to be *furious*.

Angie's heart beat wildly as she hurried to the door. Garner looked tanned and fit and totally infuriated, and she loved him so much, she was about to burst.

She opened the door and said, "Yes?"

"There you are." He reached for her and clamped her to his side. "I ought to sit down right here on the front steps and put you over my knee."

"So you can spank me? You and what army?"

But she didn't fight him as he carted her across the lawn. Not when she'd spent three months dreaming of this moment when she was back, more or less, in his arms again.

"You and I are going to have a little talk, Miss Angelina Brownwood. About that résumé of yours. You'd better have some darned good answers, because I am *not* in a good mood."

Angie's mouth twitched, but she refused to smile. "Fine. Where would you like to hold this … discussion?"

Garner smiled dangerously and opened the door of his Blazer. "We're driving to the lake, where else? I don't want any other would-be employers to interfere."

"I don't see any would-be employers around." She let him half-lift, half-shove her into the Blazer.

"Good, because there had better not be any," Garner snapped. "How, by the way, did you get Van Holden to agree to act as President of BrownWare? He strikes me as a man who can't identify a chair unless it's sitting in front of a computer."

"It wasn't easy." Angie gripped her hands together in her lap. "I've spent most of the past three months dragging him off his computer long enough to learn a few aspects of the business other than programming."

"In the middle of updating VP-Base?" he asked, turning down the road that led to his lake.

"We've got lots of young, eager programmers. Peter's job is to guide them. He doesn't need to do all the programming himself, regardless of what he may think."

"Are you sure you should have left? This is bound to be a critical time."

Angie stared out the window, blind for once to the branches brushing the windows. If this was a suggestion that she take herself back to California …

"Peter understands BrownWare and VP-Base better than anyone, and Daddy will be back in another month," she said.

"Your father's himself again?"

"When I told him what he was like before the surgery, I don't think he believed me." She sighed. "I don't understand why I didn't realize the problem sooner."

"You were too mentally and physically exhausted trying to prove yourself to him."

Beside him, Angie stared out the window. It had taken her several weeks of soul-searching to reach the conclusion Garner had just stated. "You're right. When I left Cal Tech with a Master's instead of a Ph.D., I felt like a failure. Daddy was obviously disappointed, so I began working every hour I could, trying to make him proud of me again."

"And instead of making him proud, you couldn't please him, because he slowly became more and more irrational," Garner finished. "Well, you've just had the chance of a lifetime to prove yourself. How'd you like it?

"It was better this time," she said quietly.

"Was it?" Garner turned down the graveled road leading to the lake and floored the accelerator. Tree branches and shrubs brushed the sides of the vehicle.

Angie grabbed for the dash when the Blazer hit a pothole. Her head almost hit the roof, and her glasses slid down her nose. Garner seemed tense and angry, but she could discern nothing from his conversation.

The Blazer burst out of the woods and into the clearing before the lake. Angie shoved her glasses back up and stared around appreciatively. The woods were the white-green of late summer, and the lake looked dark and cool.

She didn't have long to admire her surroundings. Garner leaped out, slammed the door behind him, and stalked around to jerk open her door. He plucked the glasses off her nose and stuffed them in his shirt pocket.

"The glasses are part of my outfit." Angie found it difficult to remain calm while Garner more or less frog-marched her toward his cabin. "I look too young without them."

"Angie," Garner said, biting out each word, "I know how old you are. I don't need glasses to prove it to me."

"Oh, yes?" She waited while he unlocked the door. "Is that why you were so eager to push me out of your office and back to Palo Alto? I'm now too old for the job?"

Garner marched her inside and slammed the door behind him. The small living room's chief furnishing was a large, brown leather sofa. He sat her on it and took up a position in front of her.

"All right, Angie Brownwood," he said. "Now, suppose you tell me just what the devil you mean by that résumé? Why is a hot-shot software executive like you hankering after a lifetime secretarial position in some guy's office in this little town?"

"Did I indicate I was interested in a position in just any man's office?" Angie sniffed. "No, I did not. I was very selective—"

"That's not what I meant," he said.

"You don't have to yell."

"I'm not yelling." Garner lowered his voice. "I want to know why someone with your training wants to deliberately give up a dream position to move to a small town like this and take a dead-end job as a secretary."

"I didn't say I was looking for a dead-end job," Angie said with enormous dignity. "I said I was looking for a lifetime job."

"There's a difference?"

"Of course, there's a difference." She sat primly straight, with her knees together and her hands laced in her lap. Garner was proving unexpectedly difficult, and she wasn't quite sure how to deal with him. "You see, the problem is there aren't that many positions open in Smackover for hot-shot software executives."

Garner shoved his hands in his pockets. "If there's one, I'll be amazed."

"Exactly." She nodded. "So a wise job-seeker fits her skills to the jobs that are most likely to be available."

"Angie, I am not interested in why you settled upon being a secretary. Believe it or not, I can even see a certain sense in it. What

I want to know is what are you doing back here in Smackover when you could still be running a world-famous software company?"

"Being interim president of BrownWare was a challenging position," Angie agreed.

Garner visibly gritted his teeth.

"But I'm tired of that sort of challenge," she continued. "I'm ready for a whole new type of challenge."

Garner said nothing. He stared at her with narrowed eyes.

Angie studied him. "I enjoy being a secretary. It's fun to learn things out of books and brush up on my grammar skills."

"How long do you think you'll find it fun? How soon will you be looking around for a new challenge?" Clearly, Garner didn't believe her.

"The trick is to stay on the lookout for new areas of challenge," Angie said. "For instance, I've re-signed up for courses at the El Dorado Business College in business English and shorthand. After I've mastered those, they've got courses especially for legal secretaries, even paralegals." She smiled happily. "They've got lots of interesting courses."

"Well, that makes a lot of sense," Garner snapped. "And just when are you going to have time to make a living if you're spending all your time taking courses?"

Angie regarded him in all seriousness. "I'll have time to *do* some living. There are lots of things out there to study besides computers. Well, I'm still a young woman, and I intend to do something about my dream."

"Your dream?" Garner stared at her in bafflement. "What's your dream?"

"I am going to rebuild my life," she announced. "I'm going to learn about nutritious diets and jogging. I'm going to learn about fishing with a rod and reel. I'm going to learn about yards and birds and home decorating. And most of all, I'm going to learn a lot more about making love to a man."

"*What?*" Garner thundered. "Oh, no, you aren't, Angie Brownwood. If you think you're going to make love to any man but me, you're out of your mind."

Angie deliberately widened her eyes. "Who says?"

"I do. And furthermore, you aren't working in anyone's office except mine."

"Oh, really?" Angie put up her chin. "And what makes you think you can tell me where I can work and who I can make love to?"

"Because you belong to me, that's why," Garner yelled.

"That's funny." Angie frowned thoughtfully. "I don't recall you saying anything about belonging to you before I left for Palo Alto." Garner froze. He stood staring at her, looking as if she had just thumped him on the head with a brick.

"My apologies, Miss Brownwood," he said at last, and took a step closer. "I should have realized you're a woman who likes to do things by the book."

"Books exist to teach people how to do things." Angie watched him uncertainly.

He smiled suddenly, that rising-sun smile she loved seeing on his face. "And you're an expert at using them, aren't you?" He reached her side and knelt swiftly on the floor by her feet. "If you insist on going by the book, then who am I to refuse to accommodate you?" He reached for her hand. "Angie, I love you madly. Will you marry me?"

Angie wondered if she'd heard him correctly. "You love me madly?"

"Of course, I do." He laughed, a sound of pure male triumph. "What's more, you love me. Otherwise, you wouldn't have set this up. You knew I'd take one look at that résumé and come charging over to raise hell with you about it."

"If you already know it all, then why should I answer you?"

"Because if you don't, I'll probably drown my sorrows in a plateful of buttered grits." He tugged her hand. "Just answer the question. This floor is hard, and my patience is waning."

Angie gave him a beaming smile of happiness. "In that case, I'll marry you."

He remained where he was. "And?"

"And I love you, too," she said, laughing.

"That's more like it. I need you so much, Angie." He rose and sat beside her on the sofa, drawing her into his arms. "I love you so much. Life hasn't been worth living since you left."

"Life in Palo Alto was never worth living," Angie said drily. "Not if I have to show up at BrownWare every morning and make like Hitler to get Peter to pay attention to the business instead of the programming." She lifted her face, seeking his kiss.

Garner held her tighter, looking anxiously into her eyes. "Are you sure you should have left before your father was able to take over?"

"I'm sure." Angie leaned forward coaxingly. "The new VP-Base is due to go into beta-testing next week. All Peter will have to do then is issue press statements and cope with the bugs that crop up. And finish programming the Ra-thor and Lenora game."

He regarded her doubtfully.

"Have some faith," she said, loving him all the more for his worry. "I wouldn't have left if everything hadn't been in good shape."

He focused on her, grinning. "You might have. I can be awfully irresistible."

Angie attacked him, breathless with laughter. They rolled off the sofa and onto the floor, laughing joyously. The action wreaked havoc on Angie's little blue suit, but she didn't care. Some things were more important than clothes, even clothes that were a part of her secretarial wardrobe.

Garner succeeded at last in rolling Angie to her back and pinning her hands above her head. He stared into her eyes. "Angie, I love you. You made me glad to be alive again. I'd forgotten what it felt like to be happy."

"So had I," she whispered. "I used to feel so old."

"You aren't going back to Palo Alto, I don't care what happens. Your knight in shining armor has spoken." He let go of her hands and wrapped her in his arms. "Kiss me, sweetheart."

Angie joyfully wound her arms around his neck and kissed him. She gave him entrance into her mouth and savored being inside his. She'd never experienced intimacy like the kiss they exchanged.

"Why on earth did you wear an outfit like this?" Garner struggled to peel her blue jacket off. "You knew I'd want to take it off you first thing."

"How could I know that?" Angie shivered at the feel of his hands on her through the thin silk of her ecru blouse. She arched her neck, encouraging him to unbutton the blouse. "For all I knew, you might have wanted me to come back to work and get a letter out immediately."

"Oh, I do want you to come back to work immediately." Garner unbuttoned her blouse with fingers that shook with eagerness. "But today, we're taking the day off to celebrate our engagement."

"Are we engaged?" Angie felt breathless, as if she'd been running a marathon.

"I asked you to marry me, and you accepted. Of course, we're engaged. We'll be married as soon as we can get a license. It's henceforth my duty to see to it that you get the proper sleep," he kissed her eyelids, "the proper exercise," he reached down and slipped her shoes off her feet, "and the proper food." He kissed her, nipping lightly at her full, lower lip and massaging her throat with his long fingers.

Her eyes opened, even though she felt dazed with pleasure. "And it's my duty to see that your office runs smoothly. I never saw an office that needed me more than yours does."

"You're right about that." He kissed her throat. "My office needs you almost as much as I need you."

"How can I turn down the chance to make such a difference in the world?" Angie asked, and opened herself to the man she loved. "Like I always say, doing things by the book can be so rewarding."

The real reward was Garner's love, and Angie never intended to lose it. At last, she had her new life back, along with a lifetime position as Garner's wife and secretary.

Angie looked forward to a life filled with joy and laughter, not to mention a whole series of new and even more exciting challenges.

About The Author

Kathryn Brocato is a lifelong reader and writer of romance who lives with her husband, dogs, and chickens in Southeast Texas. Learn more about her at *www.kathrynbrocato.com*, and visit her Facebook page at *http://www.facebook.com/pages/Kathryn-Brocato-Author/130436237088005*.

More from This Author
(From *The Look-Alike Bride* by Kathryn Brocato)

Suckered again, Leonie thought. Why did she even try?

She didn't know why she tried to evade her sister's requests. Probably it had something to do with her desire to assert her independence—for all the good it did. Leonie always resisted, and she always wound up doing what Zara wanted in the end. No doubt, her spinelessness had something to do with younger-sister syndrome.

That was why she stood in the big open living room of Zara's lakeside cabin amid a batch of suitcases carried in for her by two nondescript government agents, dressed as airport shuttle drivers. Then they saluted her as if she were some kind of important official, and swiftly left.

Her current job: Pretend to be Zara.

She had done it before, but never for longer than a few hours. However, this particular job involved a hefty paycheck, which Leonie admitted she needed, and one month of impersonating her sister in an area where no one knew Zara, except by sight. She had been assured the job was perfectly safe, merely a precaution in the unlikely case hostile entities checked on Zara's whereabouts.

"All I can say is, this had better be as safe as they promised," she grumbled.

Leonie studied the suitcases, interested in spite of knowing she'd probably be heartily bored within a week. Experience told her she wouldn't care for most of the clothing inside. Zara's taste in almost everything was totally different from hers. Still, she'd have fun being a secret agent who looked like a Barbie doll for a month.

"I'm a pushover," she told the scruffy collie at her side. "That's all there is to it. A marshmallow-filled pushover."

Butch shoved his long muzzle into her palm.

"A broke pushover, too, which is the only reason I'm doing this." She brooded a moment. "You'd think I'd know better by now. Roddy Hillister should have taught me a lesson."

For a moment, Leonie toyed with the thought that this might be the perfect opportunity to have a vacation romance. She had always dreamed of a lover who would be hers for a lifetime, but sometimes a woman had to take what she could get. Maybe she could use playing Zara for a month to her advantage and make one of the many men always chasing her sister happy.

"Then Zara can deal with the repercussions," she told the collie. "That would teach her."

The collie's tail waved gently, as if in commiseration. He had spent the previous evening visiting the vet and the groomer and had metamorphosed from a matted ball of fur into a recognizable collie despite his moth-eaten appearance.

The vet surmised the dog was about two years old and healthy, although severely neglected. He thought Butch had survived on his own by foraging through garbage cans until Leonie acquired him. Even though a groomer had spent three hours trying to untangle the dog's coat, Butch still resembled a ragged orange-and-white blanket.

"It's too bad I don't have a job already lined up." She scratched gently behind the dog's ears. "You may have to get a night job guarding warehouses to support us when this is over." Leonie bent to pick up one of the suitcases. "We may as well get unpacked. We have a *vacation* to enjoy, courtesy of Uncle Sam."

An entire month. Leonie couldn't get over it. Zara, who was an agent for an unnamed branch of the U.S. Government, showed no compunction about interrupting Leonie's quiet life as a high school health and physical education teacher and demanding that she serve her country.

"If I had wanted to serve my country," Leonie grumbled, glaring into the suitcase open on the bed, "I'd have joined the army. Just look at this stuff. I'll look like a bimbo."

She held up a silver party dress that would fit like a second skin. It was so short, Leonie wondered why anyone bothered to call it a dress. Leonie would hide in the restroom all evening if she dared to wear what looked to her like a silver camisole in public, but Zara would be a knockout in it.

Nonetheless, that was what Zara—and the United States—wanted Leonie to do. Her job for the next month or so was to visit every place Zara would if she was vacationing at an Arkansas lakeside cabin, and knock all observers' eyes out.

Leonie smiled. She might as well enjoy this to the fullest. When she returned to teaching, perhaps she'd have memories of this once-in-a-lifetime vacation that would last her for years.

"Not that anybody who really knows her would believe for one minute that I'm Zara," she told Butch as she hung the silver camisole in the closet. "Only Zara can carry off looking like a movie star and have a great time doing it."

She assessed herself in the dresser mirror. Zara looked back at her.

Inside of one day, Leonie's ash-blond hair was lightened to a spectacular silver blonde, her eyebrows reduced to a thin, well-brushed line, and her skin, from head to toe, artificially tanned with an expensive lotion. Leonie's blue eyes were actually a shade or two darker than Zara's, but people rarely noticed that small difference amidst all the glamour Zara, or Leonie dressed as Zara, projected.

The two sisters looked so much alike, anyone would have thought they were twins, although Leonie was actually two years younger. Zara was brassy and outgoing, the sister who had her shoulder-length, ash-blond hair dyed platinum, and dressed like a movie star. Leonie, on the other hand, preferred to practice her baseball swing or kick a soccer ball around while wearing loose-fitting, sturdy jeans and T-shirts she picked for their serviceability.

Even during childhood, everything Zara did was perfect, unlike Leonie who was a walking disaster: her science project got eaten by her new puppy; and her first bra underwent an elastic collapse when she was walking down the aisle to the family pew at church.

Zara was a cheerleader and was elected homecoming queen. She graduated near the top of her class though she rarely opened a book. Leonie, however, felt lucky to graduate and had to work for all her grades. She excelled in sports and track and was well liked, but nobody considered her popular. Even the boys Leonie dated really longed to date Zara.

Once Leonie tried getting a tan and bleaching her hair, only to find everyone mistook her for Zara. Moreover, she discovered she didn't like the attention she attracted. She lacked her sister's gift for repartee and was incapable of turning a man down without hurting his feelings forever. Thus, after two days, Leonie returned her hair to its original color and deep-sixed her contract with the tanning salon. Not even moving to Houston had helped because Zara visited regularly and met most of Leonie's dates.

This time, things would be different. This time, she *was* Zara—for an entire month, and by golly, she was going to enjoy it.

Leonie studied her reflection in the mirror. She was supposed to be noticeable, so that nameless individuals involved in anti-American activities would assume Zara was vacationing at her lakeside cabin rather than tracking and sabotaging their operations.

Great, Leonie thought. Attracting the attention of people who hated Americans and wanted to kill them was just the sort of thing she preferred to avoid. For that reason alone, she deserved every bit of fun she could derive from this "vacation."

However, there was no way she could stand Zara's taste in clothes for hours at a time, so she smuggled along a tiny selection from her own wardrobe. Leonie opened a paper sack that held two pairs of well-worn jeans and several of her favorite T-shirts. Around the cabin, she would be comfortable. When she went out in public, she'd be Zara.

Swiftly, she tossed off Zara's skintight white leggings and loose, hot-pink blouse and pulled on a pair of soft, faded jeans and a sky-blue T-shirt. The only thing she had forgotten was her own well-broken-in running shoes, so she laced up Zara's, a true example of high-tech athleticism. She took the cell phone Zara's employers had provided from her purse and shoved it in her pocket. Then she whistled softly to the collie and headed for the door, confident that she looked like a cross between her usual self and her sister.

The secure landline Zara kept in the kitchen rang before she could get outside. Muttering, Leonie turned back while the dog stood waiting patiently beside the front door.

"Hello, baby," Zara cooed with her usual insouciant cheer. "How's it going so far?"

"Fine." Leonie figured Zara knew very well how it was going and opted for brevity.

"Don't be huffy. Your country thanks you. I thank you. We both kiss your feet."

"Um-hum." Zara wanted something. That much was obvious. "These clodhopper running shoes of yours won't make all that foot-kissing very easy."

"I forgot to mention something earlier," Zara went on, ignoring Leonie's response. "There's a man who stays in the cabin on the other side of the woods behind mine."

"Oh, yes?" Leonie picked up on the uncertainty in Zara's voice immediately. Zara never sounded uncertain.

"Well, he doesn't stay there all the time, but he's there a lot of weekends. His brother owns the cabin."

"That's nice." It also wasn't like Zara to beat around the bush.

"His name is Adam. Adam Silverthorne."

Leonie maintained a wondering silence. Was she supposed to faint upon hearing his name? Zara sounded as if that was exactly what she expected. Leonie had never heard her sister's voice take on that particular soft, feminine quality before.

"He lives in Dallas, so you probably won't run into him, but if you do . . ." Zara trailed off.

"Am I supposed to seduce him for the good of my country? Maybe I should impress him with that silver hankie you call a party dress."

"I'll have to slap you silly," Zara said, laughing. "Seriously, Leonie, you'd better consider Adam off-limits. He used to work for my branch, and he might—" She broke off. "I mean, he might realize you aren't me."

"Oh, yes?" Leonie decided to have some fun. "This sounds interesting. Maybe I
should—"

"Don't you dare," Zara interrupted, laughing again. "So far, Adam has resisted all my blatant hints, but I'm hoping to remedy the situation soon."

"What kind of blatant hints are we talking about? Maybe I can learn something."

Zara didn't answer. Her voice retreated as she spoke to someone in the room with her, then it returned to full volume. "If you should, by some chance, run into Adam, maybe you could give him a mysterious wink and disappear. That might give him something to think about."

"He must be something if you're so interested in him," Leonie said. "Okay, mysterious wink and vanish. Got it. Anything else?"

"Charles said you've got a dog with you," Zara said. "I thought your apartment complex didn't allow pets."

"I'm looking for a new place." She hoped she could find an apartment in Houston, or in whatever city she moved to in search of a job, where dogs were welcome. "If anyone asks, I'll say I'm keeping him for my sister in Houston."

"Perfect." Zara sounded relieved. "Gotta go, honey. Enjoy yourself. And don't worry about Adam. This isn't one of his usual times to visit. Bye, sweetie."

"How do you like that?" Leonie asked the collie after hanging up the phone. "Zara's fallen for probably the only man in the entire universe who isn't falling for her."

The dog moved his ragged plume of a tail slightly.

"Usually, men take one look at Zara and fall over their own feet trying to get a date. I wonder what's wrong with this Adam Silverthorne?"

The collie, having never met either Zara or Adam, had no opinion to offer.

"You'll probably fall for her, too," Leonie grumbled. "She's an even bigger sucker for good-looking dogs than I am." She opened the door and followed him outside. "That's a compliment, in case you didn't notice."

Leonie walked toward the lake with her dog beside her, thinking hard. Assuming Adam Silverthorne visited the area while she was there, Leonie decided she better leave him off her list of men suitable for a fling.

Unless, of course, Zara would appreciate having Leonie do the hard work of attracting him. Leonie grinned at the thought, knowing full well that if Adam Silverthorne ignored Zara, he certainly wasn't going to give her younger sister a second glance.

Butch clearly found the forest-surrounded lake fascinating, but he was a well-mannered dog and remained close to Leonie's side in spite of the peculiar way she chuckled to herself.

Zara's lakeside cabin fronted Lake Ouachita in the Ozark Mountains of Arkansas, near Hot Springs. Why Arkansas, Leonie didn't know. She'd have thought her sister would prefer a cabin in Aspen or beside Lake Tahoe where there were lots of men and activities. But Zara claimed to love her Arkansas hideaway, even though she rarely spent any time there. Recently, Leonie had begun to suspect the cabin had been bought for some other purpose, probably something to do with Zara's job. Or maybe even to chase this Adam Silverthorne, she thought, grinning to herself.

Leonie walked to the shore of the lake and peered out over the shining waters. Lake Ouachita sat amid rolling Ozark foothills covered with trees and studded with quartz deposits that contained big crystals. Perhaps she'd go on a hike in search of quartz crystals, but not in these shoes.

She walked out on the narrow, wooden pier that extended about twenty feet into the lake and bent to test the water with one hand. It felt warm, just right in fact. She would take a swim later so she could stay in shape.

Butch showed no interest in the water or the pier. He remained firmly on shore, watching her anxiously.

"You aren't scared of water, are you?" she asked.

He ignored the gently lapping water and stayed at the end of the pier despite her coaxing.

She ambled back to shore, stroked the dog's head, and turned toward the forested area that lay behind Zara's cabin. "I don't blame you. After all, you aren't a Labrador retriever."

The woods were green, cool, and full of interesting, well-marked trails. The middle trail, according to Zara, led through the woods to a set of cabins that fronted another cove of the big lake, one of which belonged to Adam Silverthorne's family. She might as well familiarize herself with one of the other trails. Then she and Butch could head back to the cabin for a well-deserved lunch and afternoon nap.

The United States Government was paying the rent on her Houston apartment for the next two months. That would help, but Leonie knew she needed to be searching for a job. School would start again in two months, and all the available openings for high school P.E. teachers would be filled by the time she started looking.

That would be just her luck. Perhaps she should demand that the government guarantee her a good job the next time she filled in for Zara.

"You'd better gain all the weight you can, boy," she said. "If I don't get a job lined up, we may both find ourselves on weight-loss diets we don't need."

With all the free time available, maybe she could take a crafts class. She brightened. As soon as she got back to the cabin, she would investigate. Perhaps she could learn a craft and become a flea market entrepreneur if she failed to find a teaching job.

What could it hurt to try?

•••

Adam Silverthorne congratulated himself as he stepped out of his brother's lakeside cabin and headed for the woods. He had finally chosen a time to visit when Zara Daniel wasn't lying in wait in the next cabin over. If she'd been there, she'd be knocking on his door right now, asking if he wanted to have lunch with her.

Zara was beautiful, but Adam knew her type all too well. Once he let her talk him into taking her out, he was liable to find himself engaged to marry her. That was the level of determination he sensed in the stunning Zara Daniel.

Adam had worked for the government once himself, and he'd known the moment he met her several years back exactly what Zara did for a living. She had sought him out at a party in Dallas, and he had realized at once that she had researched him thoroughly. Her well-constructed biography about being a secretary who worked for a special interest group in Washington, D.C. notwithstanding, Adam knew that although she might spend a lot of time at a computer, she didn't spend it typing other people's letters.

No, Zara Daniel was an agent, a damned good one. Just from watching her move, he knew she'd had extensive self-defense training and worked out every day. Her pose as a brazen bimbo was so perfect, Adam was unsure how much was pose and how much was Zara's own outgoing personality.

What Adam couldn't understand was why she had set her sights on him. In fact, he strongly suspected she had bought that cabin behind his brother's property because she wanted to pursue him. From a few hints she had dropped, he figured she had been assigned to lure him back into government work.

Adam smiled grimly. If that was the case, she could resign herself to a long, drawn-out siege and ultimate failure. He felt certain Zara wasn't much acquainted with either.

He strode briskly down the forest trail behind the cabin, enjoying the cool shadows and desultory bird song that surrounded him. The Arkansas forest held a charm that never failed to soothe him, even when Zara Daniel lurked in her nearby cabin, ready to pounce. Smiling with satisfaction that he'd finally be able to get some work done, he turned a corner on the narrow trail and came face to face with his current nightmare.

"Oh." Zara took a step back, clearly startled.

"Miss Daniel. Why am I not surprised?"

Although he smiled, Adam knew his voice betrayed overtones of annoyance his mother would condemn if she could hear him. She was a stickler for gentlemanly behavior, no matter what the provocation.

"Wh—?"

Zara shut up abruptly. Adam could have sworn she was about to ask who he was.

Behind her, a long, orange-and-white muzzle with even longer-looking fangs poked forward. A deep, rumbling growl filled the quiet woods.

"Hello, fellow," Adam said. Of all the females in the world likely to adopt an ugly dog, he'd have picked Zara Daniel last. Maybe she wasn't so bad after all. "Are you a new recruit to the K-9 forces?"

"He kills on my signal." Zara backed up a few steps and almost tripped over her own feet. "Steady, Butch."

Adam's eyes narrowed on her. Something seemed different about her.

Maybe it was her voice. Zara's voice was usually crisp and determined, but at the moment, she sounded nervous and uncertain. He studied her, gripped by something he couldn't put his finger on.

Yes, it was Zara Daniel all right. He'd know that long, tall body, silver hair, and those heavily made-up blue eyes anywhere.

Yet, he'd never seen her look quite so—Adam scanned her slim, curvy figure—so *normal* before. Instead of clothing designed to flaunt her well-honed feminine curves, she wore jeans and an old blue T-shirt. She'd still attract any male eye within a hundred yards, but she wasn't going out of her way as she usually did, to make sure of it.

That didn't mean he could afford to relax his rule about letting her intrude on his quiet time. His security consulting business had just landed a contract that meant his hard work over the past few years had paid off, and he had hours of work ahead of him tonight.

"No need to sic Butch on me," he said. "I was heading in the wrong direction anyway. Excuse me, please."

"Sure," she said in a faint voice.

Now he knew something was up. Normally, Zara would have instantly claimed she was going his way. He'd have needed a shoehorn to shift her from his side.

Adam knew better than to test his luck. He swiftly turned on his heels and vanished the way he had come. A little farther down the trail, he turned off and stepped silently behind a thick tangle of wild grape vines.

After waiting a good five minutes, he was even more baffled than ever. No tall, silver-blond bombshell glided down the path in his wake.

Weird, Adam thought. It was almost as if Zara had forgotten who he was. Perhaps that was it. Maybe she had been injured in the line of duty and suffered temporary amnesia.

Adam emerged from hiding and followed the path back to the cabin, thinking intently. Something strange was going on, and for the first time in his short acquaintance with Zara Daniel, he discovered himself interested in finding out more about her.

Considering the way she usually tried to attract his attention and failed, that was probably the ultimate irony.

• • •

Leonie waited until the man disappeared back the way he had come before letting out her breath in an explosive gasp. "Wow. Well, what do you think? This is why I named you Butch, by the way."

Butch, who had no argument with his new name, remained at attention, peering down the forest path.

"That's got to be Adam Silverthorne."

Butch glanced back at her then resumed his guardianship of the path.

"I don't think he'll be coming back this way for a while. We'd better make tracks while we still can."

She could see why Zara fell for the man. He was a good six-feet-three-inches tall, lean and well-muscled, with thick, dark hair and a rugged face highlighted by straight, dark brows and arresting green eyes. Adam Silverthorne wasn't classically handsome, but he was definitely all male, something Zara was bound to appreciate.

In fact, now that Leonie thought about it, Adam's movements were similar to Zara's, as if he'd spent long hours learning stealth and hand-to-hand combat techniques the way she had. That was probably why Zara was so attracted to him. Adam was the male counterpart of herself, a well-honed, covert agent for the United States Government.

Well, Leonie Daniel didn't appreciate covert agents or their crazy schedules, and she knew better than to think she'd like being involved with a man who could be ordered at any moment into a dangerous country to do whatever terrible deed the government deemed necessary. Adam Silverthorne had nothing to fear from her. All she wanted was to get back to her own business.

Leonie burst from the woods and headed for the cabin, chuckling. If she didn't know better, she'd have sworn Adam Silverthorne was scared of Zara. She couldn't blame him. Her sister could be awfully determined, and she nearly always got what she wanted.

Still, Adam didn't impress her as a pushover. If he didn't want Zara, she had no doubt he'd make it known.

Maybe he disliked hurting women.

On top of that, he looked and sounded like a man who appreciated a good dog.

Leonie decided Adam was probably a very nice man, one she'd love to get to know better. But alas, he was like all the other men she met. Once a man belonged to Zara, he was Zara's. He'd never want plain Leonie Daniel, the younger sister who enjoyed her quiet life and ordinary job and disliked the idea of too much excitement and danger.

Besides, Leonie wouldn't dream of going after the only man she'd ever seen Zara really interested in. She focused on that thought and refused to allow herself to daydream of what would happen if a man like Adam ever fell in love with her instead of Zara. It would never happen, so why torture herself?

Leonie let herself into the cabin, relieved that she wasn't followed, and reached for the telephone book. Perhaps she could call around and locate some crafts courses. Anything to create a vacation to remember where she might meet somebody who didn't already know Zara.

• • •

Across the lake, in a small cove created by trees, two men in a bass boat held fishing poles with corks bobbing innocently on the water. The hooks, however, were not baited. The men had no interest in catching any of the perch or bass abounding in Lake Ouachita.

One held a pair of powerful binoculars, while the other manned a small, spotting scope. On the floor in a metal tackle box, powerful communications equipment waited.

"It's her, all right. Zara Daniel," the man with the scope said. "And she's got a dog with her."

"Are you sure it's really her and not a double?"

"It's either her or her twin sister." He patted his scope. "This baby can pick out a dime in a gravel pit."

"She has a sister, all right. A kid sister. But no twin." The second man reached for the metal box. "I'll notify Smith—just in case." He lifted out a tiny cell phone. "This is a helluva job. Not anything like what I signed up for, if you want to know, but a paycheck's a paycheck when the unemployment checks quit coming."

"You got that right." The scope man peered at the cabin. "Ugly dog."

"I'll tell Smith you said so."

Also by Kathryn Brocato:

Old Christmas

Sutherland's Pride

Georgie's Heart

The Counterfeit Cowgirl

In the mood for more Crimson Romance?
Check out *High Octane: Ignited* by Rachel Cross and Ashlinn
Craven at *CrimsonRomance.com*.

9 781440 582370